ROBERT BARNARD

Robert Barnard was born and brought up in Essex.
After reading English at Balliol College, Oxford, he
worked for a time for the Fabian Society, and in 1961
went as a lecturer in English to the University of New
England, in New South Wales. He taught in Norwegian
universities for seventeen years from 1966, and in 1983
came back to Britain to write full time. As well as
nearly thirty mysteries, he has written books on
Dickens, Agatha Christie and a history of English liter-
ature. He and his wife now live in Leeds.

ROBERT BARNARD

UNHOLY DYING

HarperCollins*Publishers*

HarperCollins*Publishers*
77–85 Fulham Palace Road,
Hammersmith, London W6 8JB

The HarperCollins website address is:
www.fireandwater.com

This paperback edition 2001

3 5 7 9 8 6 4 2

First published in Great Britain by
Collins Crime in 2000

ISBN 0 00 7102917

Set in Meridien and Bodoni

Printed and bound in Great Britain by
Clays Ltd, St Ives plc

CHAPTER 1

Scent of Scandal

'It's worrying,' said Mrs Knowsley.

Her friend looked at her sharply. Madge was usually a cheerful individual, naturally so, anxious to see the best in everyone and everything, ready to look forward hopefully to a happy outcome of every difficulty. They were standing just inside Madge's back door, in the little side street on the edge of Pudsey, between Leeds and Bradford. Usually they stood on the step outside, but today Madge had drawn her inside.

'Why?' Lizzie Cordell asked. 'Why is it worrying?'

'Not knowing, I suppose. Wondering.'

Her friend considered this. There must be more to it than that.

'Didn't they tell you anything?'

'Said he was going through a difficult time, and needed to get away for a bit.'

'That tells you something and nothing, doesn't it? Get away from what, or from where?'

'Well, from Shipley. He's been priest there for ten years or more.'

'It's only eight miles away. Not far to move if he's going through a spiritual crisis.'

Mrs Knowsley looked at her friend.

'What are you thinking, Lizzie?'

'Maybe they needed him close – to hand, like. In case they need to question him.'

'You mean he may have done something wrong?'

Her friend looked at her pityingly.

'Well, that is what's been worrying you, isn't it, Madge?'

Madge paused for a moment, afraid to bring things into the open. Then she nodded.

1

'I suppose so ... Yes, it is ... He's a *nice* man, Lizzie. A lovely man. And a real gentleman.'

'Anyone can go off the rails, Madge – real gentlemen as easily as anyone else.'

'I know that, but ... It tears me apart, Lizzie.'

'What does?'

'To see him like this. He never goes out, except once or twice he's been out after dark. And one time I knocked on the door to his room, got no reply and thought he must be out, and when I went in he didn't hear me, but he was sitting in his chair with his head in his hands. I could swear he was crying.'

Her friend considered.

'What did you do?'

'Tiptoed out and went away.'

Lizzie looked at her straight in the eye.

'You do realize it's not your problem, Madge?'

'Of course I do ... But I *like* him, Lizzie. We talk and he seems so warm, and wise, and ... The thought of him sitting up there alone and suffering, not doing anything except mulling over what's happened, and not knowing what it is ...'

'I can see that. What do you talk about? Can't you bring the conversation round to his troubles?'

'Oh no. We just talk about trivialities. The weather, what he'd like for his dinner, that sort of thing.'

Lizzie did wonder how Madge's lodger had been warm and wise on those particular topics. She just said: 'Couldn't you bring the conversation round to more important things gradually?'

'With time, I suppose. But I want to *help* him, Lizzie. Now.'

'He's a priest, Madge. He must have ... resources in himself, or people to go to. The Church helps its own, you know.'

'Too much so, sometimes. Oh, you don't think it could be boys, do you? Children?'

'I don't know, do I? I've never even seen him. But I do think you shouldn't get too involved. For your sake, but for his sake too. If there's been wrong-doing, there's bound to be rumours, and you don't want to be part of those rumours.'

Mrs Knowsley looked distressed and confused.

'No. I suppose not.'

'Leave it to the Church. They'll sort it out. They'll give him whatever help he needs.'

Mrs Knowsley's voice took on an unusual edge of sharpness.

'They seem to be giving him precious little help at the moment.'

The eyes of both women went up to the ceiling, as if expressing both human concern with the man upstairs and a hope for heavenly guidance.

Father Pardoe sat slumped in the easy chair in his dimly lit bed-sitting room. In his waking hours there he only ever did three or four things: peered cautiously through the window at the world of activity he was used to engaging with; walked up and down the room, hoping that his footsteps could not be heard by Mrs Knowsley in her sitting room, but unable to refrain from this limited exercise; lay in the bed looking up at the ceiling; and sat slumped in the chair, as now, looking like a wreck of his once vigorous, upright self.

Sometimes he thought he would never come to terms with what had happened to him. Now and then he wondered that his own Church, the valued superiors that he had counted as his allies or friends, could be so little understanding of what he had done, and why. At other times he tried to be more clear-eyed, to free himself of the weak instinct to blame others, and to tell himself that his troubles, this terrible burden of guilt and rejection, were something he had brought on himself, by his own actions, and by his disregard of possible interpretations of them. But when he told himself that, when he mentally tried to put himself in the dock on that charge, he could never believe it with more than half his mind.

Because the other half cried out that the Church – *his* Church, *his* Bishop – was not really concerned with what he had done, but with appearance: they worried how it would *seem*, how it would be seen, what people would say. The whole business disgusted him. They had barely looked at the facts, or at the moral issues, had not wanted to discuss them. That much had been clear from the Bishop's telephone call, the memory of which still left him angry. They had been more interested in PR, in damage limitation, in keeping everything if humanly possible under wraps. It was the same instinct that had led the hierarchy in Ireland to shift priests who had abused altar boys on to other parishes where they abused more altar boys. How could *his* Church do this? How could they worry not about what he had done, only about what people would think he had done?

That people would talk he had no doubt. Probably it was already seeping out, getting passed around in whispers through the parish. He was certain that would happen, not because money was involved, but because a woman was. A young woman. An attractive woman.

He had an image of Julie Norris in his mind's eye. The short, blonde hair, the appealing, bewildered eyes, the little boy held in the crook of her arm as she talked to him in her drab, poky kitchen. The image was very dear to him, one he cherished and did not try to put away. He had no illusions that his regard for Julie was without lust. There had been other women before her, women for whom he had felt a special affection, women with whom he might quite easily have fallen into sin. But he had not – not with them, and not with Julie.

What he had done, with some of them, was try to show them, by special attentions, what they meant to him. That was surely innocent, or comparatively so? The thought struck him that what it really was was pathetic. But he was sure that at the time it had seemed to him lovely – a beautiful way to show his regard. He came to see that it could cause jealousy among the ladies of the parish, however, and once he realized this he had tried to cloak his special regard in decent wraps.

The wraps were gone now, at least as far as his superiors were concerned. Now, in the prison of this little bed-sitting room, the image of Julie came to him, but only briefly and wanly. What pushed it aside was the image of his shattered

4

career – which meant his shattered life. He was ashamed of this preoccupation, of the worldliness that it betokened, but somehow he could not resist it. His life as a parish priest was over, his reason for existence in pieces. His hopes of future advancement now appeared ludicrous, absurd. What future he had he did not know, but he faced the fact that it did not involve the respect, the flattering attentions, the warm regard that over the years he had come to take for granted. Still less could he nourish dreams of preferment – of performing the rites he held so dear, and which had been so meaningful to him, in fine vestments, in impressive buildings, with his words on national issues given local if not country-wide coverage. Vain, silly, deluding hopes, but he had nourished them.

Total eclipse, his brain told him: no sun, no moon, all dark amid the blaze of noon.

Cosmo Horrocks sat in his place in the little restaurant compartment of the train from King's Cross to Leeds and fumed. Fumed very pleasantly, however – enjoyed, relished the process. The announcement by the buffet car steward had promised an 'exciting new menu' in the restaurant car, and he had been tempted there to a proper meal, even though he would probably have his expenses claim for it knocked back by his editor. He had made his way there, to be greeted by a lumpish girl who pointed to a seat with reluctance and informed him that after his meal he would have to go back to standard accommodation. As if he was using the meal as a way of infiltrating First Class! Even if he had been allowed to claim First Class on expenses, he wouldn't have gone in it: you never heard anything worth a bean in First Class. The antechamber to death, that's what First Class on British railways was.

Then the same lumpish girl, handing him the menu and wine list, had announced that the fish was off, and so was the chicken. 'That rather lessens the excitement,' he had said, to her blank stare. What was left was the vegetarian option – inconceivable to Cosmo, who hated anything that might be regarded as crankiness – and Cumberland sausage.

Cumberland sausage exciting! He could have done better in the most squalid sort of country pub.

There was an article in this.

As always his ferrety nose twitched, alert for more material. And as so often happened with Cosmo, it came. After twenty minutes during which no food appeared, a plump woman at the next table asked when she was likely to get served, because she was getting off at Grantham. The lumpish girl marched off into the galley and shouted:

'I don't believe it! Now she tells me she's getting off at Grantham!'

The plump woman flushed with annoyance. Cosmo fumed agreeably. Grantham. The birthplace of Margaret Thatcher. He had always called it ironically in his own mind the Holy City. How could he bring that in? He had rather admired Thatcher in her heyday, but she was now a national joke, good for a kick at any time. Should be able to connect her up with the privatized railways, which were such a disaster, he thought. His mind worked at it.

But his mind was one that, unlike a train, could travel along several lines at once. The fact that an article on railway catering was in the process of construction did not mean that he had relaxed his habitual alertness, his Autolycus-like knack of snapping up unconsidered trifles – things that to other people, even to other journalists, would have meant nothing. One such apparent trifle penetrated to him now from the table behind him.

'Gone to ground, so they say.'

'Spirited away, more like. The Church takes care of its own.'

At that moment, irritatingly, the food arrived. Cosmo Horrocks began tucking into his Cumberland sausage. It was a perfectly good and tasty coil of sausage – not much use for his purpose, if he stuck to the truth. The article was for the moment put aside, and he concentrated all his attention on the next table, hoping they would take up the topic once the waitress had finished serving them. The Church was always good for a story, both in the nationals and the locals. Cosmo's professional life had been punctuated by erring vicars. Sure enough, once the waitress had moved on, the conversation was resumed in hushed tones – but not hushed enough to frustrate Cosmo's journalistic sharpness of hearing.

'Of course the wife clams up – says she'd rather not speak about it. Faithful daughter of the Church, and all that. Well, I'm a faithful son – up to a point . . .'

'Exactly. Up to a point.'

'And I've always been willing to give them financial advice, off the record if necessary.'

'I know you have. It's well known in the parish.'

'I've lost count of the times they've come to me and said: "Look Mr Leary, you're a businessman, and you know what's what: we've got this parcel of land and we want to do as well from it as we can" – that sort of thing.'

'You've been very generous. Time's money, when all's said.'

'Well, frankly, I'd rather do that than be on my knees every Sunday, let alone racking my brains to remember lustful thoughts to pour into Father Pardoe's ear. Leave that to the womenfolk, that's what I say.'

'Not that they have lustful thoughts.'

''Course not. It's well known they don't. Any more than priests do.'

Cosmo could just imagine the wink they gave each other. He was getting very interested. Priests, eh? Father Pardoe. Catholic Church, then, rather than Anglican. Better and better. He put aside his knife and fork and took out his trusty notebook. Drawing a line under the previous notes he headed the new section 'PRIEST – SCANDAL', and underneath entered the names 'Mr Leary' (not very useful, until a parish had been pinpointed) and 'Father Pardoe' (decidedly useful). After a pause for mastication the conversation at the next table (behind Cosmo's back, which made him greatly regret not choosing the seat opposite) continued.

'What do you think it is in this case? Money or a woman?'

There was a pause for thought.

'Frankly I'm guessing here, but I'd say a bit of both. There's a name that's being mentioned – by the women who talk about it at all.'

'Oh?'

'Julie Norris.'

'Doesn't mean anything to me. Parishioner?'

'Not so you'd notice. Single mother.'

There was a brief, bitter laugh.

'Single mother! We had a better word for it in our younger days, didn't we, Con? And for the child.'

'Little bastard. Aye, we did that. Anyway, there's been women before that he was said to favour unduly. But no one thought there was anything sexual in those relationships. When it comes to a twenty-year-old bimbo . . .'

'You're right. And happen there was more to the earlier businesses than any of the parish biddies was willing to admit.'

'Of course you're right, Derek, as usual. But if there was, he was clever about it. It's not all the parish ladies think like my Mary – try to put the best construction on anything connected with any member of the priesthood.'

'Oh, I know that. There's plenty of scandal-mongers, for all they "Father This" and "Father that" them the whole time till it fair makes you sick.'

'Doesn't it ever. I tell you what, it's when the children grow up and fly the nest. There's a big hole in a woman's life waiting to be filled, and it's the Church and the priest that fills it.'

'You said the problem might be a bit of both.'

When he replied the man called Con Leary, who had kept his voice very low, reduced it to a whisper, showing that in his eyes money warranted even greater discretion than sex. Cosmo strained his ears, something he was used to doing, and managed to get the gist.

'Question of a special fund, a legacy, intended for the poor of the parish. Money gone missing or been misused.'

The man called Derek whistled.

'*Really?* That does surprise me. Seemed a very frugal bloke, Father Pardoe. They call you in?'

'*No*. I tell you, I know no more about this than anyone else. I do pick up the gossip though.'

'And do they think – the gossips – that the two things are connected?'

'Yes. Whether rightly or wrongly you can judge as well as I can. But I would say parish gossip is as often wrong as it's right.'

'True enough.' Derek immediately assumed, though, that it was right. 'Well, you've certainly surprised me. Not at all what I'd have suspected of Father Pardoe. How long has he been at St Catherine's?'

'Oh – coming on ten years.'

'That's a while. He was always regarded with a lot of respect, I'll give him that. More than most of these young priests who kick up the dust and start all sorts of things that nobody wants just to impress the Bishop . . . No, I had a lot of time for Father Pardoe. Before all this blew up.'

Leary and Derek then went on to other things – things that they could talk about in normal voices. Cosmo ordered a trifle, and then had coffee and a refill, wanting them to go first, so that he could get a good look at them. Unfortunately however they went back to the First Class carriages, so they did not pass his table. When he realized this he stood up hurriedly, but all he saw was two grey-suited men, one with a bald patch at the crown of his head, with thin hair combed carefully around it, the other with a good reddish thatch, untinged with grey. If he saw them face to face again he probably wouldn't recognize them. He downed the last of his coffee refill, then turned to find his way back to Standard barred by the lumpish waitress.

'You realize you haven't paid yet . . . sir?'

That hurdle negotiated Cosmo Horrocks went back to his seat, with a small part of his brain still fuming at the catering service, but the larger part full of satisfaction at a trail well started. He now had not just the two original names – Leary and Father Pardoe – but in addition Derek, Julie Norris and Mary all down in his invaluable notebook, as well as St Catherine's. Father Pardoe was the vital one. Cosmo had Catholic contacts whom he could consult about his parish, so he wouldn't have to go through the Leeds Diocesan authorities. Once the parish had been identified, the name Julie Norris would be crucial. He had started by thinking that this was going to be a 'Vicar elopes with cleaning lady' story, but in fact it was even better: vows of chastity besmirched; a randy bimbo who could be portrayed as a cruelly wronged ingenue if necessary; and a financial angle to boot. A story like this could make his year.

Cosmo Horrocks was never happy – he did not have the innocence or optimism that such an uncomplicated emotion demanded. But as he sat back, eyes closed, for the rest of his journey to Leeds, he felt relish, anticipation, tinglings of excitement – all the familiar emotions of a born muckraker.

CHAPTER 2

Old Hand and New Hand

Cosmo Horrocks sat at his desk in the newsroom of the *West Yorkshire Chronicle* meditating mischief. In his hand was the first draft of a story by one of the paper's new recruits. That was merely an hors d'oeuvre: it would be so easy to savage it was hardly worth his while. No cub reporter had ever had a kind word from Horrocks, and this one had committed the additional sin of being a university graduate. Child's play. But simultaneously he was meditating his next move in what had begun to be called in his mind the Priest and the Bimbo story. First identification, then establishment of basic facts, then stirring it. Cosmo's ideal story was one in which the very newspaper coverage became part of the story. He was pretty sure this would be the case with the Priest and the Bimbo investigation.

Terry Beale, twenty-two and looking nineteen, left his nook in the darkest and least salubrious part of the newsroom and came over towards Cosmo's desk for his verdict on his story with no expectation or anticipation on his face. Terry was bright, ambitious, and he knew his man: Cosmo boosted his own ego by being contemptuous of everyone around him.

'This heading,' said Cosmo by way of opening the skirmish, tapping Terry's print-out with a long, bony finger: 'REPORT SLAMS FAILING SCHOOL'.

'Not very vivid,' said Terry. 'But accurate.'

'They're "sink schools", especially in headlines. And when a school is in question they don't slam, they "cane".'

'I looked up earlier reports on that school. We used "cane" then.'

Cosmo sighed theatrically.

11

'Of course we did, you ape. Product recognition. The reader knows what sort of a story it's going to be even before he starts to read it.'

'Teachers haven't caned pupils for years.'

'What's that got to do with it? People recognize the word, and it gives them a bit of a frisson. You use "cane", or if you want to vary it a bit, "thrash" . . . I don't know. The greenhorns I get landed with . . . So what's the headline going to be?'

'"REPORT CANES SINK SCHOOL"?'

'You can't cane a school, you dolt! It will be "REPORT CANES SINK SCHOOL HEAD".'

'It didn't. She only took over three months ago, and it said she'd done a good job in a limited time.'

'Oh, for God's sake! What's a headline aiming to do?'

'Get people reading the story, I suppose.'

'Exactly. Accuracy's got nothing to do with it.'

Then he started in on the piece, line by line, image by image, word by word. At the end there was practically nothing left of Terry's original piece that hadn't been subjected to Cosmo's withering scorn. But Terry was not a pushover. He kept his cheerfulness and his humour remarkably well, though his was not a face formed for humour: it was pleasant looking, but naturally thoughtful and withdrawn. Any jokiness was specially assumed for Horrocks's benefit, and was undented even when he was sent away with a flea in his ear.

'You Southerners think you own the bloody world,' yelled Cosmo at his departing back.

'Birmingham,' said Terry, not bothering to turn around. Cosmo's geography was as rotten as everything else about him, he thought.

But as he sat down there came over him a depressing sense that when he had gone through his story and done everything Cosmo had said he should, it would make a much better *West Yorkshire Chronicle* report than his own original piece. Less accurate, less responsible, less balanced, but horribly punchy. And it would have nothing in it of him at all. And this led to a very familiar path of meditation.

What was he doing here? Did he want to be taught to sink to Cosmo's level? Was journalism of this kind anything but literary prostitution? He cast in the man's direction a look that was full of contempt and disgust, yet tinged with something else too: disillusion, disappointment, a sense of wasted hope.

The look was received by Cosmo from under his snake-like hooded lids. His guts gave a silent chuckle. The lad was regretting he'd ever thought of journalism as a career. That was what he liked doing: knocking the stuffing out of them while they were still on the first rung of the ladder. He loved seeing on their faces the bewildered look of a mistreated puppy.

Mrs Knowsley had made a decision. It showed in the force of her knock on the door of the upstairs bedroom. When she opened it Father Pardoe was already up and on his way to the little table on which she served his meals. His face showed surprise that she was not carrying a tray.

'Father, please don't get me wrong, but I'd like you to eat downstairs with me today. Just for this once, if it doesn't suit. We needn't talk about anything you don't want to talk about. But we hardly know each other, and we've been living in the same house for three weeks and more. Now, will you come down to the dining room and we'll eat together like Christians?'

Father Pardoe hesitated. It was not the tone of voice in which he was accustomed to being addressed. But the sort of rebuke that he might once have used to reprove it was no longer in him. He turned back to the door.

'Yes. Yes, I'd like that for once. Thank you very much, Mrs Knowsley.'

And he followed her downstairs like an obedient school-boy.

The dining room was warm from a gas fire, and from the midday sun that streamed in the window. The table had been set for two, with a white napkin beside each plate. As Mrs Knowsley bustled back and forth to the kitchen, finally returning carrying a steak-and-kidney pie, which

13

she set down beside the three tureens of vegetables, Father Pardoe had an agreeable sense of being back in time ten or fifteen years, to the era when priests usually had live-in housekeepers – widowed ladies, as often as not, who treated their employers as if they were incapable of doing the simplest household job. The dailies who had taken their place took a very much more robust view of the priesthood. Progress, of course . . . But still, the housekeepers had got a great deal of pleasure out of mothering grown men.

Mrs Knowsley sat opposite him, and such was the warmth of her personality and concern for him that within five minutes of starting in on the pie and the roast potatoes Father Pardoe found himself telling her about his family background in the Irish Protestant Ascendency.

'Though they weren't particularly ascendent, you know. Not big landowners or anything grand like that. Lawyers, solicitors, doctors – professional people. Then my grand-mother converted to Catholicism – that was a big step, particularly as it was not long after the Troubles. A very strong-minded woman she was, though I only remember her in her last years. The younger children converted with her, and then the elder ones did the same, one by one. She had six – a large family for a Protestant one. Only my grandfather stood out, but he was very good-humoured about it. The story is my grandmother introduced a priest to his deathbed, but I don't know how true that is. So I was brought up a Catholic, though it may be that most of the Irish regarded me and people like me as neither fish nor fowl.'

The ice was broken. And so, momentarily, was the despair. He went on to tell her about his training at Maynooth, his first parish in Ireland, the almost inevitable transition to mainland Britain, first on the west coast of Scotland, eventually to Yorkshire. He had a second helping of pie, told her about some of his work in the parish: the rebuilding of the church hall, the formation of the Youth Club and the young mothers' circle, the strengthening of links with other churches. Mrs Knowsley was collecting up plates when he said:

'And then this happened.'

Madge Knowsley paused in her piling up crockery.

14

'I said you didn't have to talk about anything you didn't want to talk about,' she said, taking the pile into the kitchen and coming back with fruit salads in little glass bowls.

Christopher Pardoe began eating, his mind elsewhere. His training and experience told him to do nothing on impulse. Hitherto he had relied heavily on his judgement of people, but that had been shaken. However in the end it was not the feeling that the ice had been broken, not the warmth or the good food or the sheer relief of having someone to talk to that decided him. It was his judgement of Madge Knowsley as a person – Madge, who sat opposite him, not waiting, not hoping, but eating quietly, and there if he needed her.

He put down his spoon and told her the whole story.

The newsroom of the *West Yorkshire Chronicle* was in the throes of its mid-morning frenzy, with stories for its late editions being hastily cobbled together and occasionally checked. In the middle of the scurrying hither and thither, Cosmo Horrocks's desk represented an oasis of calm. The story Cosmo was working on demanded consideration, even meditation. It was not for a day but for a week, a month – a long and satisfying time-span in his world.

He had been thinking which of his Catholic acquaintances he should approach, and had come up with Brian Marris – a one-time reporter on the *Bradford Telegraph and Argus* who had gone into local government and was now someone of power in the Parks and Gardens Department. Not generally a person of any great use to Cosmo, but he was honest, and a Catholic, and he might be tricked into telling him what he wanted to know.

'Cosmo – long time, no see,' came Brian's voice when his secretary put Cosmo through. The lack of bonhomie in the tone suggested he had not felt it as a deprivation.

'That's right, Brian. We must get together some lunchtime.'

'What can I do for you, Cosmo?'

Business-like, that was Brian Marris.

'I'm just putting together a possible series of little pieces, Brian, on Victorian churches in the area.'

'Hmmm. *Chronicle*'s going up-market, isn't it?'

'Just something for the cubs and juniors to work on. If they do a good job it might see the light of day. Now, there's Leeds Parish Church, of course —'

'Just pre-Victorian, that.'

'We may be going up-market, Brian, but we're not becoming pedants. We can say nineteenth-century, anyway. Then there's that High Church place off the York Road that's going to rack and ruin, and the big barn of a place in Birstall. Now, I thought we ought to have a few Methodist or non-conformist places — that Baptist one halfway down the hill in Haworth, for example. And of course some Catholic ones.'

'There's one or two very fine ones.'

'Someone mentioned a St Catherine's.'

'St Catherine's in Shipley? I shouldn't have thought —' For a second or two there was silence at the other end. 'Cosmo, are you up to your old tricks?'

'Old tricks, Brian? I don't know what you mean.'

From now on there were pauses every time it was Marris's turn to speak. He knew that with Horrocks every step had to be thought out in advance if you were not to find yourself treading in dung.

'Well, let's just say I'd be very surprised if any series on Victorian churches ever saw the light of day in your columns,' he said at last.

'I told you it was touch and go if it would. With the juvenile shower we've got at the moment I'd say it was odds against . . . So there is something going on there, is there?'

'I know nothing about it, Cosmo.'

'You know there's something going on, so that's a start. It's very seldom someone knows there's something going on without having some inkling of what it is.'

'Is it, Cosmo? I bow to your experience.'

'I gather Father Pardoe has suddenly taken a rest for spiritual renewal.'

'Has he? That's not unusual.'

'It is when it's a pack of lies and he's really under investigation by the Church.'

'I told you, I know nothing about it.'

16

'Come off it, Brian. You live at Greengates – just down the road. I can tell you've heard something.'

'When I say I know nothing about it, Cosmo, what I mean is I have no intention of talking about it to you.'

Cosmo let out a rich chuckle. That's what Brian thought!

'I rather interpreted it as that. Unfriendly, that's what I call it. You were always in the thick of things, Church-wise, Brian. I should think you even know the name of the bimbo concerned.'

Again there was silence at the other end. But he hadn't rung off.

'Well,' resumed Cosmo, in a reasonable voice, 'let's say it wasn't Monica Lewinsky, and it wasn't Paula Jones. But would I be getting warm if I suggested Julie Norris?'

'Cosmo, if you know so much –'

'I'm guessing she isn't the sort of single mum who'll be in the telephone directory. I'd guess she lives in a grotty flat in a slum estate, full of nappy smells and greasy fish-and-chip paper – would I be right?'

'I'm not involved with the girl, Cosmo.'

'I'm not suggesting you are, Brian. Happily married as they come, aren't you? That little episode with Mandy Miller on the switchboard at the *Telegraph and Argus* is long behind you, isn't it? I shouldn't think your lady wife ever even got suspicious, did she? Lucky man, you are, Brian . . .'

He still hadn't rung off. Cosmo could almost hear the sound of thinking. In the end the reply he wanted came:

'They say she lives on the Kingsmill estate . . . God, you are a bastard, Cosmo. I pity your wife and daughters.'

Cosmo barked with laughter.

'Don't bother, Brian. You can't pity them more than they pity themselves.'

This time the phone at the other end was put down, and violently, but Cosmo's smile as he replaced his own receiver showed that he knew he'd won a famous victory.

Later that day, when the last editions were on the streets, Terry Beale and several of the other juniors on the paper – anyone in fact, under the age of twenty-five – went along to O'Reilly's, the nearby Irish theme pub, which was about as

17

Irish as Cleethorpes, and had a convivial pint, as they often did at the close of their day. Terry, though, stuck to his usual orange juice.

'What was old Cosmo up to today?' Carol Barr asked Terry. They had a common history of suffering at his hands.

'Cosmo? You mean apart from rubbishing my piece?'

'Don't make a big thing of that, Terry. We all know he rubbishes everybody's pieces.'

'True. I'm not claiming most-picked-on victim status.' He thought for a moment, then added: 'But the thing that hurts is that, from his point of view, and from the paper's point of view, he was dead right. What I finally turned out was a better *Chronicle* story.'

'That may be,' said Patrick De'ath. 'But Cosmo and the *Chronicle* are things of the past. Cosmo lives in a world of scoops and "Hold the front page". He's a bit pathetic, a survival.'

'Oh, and has journalism got beyond all that?' asked Terry bitterly. 'Gone onward and upward to better things? It's passed me by if it has. All I can see is British newspapers going further and further down into the sewers.'

'You're wrong, Terry,' said Patrick, draining his Guinness. 'The future isn't with the tabloids – that's why they're increasingly desperate and hysterical. The future is with the broadsheets. That's what people are turning to.'

'And could anyone say *The Times* and the *Guardian* are what they once were?'

'Cut the philosophical stuff,' said Carol. 'I asked what Cosmo was up to after he'd savaged your piece.'

'How would I know?' Terry asked.

'Don't come the innocent with me, Terry. I saw you passing backwards and forwards behind Cosmo's chair without good reason. It wasn't the attractions of his person took you there.'

Terry thought, then grinned.

'I just like to know what the old bastard is up to.'

'And what was he up to?'

'A scoop of the most traditional kind, you won't be surprised to learn. Some vicar or priest and a bimbo.'

'The vicar of Stiffkey lives on,' commented Patrick.

18

'The vicar of *where*?' Terry asked.

'Stiffkey. Pronounced Stookey, spelt Stiff-key. Which is rather appropriate. His missionary zeal took him mostly among prostitutes, and he died in the lions' cage of a travelling circus.'

'I don't believe it!'

'Gospel truth. They used him as their communion wafer. You can imagine what a field day the papers at the time had with *that* story.'

'When was this?'

'Back in the 'thirties.'

'And still it goes on. Vicars are still fair game.'

'I'm not sure that's so unfair,' said Carol Barr. 'Anyone who sets themselves up as rather better than anyone else is asking for it if they show that in fact they're pretty much the same. There's the same interest in a bent copper.'

'Only bent coppers are always found Not Guilty by juries, unless they mistreat animals,' said Patrick De'ath. 'Vicars are judged Guilty by readers without a hearing.'

'So where is this vicar, then?' asked Carol, turning to Terry. 'Local, presumably?'

'Presumably. Actually, I think it may have been a priest. I heard the words "Father" something or other. In other words, Cosmo is cobbling up the sort of traditional story that is thoroughly cringe-making and sells loads of copies.'

'That's what we're all meant to do,' said Carol.

'Don't defend the slimy little git,' said Terry, his voice becoming louder. 'What he does – the sort of story he homes in on – is beyond the pale. He's what journalism has sunk to. It's what we all will sink to if we don't go after something better.'

If his friends were puzzled at the passion in his voice, they kept quiet about it. Patrick collected up the glasses for a second round. And Carol Barr, meditatively chewing a bap that seemed to consist entirely of iceberg lettuce, wondered whether it was Cosmo, or Cosmo's story, or Terry's growing doubts about a career in journalism that had aroused something close to passion in the normally self-contained young man.

CHAPTER 3

Sink Estate

Julie Norris gazed out of the window of her ground-floor flat in the council house on the Kingsmill estate on the outskirts of Shipley, the part nobody visited or went through. Immediately opposite was a patch of waste ground. The tenants of one half of the semi-detached that used to be there had misguidedly bought their house when the council offered it to them at a knockdown price. When one died and the other was taken into a nursing home the property proved impossible to sell. Before the place had been on the market a month the local youth had moved in, smashing first windows, then doors. In no time the place was a total wreck. Before long the house became such a local eyesore and scandal that the tenants next door had to be moved elsewhere, and the shell of the two homes eventually demolished. Now the space where they had been was the dumping ground for ragged armchairs and sofas, old televisions, bags of household and garden rubbish, and all the detritus of modern living.

Gary, playing on the floor in his usual boisterous manner, caught his thumb in the door and started to howl. After a minute or two of hoping he would stop of his own accord, Julie turned, crouched down, and took him in her arms.

'Bye, baby bunting,' she crooned, remembering the old rhyme, 'Daddy's gone a'hunting.'

But she didn't know what Daddy had gone a-doing, nor, with absolute precision, who Daddy was.

That was one thing she had vowed would never happen again. That was a period in her life she felt very ashamed of. She did know exactly who was responsible for the current bulge in her belly, though she had little recent information

20

about him. She had not seen him since the day she had told him her news.

God, she was a lousy picker!

When Gary had quietened down she put him back on the floor and went around dispiritedly picking up this and that from the chaos that was her living room. It was not a room that repaid tidy habits. Whatever you did, it never looked anything but a dump. When she had collected up a pile of things she was in a quandary: she could put the bits of underwear and toddler's clothing in with the dirty washing, but all the other things defeated her, and she put them in a pile on the floor in the corner of the kitchen, where Gary would before long retrieve and redistribute them. A feeling washed over her, as it frequently did, that she had got herself into a situation that she was quite incapable of solving or making less depressing.

There had been better days until recently. Father Pardoe – Christopher – had made a difference, made her look at herself in a better, a more hopeful light. His kindness, his concern, his involvement with herself, had been so unexpected but, once she understood, so welcome, that it had been like a little beacon of light. Now he was – somehow – no longer there, not in Shipley at all so she had heard. She was aware that rumours were going round among the Catholic faithful, and though very few of the faithful lived on the Kingsmill estate she was aware that rumours, less hushed in the telling, were going around there too. His visits had been observed by the neighbours. Of course they had been observed by the neighbours. Everything was observed by the neighbours. Especially by that cow at the back.

The fact that Christopher was in trouble because of her was painful to Julie, whose conscience took unexpected forms but was definitely operative. People who were kind to her – consistently kind, not kind to get what they wanted from her – aroused feelings of intense gratitude. Her parents had thrown her out at seventeen, and had been looking for an excuse to do it since she was fifteen. Just like me, she thought bitterly, but looking tenderly at Gary, to give them one.

She jumped when the doorbell rang. She very nearly didn't

answer it. What was the point? Any friends she had she met at usual places of resort – clinic, supermarket, laundromat. For the most part she did not call on them and they did not call on her. Why leave your dump to go to another person's dump? The ring at the door could only be a crank religionist or the more hopeless sort of door-to-door salesman. But when, after a second ring, she went to answer it, it turned out to be neither.

'Are you Julie Norris?'

'Yes.'

'I'm Cosmo Horrocks. You may have seen the name in the local papers. I'm Reporter-in-Chief on the *West Yorkshire Chronicle*. I wonder if you'd like to comment on the rumours.'

She looked at him in bewilderment. The man standing eyeballing her was of middle height, wiry of frame, wearing what she recognized from experience as cheap clothes in need of a dry clean. His hair was meagre, plastered across his pate, and his face was set in what was intended to be an expression of sympathetic interest, though even the inexperienced Julie could discern underneath the suppressed sneer. What sort of man was this? A more sophisticated person than Julie might have decided that he didn't look like a Chief-anything-at-all, but she was hardly aware what a reporter was. She took no newspaper, and her only contact with the press came when she cast her eye over the tabloid headlines in the newspaper racks at the supermarket.

'I don't know what you mean.'

She was a poor liar, at least in situations she was unused to. She had certainly pulled the wool over the eyes of benefits claims officials in her time, but this was unexplored territory.

'Oh, you know all right,' said Cosmo, the sneer winning out easily over the sympathetic expression. 'I can see it in your face. I'll spell it out, shall I? I mean the rumours about you and Father Pardoe of St Catherine's.'

The confirmation of her worst fears pulled Julie up short. She was suddenly conscious that this horrible little man's foot was in the door. She might have thought Cosmo's acting out of the cliché behaviour of newspapermen was funny, if she had known the cliché. Knowing nothing about newspapermen she felt threatened. But she knew she had to be cautious, for Christopher's sake, and she dredged up some of the verbiage from her childhood. Her home had been at least nominally Catholic.

'Father Pardoe is my priest. He knows I've been going through a difficult time with the baby and . . . and all that, and he's been helping me and giving advice.'

'Oh yes? Spiritual advice?' asked Cosmo with a leer.

'Yes. Spiritual advice, and practical advice too, if I needed it.'

'And what have you been giving him?'

'I beg your pardon?'

'You heard. Have you been giving him something in exchange, like the rumours say?' He looked at her bulge. 'I see there's another on the way.'

Julie's reaction was pure instinct. The flat of her palm flashed out at him, pushing hard on his chest so he fell backwards off the step and on to the pathway. Mid-fall her heel went into his groin. She slammed the door shut.

'I could sue you for assault!' came a shout from outside. But it didn't sound like a threat, more like crowing triumph. 'I only want to give you a chance to put your side of things, you know. I'm doing you a favour.'

Julie knew enough about life to see through this. She knew that people never knocked at your door to do you a favour. She went back into the living room, and just to have clean human contact again she scooped Gary up from the floor and jogged him up and down in the crook of her arm. In a trice he was gurgling with laughter and putting his little fingers into her face. She was just regaining her cool when a reflection in the glass door into her kitchen sent her spinning round to the window.

The foul-looking man was gazing through at her and the baby, and by the look of him noting every detail of her still messy living room: the nappy on the chair, the toys left anywhere, the dirty towel draped over the back of an armchair. And when he saw he was observed he had the cheek to raise his hand in greeting and smile his knowing, triumphal smile. Julie felt like vomiting.

If she had had curtains she would have drawn them, but she only had them in the bedroom. As it was, all she could do was to take Gary through into the poky hallway, shut the door on the prying face, then sit down with her son on the uncarpeted floor and have a good cry.

By now Father Pardoe and Mrs Knowsley were friends. It made all the difference in the world for him, to have someone on whom any- and everything could be unburdened. Of course he had friends in the parish. Had had. No one, apparently, had sent letters to the Presbytery for forwarding to him. In any case, that was Shipley, this was Pudsey. He now had in his exile, his incarceration, someone who was in his confidence, on his side.

It was a friendship without complications or tensions. Mrs Knowsley almost never asked him anything, unless it was about the trivialities of day-to-day living, or unless it followed on from something he had told her. This was not, Pardoe knew, because she was incurious, but because she was tactful. Anything she learnt had to be told her voluntarily.

Pardoe still took some of his meals alone in his room, but he came down quite often for the midday meal, which was the main one of the day. After it, as a rule, he took an afternoon constitutional, which was a new departure. He never saw anyone whom he knew, and the fresh air was good. His prison was at least becoming an open one. He was losing his instinct to hide from the world.

It was one day at the end of midday dinner that Father Pardoe, pushing away a plate that had contained apple crumble, said:

'I think I'll take a little walk. I often find it gets my thoughts in order.'

'I'm sure it does.'

'Though it's difficult getting one's thoughts in order when you have no idea what's happening in the one thing that you want to think about.'

Mrs Knowsley paused in her piling up of plates.

'Hasn't the Bishop kept you informed about what's being done?'

'I haven't had a word.' He tried, out of habit, to put the best gloss on his superior's actions, or lack of them. 'He's informed me that the matter is being investigated by a committee. I suppose he thinks that anything he writes before they've reported back may arouse false hopes or fears . . . But it's like living in a vacuum.'

Mrs Knowsley said nothing, and took the plates into the kitchen. She was often out when the post came – at the shops, or visiting her daughter half a mile away. But when she did take up the post to her lodger she had noticed that any letters he got generally came from Ireland.

On an impulse she went out to him in the hall, where he was pulling on a mac, having looked out at the uncertain early May skies.

'Wouldn't it be an idea –' she said tentatively, 'tell me if I'm talking out of turn – to write to the Bishop giving an account of your dealings with this –'

'Julie. Julie Norris.'

'Right. With this Julie Norris from beginning to end. Just like you told me.'

'I've assured him all our dealings were entirely innocent. That wasn't enough for him.'

'That's not quite the same thing as saying exactly what they were, and how they came about.'

She was holding her ground, being surprisingly firm. And her view made sense, as he knew from his dealings with his parishioners.

'No . . .' He was still dubious. 'The question is: will it do any good?'

'There's another question too: will it do *you* any good? I think it might make you feel better. Even if you never send it, it will get your thoughts in order, and you will have words and arguments in your mind that you may want to use when you go before this committee.'

Father Pardoe nodded, thanked her for her interest, and went out into the spring drizzle.

He was a man for whom writing had always been a pleasure, or at least a satisfaction: sermons, letters of sympathy, letters expounding a view or advocating a course of action. As he walked forms of words came to his mind, ways of putting some point about his relationship with Julie, or describing some action of his that might be misinterpreted. He had to tell himself that if he did write a full account simplicity would be much the best literary approach to adopt.

That evening he turned off his little television after the *Channel Four News*, poured himself a modest finger of Irish, and took up his pen.

'My Lord,' he began.

I have decided to write for you a full account of all my dealings with Julie Norris and her family. Of course it will be for you to decide whether to pass it on to those people investigating my actions. I believe that if you do they will find my account entirely consistent with what they have discovered from any other reliable persons about the relationship.

I have been conscious of Julie as a nice, bright child since I first came to St Catherine's, but for many years I hardly did more than swap greetings or trivialities with her. I became more immediately involved two years ago, when I heard to my distress that she was pregnant, and that her family were threatening to throw her out of the family home.

I should say that I had never found her parents particularly congenial. They were at best occasional attenders at St Catherine's, so my acquaintance was little more than superficial. I was not surprised by their actions, but I did think they were deplorable. Julie was only seventeen, and such a response to her situation could well have made her contemplate abortion. I visited them in their home (which Julie had already left) and remonstrated with them, but they were adamant not only about the expulsion, but insisting they would have nothing further to do with their daughter. I soon heard that Julie had moved in with the family of the child's father, though this turned out to be misleading: this was a temporary measure, while she waited for the Council to provide her with emergency accommodation. In any case, I gathered that the boy (he was scarcely more) disputed his paternity.

I next saw Julie when she was wheeling Gary, her baby son, in an old pram through Shipley market . . .

Christopher Pardoe paused. A picture of Julie and all the circumstances of their meeting flooded his mind. She had seemed to him so incredibly lovely, and the memory of her appealing fragility still stopped his breath. He could say nothing of this to the Bishop, of course: he would stick doggedly to fact. But wasn't this reaction the most vital fact of all?

The next day he said to Mrs Knowsley, à propos of nothing:

'I'm not entirely ignorant about sexual matters, you know. The authorities at Maynooth winked at what went on when the seminarians went away for the weekend. They knew they got up to pretty much the same sort of thing as other young men who were let off the leash for a day or two.'

'Now you are shocking me,' said Mrs Knowsley, but quite calmly.

'I expect they thought it enabled them to sow their wild oats early, and get rid of the tensions,' said Pardoe.

But it didn't get rid of them. It didn't.

The Learys were a family that still had breakfast. Not something grabbed on the wing or munched from a wrapper, but a sit-down meal, albeit often a hurried one. The Learys rather prided themselves on 'still' doing things that other people no longer did, or Conal Leary prided himself on it, at any rate. The children's expressions around the table did not suggest one hundred per cent agreement. And bacon and eggs only featured at these meals at weekends when the children – Mark and Donna – did not have anything pressing on. Otherwise they ate whatever was fashionably deemed healthy by their generation. Their parents too had cut back to cornflakes or porridge, followed by toast and marmalade. Conal had been quite a sportsman in his time, and still played mean games of golf and squash. He believed in keeping in shape.

27

'What are you two doing today?' Conal asked his children – the sort of traditional father's question nowadays heard more in soaps than in real life. Donna shrugged, but Mark answered.

'After school I've got nets practice.' The cricket season had just started, and Mark had been waiting for it all year, impatient to consolidate his burgeoning prowess. He was a first-rate sprinter and hurdler too, but the cricket season was the highlight of his year.

'You, Donna?'

She shrugged again. It was an expression of thirteen-year-old ennui that she often had recourse to.

'Dunno. Hang around with me mates after school, I suppose.'

'It's Youth Club night at St Catherine's, isn't it? Will you be going along?'

'Shouldn't think so. It's hopeless now Father Pardoe's gone.'

'He's not gone, dear,' said Mary Leary. 'He's just away for a period of spiritual refreshment.'

A suppressed snigger greeted that, and then Donna said:

'Anyway, his stand-in's hopeless. A real wally. Something from another planet. There won't be anyone there.'

'Will you be going, Mark?'

Mark had spooned into his mouth the last helping of a calorie-rich cereal, and was standing up.

'No way. I've got a history essay to write.'

Mark was the traditional one in the family. He was going to do well at sport, well in exams, well at university. That was the male role, expected of him as the next generation in a traditional family. Whether Donna was going to be satisfied with the traditional female role was another matter. She was just beginning to look at how the family was run, how her father clung obstinately to the patriarchal role, how Mark was in training to carry it on – very conscious it was to his advantage – and she was just starting to say, if only to herself, 'No way' and 'That is not for me'.

When Conal Leary came down ten minutes later in dark grey suit and claret-coloured tie, ready to drive off to the electrical goods firm he had inherited and expanded, his wife was washing up. He kissed her on the neck, murmured 'Bye, Mary,' but then lingered.

'Seems like the children know all about Father Pardoe,' he said.

'Then they know a great deal more than I do,' said Mary firmly. 'Because I know practically nothing.'

'I mean that he's suspected and under investigation.'

Mary's mouth set firm.

'The children liked Father Pardoe, and thought he did a good job,' she said. 'I hope they keep an open mind when they hear talk.'

'Oh, we're all keeping an open mind. Still, there's –'

Mary's voice became higher and sharper.

'If you're about to say, "There's no smoke without fire," then save your breath, Con, because there frequently is. Rumours start in the silliest ways – because people have got the wrong end of the stick, or misheard something, or are just spreading malicious lies. As far as I'm concerned Father Pardoe is an honourable man and a good priest, and I'll be very surprised if I have to revise that opinion.'

'Derek says –'

'I don't give tuppence for what Derek Jessel says!'

'Well,' said Conal, turning away, 'if Pardoe wants a defending counsel in front of the investigating committee he'll know where to come.'

'I'm rather afraid he won't be given the chance of having one,' said Mary Leary sadly.

Conal went off to the office feeling vaguely dissatisfied. Ten years ago Mary would not have spoken out like that. Then she had acquiesced in all his decisions, including his use of birth-control methods after the difficult birth of Donna. Often she must have had her doubts, but she had gone along with whatever he decided and had kept her own feelings to herself. By and large she still did, but there came a point when she – the word 'rebelled' came to his mind, but he substituted the phrase 'stood her ground'. If she disagreed in certain vital areas she made it plain. And Conal didn't like it.

Mary, starting to go the rounds of the house doing the usual household tasks, wondered if her husband had noticed how she had tensed up when he kissed her neck. It wasn't often thus, but she knew the topic of Father Pardoe was going to come up, and it made her blood boil how Con had appointed himself judge and jury in that matter, and now to boot he had been spreading the word about what he was accused of among his buddy-pals in the parish. The hypocrisy of it was glaring. He had convinced her often enough in the past that – as far as he, Conal, was concerned – there *was* smoke without fire. That the ladies whose names were mentioned in tandem with his meant nothing to him, and that it was all ugly rumour-mongering. If Con did not make the connection with Father Pardoe's case, then he was stupider than she had taken him for.

Of course the connection was only a partial one, because she had never in her heart of hearts believed in Conal's innocence.

CHAPTER 4

Happy Families

When Cosmo Horrocks had got all he thought he journalistically could out of Julie Norris and out of the contemplation of her grotty flat, he legged it as fast as he could out of the Kingsmill estate. Once beyond its boundaries, however, he cast his eye round for the nearest pub, conscious that, since there were seldom any pubs on council estates, the residents who liked a tipple would make for the closest watering hole outside. There it was – the Lord Grey. And there, heading towards it, was one of the women he had asked about Julie's whereabouts on the estate. He nipped across the road, pushed open the door that led straight into a dismal and dirty public bar, and went over and stood beside the woman.

'I found Julie Norris,' he said. She turned and contemplated him with a dyspeptic eye.

'Did you now?'

'Care for a drink?'

She considered – a painful process.

'Not a rent collector or a debt collector are you?'

'No I'm not. Is that why you wouldn't tell me where she lived?'

''Course it was. Come on, you can buy me a sweet sherry.'

'Pint of Webster's, a sweet sherry and a tuna sandwich please. No, I'm not here to do her any harm. I thought she was a lovely girl. I'm here to do her a favour.'

The woman nodded unsuspectingly.

'Well, I'm glad to hear it, because she could do wi' one. Such a nice girl – pretty too, if she'd take the trouble.'

'She would be – a real stunner,' said Cosmo, with all the enthusiasm of a child whose greatest pleasure was tearing the wings off a particularly beautiful butterfly. She took his words at their face value, just glad to have someone to talk to.

'Mind you, I blame the parents. You can't justify throwing out a girl of that age, baby or no baby. Typical, though.'

'You know them?'

'Oh, I know them, or knew them. Used to live on the estate, didn't they?'

She had the odd North Country habit of imparting information in question form.

'*Really?* I didn't know that.'

'The posh end, o' course.'

'Posh end?'

'That was when there was a posh end – over towards the Cottingley Road. Nowadays it's all pretty much of a muchness. The Cape of No Hope they call us. Too bloody right. We never had much, and now we've got none.'

'How long ago was it when they lived here?'

'Oh, matter of about twenty years I suppose. They moved here when she was pregnant wi' Julie. I mind seeing her as a babby screaming her heart out in her pram in the front garden. O' course they moved out like a flash soon as they could. Anyone would. Said they wouldn't want a child o' theirs growing up on the Kingsmill. Snobby pair. Still, you could see their point, even then. It's just that they're so –'

Cosmo didn't supply her with a word. He intended to make his own judgement of Julie's parents, and he didn't expect it to be any more favourable than this woman's.

'So they moved away, did they?'

'Oh yes. He'd got promotion, managing a menswear shop, so they took out a mortgage on a house in Beckham Road. They'd have got it for seven or eight thousand then. Be worth six or seven times that now. But then – some people have all the luck, don't they. What I always say is –'

But Cosmo, who had been shifting from leg to leg for some time, now made his thanks and beat a retreat to a table by the window. He didn't enjoy talking to people, only milking them.

'Here, what did you say you did?' called out the woman.

Cosmo settled into a chair with his back to her and said nothing. Once settled down he sipped his pint and took a bite from his sandwich, then took from his pocket a list of the Shipley Norrises, which he had photocopied from the telephone directory, feeling pretty sure that Julie would not have changed her name either from choice or by marriage. His nicotine-stained finger went down the short list. There it was: S. Norris, 23 Beckham Road.

'Got you!' he thought.

The triumphal reaction was not because of any particular animus against the Norrises, still less from disapproval of their action in casting off their daughter. He would do the same to his daughter in the same circumstances, or with even less provocation. His exultation was the result of a feeling that the Norrises were going to fit very nicely into what he in his own mind called (though no one else did) a 'Horrocks story'. They somehow had the feel of stupid people who could be magnified into monsters.

When his sandwich was eaten and his pint down to its last quarter, he took out his Bradford *A to Z* and searched for Beckham Road. There it was: maybe ten minutes' walk away. He downed the dregs of his beer, wrapped his mac around him, and set off.

Beckham Road was without doubt several notches above Kingsmill Rise, but it was otherwise an unremarkable stretch of pre-war and post-war detached and semi-detached houses. Number 23 was detached, and decorated with the usual nailed-on bits of timber. Half of the front garden was a neat square of rose bushes, with the other half a gravelled patch in front of the garage. Cosmo took it all in with his jaundiced camera-eye, labelled it with the word 'unremarkable', then rang the doorbell.

The woman who opened the door had thick, round glasses, behind which her eyes glistened dully. Her mouth was so narrow it seemed inadequate to take a good bite with, and her nose was red and pointed. Her expression seemed to say that she had had experience of the world and its ways, and they were not her ways, thank God.

'Yes?'

'Mrs Norris? You won't know me, but I'm Cosmo Horrocks of the *West Yorkshire Chronicle*.'

'We don't want to take out a subscription.'

'You misunderstand me. I'm a reporter.'

'We wouldn't want to talk to –'

'It's about your daughter Julie.'

The door, which had been in the process of shutting, stopped. She peered at him, her expression more concentratedly vinegarish.

'What about her?'

'I really think you ought to talk to me, Mrs Norris. Your daughter is in trouble.'

'That's nothing new.'

'Yes, I've seen the . . . little one. But by trouble I mean she's likely to be the subject of a story in my newspaper, and, so as not to be unfair in any way, I'd like your side to be heard too.'

It was one of the oldest ploys in the book, and it worked. She was silent for a second in outrage.

'My side. What's it to do with me?'

'You and your husband, really,' said Cosmo, smiling his piranha smile. 'You were agreed about throwing her out of the family home, weren't you? A lot of people are commenting on that. They think that's where the trouble started. They're saying you were hardly supportive when your daughter needed you most.'

Mrs Norris was clearly in waters deeper than she could swim in, and she knew it. After much thought she said:

'I'd better ring my husband.'

'Can I come in? I'm sure he'll want to talk to me and put your side.'

The ploy worked again, and after a pause she nodded. He walked down the hall to the sitting-room door, which she held open. He went just inside the room and stopped when he heard the phone being dialled. Her voice came satisfactorily clear.

'Says it's about our Julie. Says she's in trouble . . . That's what he said, but he says we're being blamed . . . Can't you come back? Just to find out what it's all about?'

Her pleas seemed to go home, because when she had put the phone down she poked her head round the door, said, 'He'll be here in five minutes,' then shut the door on him and went back to the kitchen. Cosmo sent his camera-eyes once again around his new environment, his temporary prison. The room was horribly clean and tidy, and it had a dank, cheerless air. There were one or two signs that it was used, but it seemed to have been disinfected after use like an operating theatre. On the sideboard was a photograph: a family group of three, but the youngster was a boy. Five minutes to the dot later, a Ford Fiesta drove up outside and a squat, chunky, peppery man marched down the drive, into the house, and then swung open the sitting-room door.

'Now, what's all this?'

'Ah, Mr Norris. I'm glad you've agreed to talk to me.'

'I've agreed to nothing,' the man barked. 'I want to know what this is about.'

'Shall we sit down?'

'Not before you tell us why you're here.'

Mrs Norris had drifted back down the hall to the doorway, a dimly disapproving presence who was now looking at her husband admiringly. They stood together confronting him. Cosmo was unabashed.

'Right you are. Well, I don't know if you've heard that Father Pardoe at St Catherine's is under suspension.'

They shifted a little, looking embarrassed.

'We hadn't, no,' said Mr Norris. 'We're not . . . not very in with the Church these days.'

'Well of course he's your daughter's priest as well –'

That brought a reaction.

'Julie's priest?' barked Norris. 'Don't make me laugh. Any priest ought to run a mile from the likes of her.'

'It does seem as though he would have been wiser if he had.'

That took them aback. They came further into the room, looked at each other, and sat down. Cosmo, smiling like a shark who's had one leg and looks forward to the other, sat down facing them.

'You mean Julie has –?' Mrs Norris ventured.

35

'She's pregnant again,' said Cosmo, who tried not to answer questions. 'Did you know that?'

'We wouldn't,' said her husband. 'We don't keep in touch, do we, Daphne?'

'It doesn't surprise me,' said Daphne Norris.

'I'm not saying it's Father Pardoe's,' said Cosmo. 'But I am saying that the reason he's been suspended is the relationship he's had with your daughter.'

'Well I never,' said Norris. 'I've never heard the like, have you, Daphne?'

'Seducing a priest. She'd stoop to anything, that girl.'

'We don't quite know who did the seducing, do we?' Cosmo pointed out. 'Or if either of them did. Takes two to tango, doesn't it? So all this comes as a complete surprise, does it?'

'If you're any sort of reporter you'll have noticed that,' said Mr Norris, who retained a shadow of his old aggression, apparently part of his personality.

'*Except*,' put in Daphne Norris, 'if a girl gets pregnant at seventeen, you know she's on the slippery slide already and likely to go downhill fast.'

'And if people are going to say we caused it by chucking her out, then I'd say they've got it the wrong way round,' said her husband. 'We chucked her out because we could see it coming.'

'The scandal will kill me,' moaned his wife. 'And what are the other boys going to say to Leonard at school?'

'Leonard?'

'Lennie, our son,' said Mr Norris, all aggression slipping away from him. 'She resented him right from the start, didn't she, Daphne? Saw what a bright, clever little chap he was, and resented it when people commented on it. She was a right obstinate baby, from the time she could walk and talk. Wouldn't give up her room to Lennie when he needed the extra floor space for his train set. He had to make do with the poky one – hardly more than a box. Made my blood boil, didn't it, Daphne? But like I say she could be sullen and stiff-necked, and she really dug her toes in.'

'Until she got pregnant, Simon. And then we'd really *got* her.'

Cosmo turned his attention to Daphne Norris.

'Got her?'

'Got a hold over her,' she said, unembarrassed. 'A lever. Before that she'd stood out against us like a mule.'

'I see,' said Cosmo, though, rarely for him, he wasn't quite sure that he did. 'So when Julie got pregnant –'

'We laid down a few ground rules,' said Simon Norris, 'and when she didn't agree to them, then out she went. So you can say to these people who say we caused her problems that we didn't encourage her to get pregnant, and we didn't make it easy for her to get pregnant. We were as strict with her as you can be these days. And when she told us she was having a child, and when she still stood out against us –'

'Were you encouraging her to have an abortion?'

'We were not. We're Catholic as you know.'

'Not practising Catholic, though,' said Cosmo, making a little note in his book.

'Well no, not practising. And if she'd wanted to have an abortion, we might not have stood in her way. But the point I'm trying to make, if you'd stop interrupting, is that *she* got pregnant, *she* wouldn't play ball with us, so it was *her* doing if she had to leave here. She went to live with her boyfriend's family, which was pretty daft because he denied he was the father. And then she badgered the council, so I've heard, till they gave her a flat on the Kingsmill estate, of all bloody places.'

'We know all about the Kingsmill,' said Daphne. Her husband frowned.

'Well – er – we don't need to go into that. Anyway, there she is, and there it's my bet she'll stay, and it's her fault, especially if she still hasn't got the wit to avoid getting pregnant a second time. And anyone who says it's our fault doesn't know their arse from their elbow, pardon my language, because she dug her own grave and she can bloody well lie in it.'

'By loose behaviour,' put in Daphne primly, in corroboration.

'And I can quote you on that, can I?' asked Cosmo.

'You can,' said Daphne. 'It'll be pretty self-evident to all who see her.' Her ears pricked up when she heard the front door. 'That'll be Lennie.'

Lennie had clearly noticed there was company in the front room, because he stopped outside the door and then swung it open.

'What's he doing here?'

He was dressed in the standard dress for thirteen-year-olds of yellow and black anorak and Mitsu trainers. His black hair was cut spiky and short, and his white face was pitted with acne around the jowls. He had the unendearing swagger of a child who knows he is the boss.

'Oh, nothing, Lennie,' said his mother. 'He's just come about Julie.'

'Julie? That slag?' He turned to Cosmo. 'You're not trying to persuade them to take her back, are you?'

'No, I'm not,' said Cosmo, who would have preferred to kick him in the face.

'Because she's not coming back here and pushing me out of my bedroom. You don't want her back, Mum, do you?'

'No, Lennie darling. There's no question of that. Julie's in some kind of trouble –'

'Well, that's no surprise. But it's not our business. Have you told him that?'

'Yes, we have, Lennie.'

'And you got the message?'

'Yes,' said Cosmo obediently.

'Well, that's all right then.'

And he banged the door shut and went up the stairs two at a time. Mr and Mrs Norris looked at each other, apparently pleased with themselves. They'd done what Lennie wanted. Cosmo was used to the extremes of human oddity and perverseness, and he was beginning to get the idea that Julie had been thrown out of this house so that her kid brother could have a room big enough for his train set. He, schooled in the tabloid gutter, could believe such an absurdity. It was another piece in what was proving to be a very interesting little jigsaw.

*   *   *

38

'Just fetching something I'd forgotten,' shouted Derek Jessel as he came through the front door and scaled the stairs.

The fact that the something he'd forgotten was condoms he did not mention. When he had slipped a packet into his briefcase he dashed down again, but paused at the sitting-room door. Then he poked his red shock of hair through the door and said to his wife:

'Heard something about your Father Pardoe today.'

Janette Jessel sighed. She was eating soup and a roll, as she generally did at lunchtime, and she did not look up.

'He's no more mine than he is yours,' she said, 'but go on: tell me, because you will anyway.'

'A priest is always a woman's rather than a man's person. He's all the women's pet. Anyway, Ben Lucas has been going regularly to this quack in Pudsey, acupuncture or something, and he's seen him twice, walking off his mid-day meal. Apparently that's where he's holed up: Burton Avenue.'

'Well?'

'Odd place for a spiritual retreat.'

Janette Jessel turned away and looked out of her back window in irritation.

'It's pretty generally known there's some kind of enquiry going on. That doesn't mean he's guilty. I'm absolutely sure he's not – and that's based on knowing him a lot better than you do.'

'Oh, I wouldn't quarrel with that. Still, it's pretty funny spreading a lie like that, isn't it? The Church and all that?'

'That sort of thing happens when you're trying to be kind. If you'd been caught fiddling the books you'd be quite happy if they spread the story that you'd been overworking and needed a rest, wouldn't you?'

'No chance of that,' said Derek, a false heartiness in his voice. 'Straight as a die, you know me.' But he thought it was prudent to take himself off before she could reply.

Left alone, Janette put the spoon down beside her half-finished soup and wiped the corners of her eyes. It was the hypocrisy and double-dealing of her husband that she . . . she nearly thought 'hated' but substituted in her mind the word 'despised'. There must be some sort of jealousy of Father Pardoe based on women making a lot of him, fussing over him – above all looking up to him and respecting him. That's what must rankle: the respect. When she thought about Derek's own personal conduct – his lying, his women, the dodginess of his business dealings – then the contrast with Father Pardoe made it even more stunningly clear that he *must* have been wrongfully accused.

She had once been in the house when Derek had thought she was absent, and she had heard him talking on the phone to Conal Leary – his fellow adulterer and bullshit artist, a man absolutely after Derek's own heart. She'd heard Derek talking about one of his women – she couldn't now remember which, and it really didn't matter. After a bit Leary must have mentioned her, because Derek, laughing, had said:

'Janette? What can she do? Anyway, she's got nothing to complain about. She's got a good Catholic marriage.'

The phrase had gone through her like a knife – still did when she thought about it.

CHAPTER 5

The Faithful

Sunday Mass at St Catherine's was drawing to a close. Father Greenspan, standing in for Father Pardoe as he had for the past four weeks, thought it had gone beautifully. He was a slim man in his late twenties, with dark curly hair and plump cheeks, which gave him the look of a cherub. His religion was for him a thing of beauty – of sights and sounds that plucked aesthetic chords, aroused pale earthly intimations of future heavenly experiences beyond our understanding. The church at Shipley – mid-Victorian Gothic at its less inspired – gave few such intimations of itself, but Father Greenspan was conscious that the way he orchestrated and led the worship there was providing his flock with an experience superior to anything they had known under the leadership of Father Pardoe.

For Father Greenspan was ambitious not only for the greater glory of God, but for the advancement of himself. In fact, the two things inevitably went together in his mind: it followed that, for the Lord's praise to be magnificently conducted, he himself must gain advancement to a position of influence. At his age a permanent position at a parish as important as St Catherine's was hardly to be thought of, and yet . . . and yet . . . The shortage of new priests was chronic and endemic. God's ways were beyond scrutiny. And what a good thing it would be for the parish!

He advanced a few steps to give the blessing, like a Victorian prima donna preparing to sing the final rondo.

'Silly bloody pillock!'

Conal Leary, on one of his occasional attendances at church, hissed the words to his wife. Mary Leary hushed him, and suppressed that part of her mind that agreed

41

with him. The disloyal thought had occurred to her earlier in the Mass that Father Greenspan reminded her of a camp hairdresser. She thought it must be Marco at Snip 'n' Set, a few years back. He hadn't lasted long. Not at all suitable for Shipley. She shut her eyes to obliterate the picture of Father Greenspan and to concentrate on the words.

Mass over, the congregation moved towards the main door, the Leary family towards the rear, having sat as usual towards the front in a pew that Con's father had considered his own private property.

'Current laddo's a bit of a ponce,' muttered Con Leary in his wife's ear. She agreed, but gave the tiniest of nods. 'Not a patch on Father Pardoe.'

'No.'

'Currently holed up in Burton Avenue, in Pudsey, so Derek Jessel tells me.'

Mary Leary made no reply, not even a shadow passing over her face. But as they slowly advanced, greeting friends, she thought she heard the name Leary, and then definitely heard the words 'involved with the Norris girl too', whispered, but distinct. This time an expression of pain did briefly come into her eyes, but she put it from her. Probably the sort of silly rumour that was accumulating around Julie Norris's name. And even if it were true, rumours about her husband had reached her so frequently that she had developed a hard carapace to cope with them.

Father Greenspan was quick to leave the church by the back door and mingle with a selected few among the faithful in the churchyard. The young he had given up: he knew he did not go down well with hormone-happy teenagers, and he did not regret it. It was their parents and grandparents who mattered in the parish: they were the people with the clout. And it was the men, ultimately, who mattered most, and he tried hard with them, though he had to admit in his innermost heart that he found things easier with the women, and particularly the older ones.

'He tries hard, poor lamb,' said Janette Jessel to Mary Leary, standing in the nearly warm sunlight. It wasn't necessary to specify who she was talking about. They looked in his direction: he was talking to Conal Leary.

'He tries a bit too hard,' said Mary Leary. 'During Mass I suddenly thought of Marco at Snip 'n' Set. He'll get nowhere with Conal, I'm afraid.'

'He doesn't take to him?'

'Not a bit. Nor the children either.'

Janette shook her head.

'He should be in a small parish at his age. Learning what it's all about. Shipley isn't exactly the deep end, I know, but he's out of his depth.'

'But you can't get the priests these days, can you? There's so few have the vocation.'

'No, it's sad.' Janette took a deep breath and voiced her fears. 'I sometimes think that Father Pardoe may be the last of the old-style priests we have.'

Mary's face twisted into a grimace.

'Please God that isn't so. And please God he comes back to us, and soon.'

Mary's eye was caught by a far corner of the churchyard, where her son Mark was talking to Lennie Norris. Janette's eyes followed hers.

'I didn't see the Norrises at Mass. It'll be the first time in months if they were there.'

'It wouldn't worry me if it was months before we saw them again. Personally I blame them for . . .'

She didn't need to say what she was thinking. Janette took a tougher line.

'I *would* blame them if I thought there was anything in it. But I'm sure there isn't.'

'Of course you're right. It's pure malice. I'm sure that's the conclusion they'll come to.'

'They, whoever they are.'

Their eyes, leaving the boys, lighted on their husbands, now chatting together nearby. But on that subject they never talked, prevented either by their loyalty or their shame. Feeling awkward about their silence they soon separated and went their ways home.

Father Greenspan was talking to Miss Preece-Dembleby,

one of the parish stalwarts. He was impressed by the double-barrelled name, and skimmed over in his mind the fact that it was the sort of improbable double-barrel that Prince Charles seemed to have a penchant for. The word 'lady-like' might have been coined for Miss Preece-Dembleby. She was perhaps not a lady – ladies being thin on the ground in Shipley – but she was very like one, and was generally treated as one.

'A truly lovely service,' she was saying, in her clipped, carefully enunciated tones, 'and beautifully conducted. But of course that goes without saying, doesn't it? Beautiful services don't come about of their own accord, do they?'

Father Greenspan cast his eyes down to survey the soil. 'They have to be led,' he said.

'Of course they do. You make sure everything is fitting and reverent and grateful to the eye.'

'Your appreciation is very valuable to me.'

'And how is the Youth Club coming along?' Miss Preece-Dembleby suddenly asked. 'One wouldn't want Father Pardoe's good work to decay while he is in retreat.'

'Oh, quite nicely, *quite* nicely . . . I must go and have a word with –'

And he hurried away. He was very fond of Miss Preece-Dembleby, but she did have a habit of asking inconvenient questions out of the blue. Older and wiser parishioners could have told him that he had been deceived by her etiolated figure and prissy manner, and had failed to notice the spark of shrewdness in her eyes.

Miss Preece-Dembleby, her mouth and eyes thoughtful, watched him dither as to which of his congregation he had to have a word with, then turned and left the churchyard to take the road home. Her way coincided for two streets with Janette Jessel's, and she soon caught her up.

'He won't do,' she announced, as she came up beside her. As with Mary Leary, Janette knew at once who she was talking about.

'No, he won't,' she said.

'He's simply a lightweight, to put it at its kindest. No earthly good in a parish like this.'

44

'I'm afraid he reminds Mary Leary of Marco at Snip 'n' Set.'

They both laughed.

'I hope you have absolute faith in Father Pardoe being cleared of those wicked slurs?' Miss Preece-Dembleby demanded.

'Absolute!' her companion averred. 'Provided –'

'Yes?'

'Provided they really try to get to the bottom of them. Provided they really want to find out the truth.'

'Why would they not?'

'Because they might just be running scared at the thought of sexual misconduct. After so many nasty cases.'

'But Father Pardoe is a man of *substance*, a man one can trust,' Miss Preece-Dembleby said indignantly. 'They would be going against the whole wisdom of the parish, our knowledge of him over a decade and more, if they simply assumed the worst. But I do understand your feeling that the affair is being mishandled.'

'Why is it taking so long?' Janette demanded. 'And why do we know of no one in the parish who has been questioned?'

'Why indeed?' Miss Preece-Dembleby agreed, nodding vigorously. 'And *who* is looking into the matter, and why all the secrecy? It's pulling the parish apart, you know.'

'It's so . . . so unusual,' said Janette. 'I've never been in a parish where anything like this has happened. Who should one go to?'

Miss Preece-Dembleby thought.

'We have so little scope in our Church for the involvement of the laity. I have a shrewd suspicion that if we tried to make our opinions felt through Father Greenspan, they would get no further, whatever he might say.'

'Yes. It's awful to mistrust a priest, but –'

'But –' agreed Miss Preece-Dembleby. 'That being so, I suppose the only course is to approach the Bishop.'

They both thought about this unusual step.

'A petition might be too radical,' said Janette. 'It would smack of . . . rebellion.'

'Yes, we couldn't have that. The Bishop would be very

angry.' Miss Preece-Dembleby thought. 'Perhaps a letter. With a note at the bottom saying it had been read to so-and-so and so-and-so, and they agreed with its contents.'

'That's a *really* good idea,' said Janette. 'Sort of like a petition but not actually one. You would write it, wouldn't you? I would be hopeless.'

'I could have a try.'

'And we'd need to get some men on the list as well as women. It would look bad otherwise.'

Miss Preece-Dembleby screwed up her mouth in distaste. 'Oh dear – men,' she said.

It was much later in the day, after three drafts and three phone calls to Janette had resulted in a letter she regarded as tolerable, that Miss Preece-Dembleby let her thoughts stray to earlier in the day and to two persons of the male sex. As she had emerged from church she had seen the Norris boy arriving at the churchyard, down the street that led from his home. Later she had seen, in the farther reaches of the churchyard, him and Mark Leary deep in conversation, and she had been puzzled by the sight. Thinking it over, sipping a glass of sherry, she decided there were two things that were somehow not quite right about it: their disparate ages and their disparate tastes.

Cosmo Horrocks had never gone in for 'at home' pieces, and if he had been any sort of celebrity he would never have invited a journalist to bear witness to him in his domestic role. Too risky by half. You never knew what children would say. Half the time they just blurted out the truth. However hard you'd borne down on them, however well you'd kept them under your thumb, somehow they wriggled out from under if there was the stimulus of visitors.

Sunday lunchtime was one of the few times that the Horrocks family functioned as a family. It usually began with Cosmo in unusually good humour. Sometimes he let it end like that too. Predictability was not the name of his game. Still, he engineered a storm often enough for his elder daughter to have given up working to keep the peace. The tension in his wife's mouth and eyes, the sometimes white-knuckled grip she had on plates and tureens, showed that she never took his mood for granted. And if today he was unusually sunny of disposition she knew that must be because he was on to a good story. She had met him first when she was part of such a story, and had married him in the afterglow of his good mood. Sometimes she wondered how she had stood it for twenty-one years. Early on she had been grateful to him, believed he had 'rescued' her. But to rescue someone you have to bring them to something better.

'Very good,' said Cosmo, pushing away his plate of roast beef with all the traditional trimmings. 'As good as Mother made. Except that my mother was a lousy cook, made the worst cup of tea in London, and could even spoil a mug of Nescafé if she put her mind to it. No, I wouldn't compare you to my mother.' He turned to Samantha and Adelaide. 'You'll be judged against your mother's standards when you grow up and have families of your own.'

Adelaide nodded with the solemnity of a twelve-year-old, but Samantha in a neutral tone that did not conceal the scorn in her voice said:

'Women aren't judged by their cookery any more. They've got more things in their lives than that.'

Samantha was of an age when she would, in her words, take no more crap from her father, not even to please her mother, not even for the sake of domestic peace. What can he do to me? she asked herself. You can't spank a seventeen-year-old girl and get away with it. She'd be down to the police station like a shot – having kneed him in the groin first.

'Oh, swipe me!' sneered Cosmo. 'I've been put down by Rodley's Germaine Greer. If women aren't judged by how they do household duties then more's the pity I say. They should have clung on to the things that they can do and not gone hankering after the things they're hopeless at and always will be.' He turned to his wife, his good humour apparently reasserting itself. 'She's been listening to that daft teacher of hers, whatever her name is.'

'We can hardly tell her not to take any notice of her teacher,' said Cora, her face a mask, her hands gripping the plates she was taking out to the dish-washer.

'Can't we?' Cosmo shouted at her back. 'With the sort of mentally subnormal types who go into teaching these days it's the best thing we could do. Most of them are only doing the job because nobody else would employ them.'

'Miss Daltrey is a very good teacher,' said Samantha sulkily. 'You wouldn't know because you never go to parents' evenings. She's the best in the school – everybody says so.'

Cosmo twisted his mouth into a sneer.

'When everybody says something it's got to be wrong. She sounds like Miss Jean Brodie to me: gets the girls thinking they're all God's gift to humanity, and uses her position to fill their minds with poisonous bullshit. That's the most dangerous sort of teacher there is.'

'She doesn't do anything like that,' said Samantha, matching him in contempt. 'She makes us so interested in history that we want to work hard at it and get books out of the library to follow things up. Then we make our own judgements.'

'If she's got you working hard it's a wonder she hasn't had her union on her back. Kids working hard is the last thing they want. It might mean teachers having to take home some marking.'

'So what's the story you've got in the pipeline?' his wife asked, cutting the turnover she had brought in from the kitchen. Cosmo hardly bothered to show that he registered the attempt to change the subject.

'Oh no you don't,' he said. 'You won't get anything out of me about *that*. It's about a person in a position of trust who has abused that trust, with some unsavoury goings-on with a much younger person. Hmm. Sounds familiar that. More I shall not say, except that it'll give the people of West Yorkshire something very juicy to mull over with their Barnsley chops of an evening. And perhaps not just Yorkshiremen. It could be something the nationals will be interested in too.'

Cora Horrocks was just about to say it sounded like something the *Sun* or the *Mirror* would snap up when the telephone rang. Cosmo got up to take it in the hall. It would be for him. It always was. Cora had no circle of her own, and the girls' friends had been put off from phoning them by some choice words from Cosmo when he was home. All the women in the dining room sat listening, looking down at the plates as if saying grace.

'Yes . . . Yes, it is . . . Yes, I am . . . Pardoe, yes . . . Yes, I would be interested.'

Cora Horrocks had registered the name with a blink. She had picked up snippets of information about Shipley since Samantha had started going to school there. Quite a lot of her school-mates were Catholics, and she had had a crush on Mark Leary at one time, before either despair or disillusion had set in. Then Cora realized, at a harrumph from her husband, that his tone was about to change.

'Look – don't you play games with me. There's many have had their fingers broken trying to do that . . . I didn't say I wasn't willing to pay for information, I said I wasn't willing to be played with . . . You're getting right up my nose, do you know that? . . . Suit yourself. I'll be here or at the *Chronicle*'s offices.'

When he had banged the phone down they heard him press four digits: 1471, no doubt, to find the caller's number. If he got one it did not give him satisfaction. He came back into the room fuming.

'B-*loody* hell! I don't know what things are coming to.'

'Who was it?' asked Samantha.

'Never you mind. I don't. I'll get the information whether he comes clean with it or not.' He sat at his place, the remains of the apple turnover staying uneaten. 'If anyone rings me later, call me straight away and keep him talking. If it is a he. They're crafty – they leave you not quite sure.' He lit up a cigarette and puffed smoke at them. Frustrated by the call his mind reverted to an earlier topic, but this time in more sulphurous mode.

'By heck, teachers have got a lot to answer for. They don't teach facts any more, not information, let alone standards of behaviour. Oh no. They just perform for kids, scatter their personalities before them, give them the beautiful example of their own ego-crazed selves. Like that Miss Daltrey of yours,' he added, turning to Samantha.

'I thought we'd get back to her. She doesn't do anything like that. You don't know a thing about her.'

'What's the betting she's a lesbian?' he said, turning to his wife. She intensely disliked his parading his muckraking instincts when his daughters were present.

'Cosmo! Give it a rest. Not in front of the children.'

'That's exactly who it should be in front of,' he snarled. 'They'll be her victims. If it hasn't happened already.' He turned back to his elder daughter. 'Well, has it? Has she made advances? Are you sleeping with her – is that where you go? Or is it nothing more than a grope behind the cycle sheds so far?'

'What's Daddy talking about, Mummy?' asked Adelaide.

'Just a joke, dear.'

'This is no joke. I'll *have* her, if there's anything going on. She'll think twice if she knows a journalist's on to her. So you can tell her that: I'll *have* her.'

'I won't tell her because there's nothing going on,' said his daughter, standing up. 'And I don't know why you're pretending to get so hot under the collar about it. You wouldn't care if I was fucking Mick Jagger – except you'd like that because you'd get a good story out of it.'

Father Pardoe finished the letter to his Bishop after five attempts, all of which he had read to Mrs Knowsley. Madge he called her now, though she was unable to call him anything but Father Pardoe, or just Father. She was not much use when he read her the first attempt, confining herself to assent and enthusiasm and then agreeing to his self-criticisms. But she gained in confidence, and when she heard the later attempts she would, eventually, when she had thought about it, tell him about the passages that she'd had doubts about. Often her points were shrewd.

Eventually they had reached a point where a draft satisfied them both, convinced them that all the necessary points had been covered, and had been presented in the most honest and convincing words. Above all the *tone* had been right. Pardoe had always been careful to get the tone right when addressing different congregations and groups. He thought he should be equally sensitive when addressing his superiors in the Church.

He tapped out the letter on the decrepit old manual typewriter he had brought with him. When Madge looked it over she said it was fine, except that it looked rather dirty, with the holes in the d's, g's, e's and a's all clogged up with dirt. A trip to the stationer's in Leeds in search of a cleaner convinced Pardoe that they regarded electric typewriters as ridiculously passé and manual ones as prehistoric. Mrs Knowsley took the letter for her daughter – sworn to total silence on the subject – to put on her grandson's word processor. So there was someone else who knew. Pardoe took it out with him on his walk next day and popped it into the nearest post-box.

'So *that's* off at last, Madge,' he said to Mrs Knowsley. He saw her hesitate.

'Would you mind very much if I asked you to call me Margaret?' she said, out of the blue.

'Not at all. Why should I?'

She smiled, oddly nervous.

'Madge started at school, but I've always hated the name. My parents were Scottish, and they called me after St Margaret.'

'Wife of Shakespeare's Malcolm. A good choice of name. So – I'll always call you Margaret, Margaret.'

They both laughed. It was a bond between them, making relations not more formal but less. He knew all her friends such as Mrs Cordell called her Madge, and now he knew she didn't like it but wouldn't tell them so. It meant that just by naming her he was doing something special, and something private to them.

On the third day after he had posted his appeal, he collected the post and said: 'Nothing from the Bishop, Margaret. He's obviously not going to be rushed.'

'Do you think,' she began hesitantly, 'that you should – not go and see him –'

'No, I couldn't do that. Not straight after writing.'

'– but put yourself in his way. So he has to say something, or make some gesture.'

Pardoe frowned.

'Oh, I don't know –'

'It's just a suggestion. I saw in the local free sheet that he was going to Greengates for a service blessing the new church hall there, and it occurred to me – well – there's no reason why you shouldn't turn up there, is there? Maybe you'd have gone anyway, if things had been normal, Shipley being so close.'

'I probably would have been there.'

She left the suggestion with him, with her usual tact. When he thought it over, Father Pardoe did see all sorts of reasons not to return to his own patch to encounter the Bishop. He was supposed to be on retreat, and though word must certainly by now be spreading, his return there would cause all the wrong sort of gossip and whispering, which his counterpart in Greengates could well resent as a distraction from the celebrations. But he needed to go to Mass, had done so unobtrusively in Pudsey and elsewhere since he had left Shipley. He could see no reason why he should not attend it next Sunday in Leeds. From his own Bishop. There surely couldn't be any reason against his doing that.

CHAPTER 6

Confrontation

When Julie Norris got the letter from the Bishop's office asking her to give evidence to the committee investigating Father Pardoe – not in those terms, but in terms less calculated to scare her off – her first thought was that this was Trouble, and that Trouble was something she had had more than enough of. Her second thought was that the trouble was Christopher Pardoe's, not her own, and that ignoring the summons would hardly help him. She went back and read the letter again, registering that they were offering her ten pounds to cover her travel expenses to Leeds. A quick calculation told her that this could net her a profit of nearly eight pounds. Julie's life since she first got pregnant had been largely composed of a similar mixture of generous impulses and sordid calculations.

The letter suggested a day and a time, and asked her to phone and arrange an alternative time if that was not convenient. Any day was equally convenient to Julie, and also equally inconvenient, granted the existence of Gary and the bulge in her tummy that she had to think of as a human being lest she be tempted to get rid of it. The day was Thursday of that week. She desperately wanted to think through what she should say – not what the truth was, because that she was quite sure about, but how she should present it to the sort of person likely to be on a Bishop's committee. She also wanted to talk it over with her friends – the girls similarly situated to herself living on the Kingsmill estate. It being Monday she could rely on there being someone to talk to at the laundromat. That was a cycle of activity that had survived in something like its traditional form in the wreckage of working-class habits that had come about in the 'eighties.

The Kingsmill estate had no shops. Council estates never did. If by any chance some were built, they soon declined into takeaways, thence into vacancy and dereliction. The nearest row of shops and services was ten minutes' walk away, north of the estate and to the south of the town centre. In that row could be found the single mothers' lifeline: a corner shop, a newsagent's, a Chinese and a pizza takeaway, a sewing-repair shop cum dry-cleaner's, and the laundromat that called itself the Washetaria.

'Hi Tracy, hi Vicky.'

She dumped Gary down with them and went with her washing to the machine, she as much on autopilot as the machine itself: she washed her big items there – the same things in the same way for the same money every week. When she had stuffed her load in and set it to the right programme she went back and sat with Vicky and Tracy. Vicky had a little girl of one whom she cradled in her arms, Tracy a four-year-old who would play around the floor with Gary until someone complained.

'I had a letter this morning,' she said, launching straight into the matter that was occupying her thoughts. They turned to look at her. A letter was sufficiently unusual in their lives to arouse interest.

'The Social cutting your benefits, I suppose,' said Tracy.

'No. From the office of the Bishop.'

'The *what*?'

'The office of the Catholic Bishop, in Leeds.'

'Didn't know the Catholics had bishops,' said Vicky.

'What's a bishop when he's at home anyway?' asked Tracy.

'He's a high-up in the Church, ignorant,' said Julie.

'Oh! It's about your priest bloke!' said Vicky. 'You said he was in trouble.'

'Yeah, it's him. They want to talk to me about him. And they'll pay me ten quid for my travel expenses to Leeds.'

The other girls chortled.

'They must be barmy,' said Tracy, contemptuous of all open-handedness while accepting it. 'Go for it, girl. It's one-eighty on the train.'

'I know. I'll have to go. Can't pass up the chance. But what'll I say?'

The other two girls' experience of life was if anything even more limited than Julie's. But it gave them set answers to every situation.

'Lie and lie again, like you was in court,' said Tracy.

'I don't mean that. I don't have to. He's innocent.'

The other two just laughed.

'We'll believe you. Thousands wouldn't,' said Vicky.

Julie turned on them, genuinely irritated.

'Nothing happened. I don't go for older blokes anyway. You know who fathered my two.'

'We know what you've told us,' said Tracy. 'Haven't had the pleasure of either of the young men. I haven't met them either.'

This time they all three laughed.

'I go for young blokes. Anyway, even if I had wanted to, he's a priest. Catholic priests don't.'

'What d'yer mean "don't"?'

'They don't have sex.'

'And birds don't fly,' said Vicky. 'And politicians always tell the truth. And them down at the Social just wants us to get everything we're entitled to.'

'They don't. I mean, priests don't. They're celibate. It's part of their oath, like.'

'Well, if all priests were celibate, what's this enquiry about that they're paying you to go and lie your socks off to?'

Julie caught a glint in the eye of one of the older customers at the Washetaria. Friend of that cow Doris Crabtree. She blinked at the other girls, and the subject was changed until, when they had all finished and were on their way home, Tracy said, 'Come in and have a coffee,' and in Tracy's flat, which bore a depressing similarity to her own, they all sat around the kitchen table and looked at Julie.

'So what am I going to say to this enquiry?'

By now the other girls had had their laugh out and treated the question seriously.

'If what you say is right, then you just tell the truth. As they say: "You've nothing to fear."'

That was Vicky, who still had wisps of naivety left.

'But you know what they do in court,' protested Julie. 'They throw questions at you, and tie you up in knots, and make out you've said the opposite of what you meant to say. That's why I don't nick things in shops – I'd rather die than land up in court. It'd be like having my dad going on at me all over again.'

'But this isn't a court, is it?'

'I don't think so,' said Julie, scrabbling in her pocket for the letter. 'They call it a committee – investigating allegations against Father Pardoe of St Catherine's. But you can see it, can't you? A long row of boring old farts just waiting to twist everything I say.'

'I suppose so,' said Vicky, who like all of them was acquiring a distrust of anything that represented authority. 'But if you tell the truth, and the truth is like you say, what can they do?'

'It's not as simple as that,' said Julie, unhappily.

'No, it's not,' said Tracy, who had been up in court several times.

'I mean, what if they say, "Are you fond of him?" The truth would be to say, "Yes," because I am. He's a good bloke, he's taken an interest in me, done me lots of favours, got me things I needed, given me help. Yes, I am fond of him, but not in that way.'

The other girls thought about this.

'If they ask you that,' Tracy said at last, 'you ask them exactly what they mean by "fond". And then if they say something fairly mild, you say, "Yes, I am fond of him like that, but I'm not fond of him romantically or sexually."'

Julie perked up a little.

'That sounds good,' she said. 'I suppose I could say that.'

'And if they do try to twist things you say, just tell them you're not answering any more questions.'

'But what if they say they won't give me the ten pounds?'

'Get it before you go in,' said Tracy.

Terry Beale was beginning to recognize the signs in Cosmo Horrocks – the signs that he was making progress with his

Catholic priest story. There was a something that came into his eyes (newspaper cliché would call it a glint) and his mouth set firmer and his shoulders squared themselves. All those signs were visible when Cosmo received a phone call on Tuesday morning, and, slipping from his desk, Terry found urgent business to do at the coffee machine situated feet away from Cosmo's patch.

'Now you're talking,' he was saying, oozing satisfaction, but not letting it get into his voice. Terry examined the intricate set of buttons for with or without sugar and milk. 'What I said was I wasn't going to be played with, and I'm not . . . Money I'm prepared to pay. That's usual . . . Right, now I'll tell you what *I* want. Takes two to make a bargain . . . Oh yes, you've got the information, but I've got the money.'

Cosmo took from his pocket a packet of small and foul cigars. Smoking was banned in the newsroom. He lit one.

'Now, what I want is the address, street, number, area, written out for me, and I want your name on the back. Don't try any silly-buggery, and don't feed me a false name. I know where you come from, and I tell you your life won't be worth living if you try to play the smart-arse with me . . . Make it a hundred and we've got a deal . . . Right, now where? I want it reasonably private, but not solitary . . . That sounds satisfactory. And when?'

Cosmo was busy writing on the pad in front of him. Now he nodded, tore the leaf out, and put it in his inside pocket.

'Right then. I look forward to completing our transaction.'

He sat there when he had put the phone down, still oozing satisfaction. Terry Beale started back to his desk, then paused. Marcia Moore, Deputy Editor, was marching through the newsroom, from behind Cosmo's back. Anti-smoking fanatic. When she got to Cosmo's back she simply bent over, grabbed the cigar from his mouth, and ground it under her shoe on the floor beside him. Then she continued her march through and out of the room.

She was expecting a few choice epithets to follow her. So was all the newsroom. They were disappointed. Cosmo continued gazing in front of him, his contentment with the

57

universe and its ordering apparently undented. He reminded Terry Beale of a cat purring because its prey is near.

'So what did he do?' asked Miss Daltrey – Cassie to her friends. It was the end of the school day, and she had just finished history with the sixth form, and was walking through the playground with her favourite pupil.

'Nothing much,' said Samantha Horrocks. 'When he came up mid-afternoon to go to his study he just stood in my bedroom doorway, fixing me with his gaze. I think he'd been reading about snakes transfixing rats or something.'

'Hmm. Well, I'm glad it was nothing worse than that.'

'What can he do now I'm seventeen but try to terrify me? It *would* have terrified me two or three years ago. Now I could just shrug and turn away.'

Miss Daltrey wondered whether to ask what Cosmo might have done to her when she was younger, but decided there was no point in raking over unpleasant memories. Instead she said:

'Good. You're growing up.'

'Oh, I'm a big girl now. He knows I could raise a stink if he lays a finger on me. I owe it all to you.'

'You owe me nothing. It was all there, in you, to start with.' They stopped by Miss Daltrey's car. 'Coming for a cup of tea?'

'Better not. I've got a mountain of reading for my English essay.'

'Shall I drive you home?'

'Definitely better not. You never know when the Mean Monster may be around.' Samantha saw a look in her teacher's eye, and said quickly: 'I'm just thinking of you. He's right, you know. He could cause an awful stink. It's what he enjoys most.'

'Of course. See you tomorrow.'

But as she drove off her expression was thoughtful. Maybe Samantha had not come as far as she thought. Maybe she was still living in a degree of fear of that man. On the other hand she was right that he could make one hell of a stink. It was his job.

Heading for home, Cassie said to herself: I've been unwise. After all the resolutions I made, to fall at the first real temptation. And she'd been sure that the girl enjoyed herself, that it had been what she wanted. Now she wondered. She was perfectly right about what her horrible father might do, yet somehow, looking at her face and body language, she wondered whether Samantha wasn't having second thoughts.

'So what was Cosmo up to today?' Carol Barr asked Terry at lunchtime in the Ne Plus Ultra, a wine bar in the Headrow that made nods in the direction of Leeds's dubious Roman heritage.

'Making an assignation,' said Terry, before opening his mouth to get it round a gargantuan ciabatta roll stuffed high with what seemed to be mainly iceberg lettuce.

'With a woman?' Carol asked. She had to wait while he chewed and swallowed, and added: 'Some people have all the bad luck.'

'I wouldn't think it was a woman. Doesn't sound like Cosmo.'

'Why not? He has a wife and daughters.'

'Poor buggers.'

'Not to mention rumours of his past down South. Who with then?'

'Could be a woman, of course. Because it sounded like it was someone he wanted information from.'

Patrick De'ath, arriving with a plate and a pint, said: 'Does he pay for gen? A pittance, I would guess.'

'How did you know who we were talking about?'

'I saw you eavesdropping.'

'Anyway, it was a hundred pounds.'

Patrick whistled.

'That sounds like more than par for the course.'

'Depends on the story, doesn't it?'

'Do you think it's still this vicar one?' Carol asked.

'Priest. Yes, I wouldn't mind betting. I expect he has a hope of selling it to the tabloids.'

'Could be. What's your interest?'

'What do you mean?'

'What I say. Why do you find Cosmo and his doings so fascinating?'

Terry shifted in his seat.

'I don't. I think he's repellent. He's the sort of reporter who gives journalism a bad name. The original sewer rat. I'd love to see him stopped.'

Patrick and Carol looked at him, then down to their food. There was something there they didn't understand.

'There's no journalistic equivalent to the Hippocratic Oath,' said Patrick. 'You can't have him struck off for muckraking.'

Julie told herself she would not be intimidated by her unaccustomed surroundings. Nor were the offices just by the Cathedral in Great George Street intimidating in themselves. But they were unusual for Julie, because the only comparable building in her limited experience since school was the Benefits Office. Here in the little outer room, the woman behind the desk looked at her with a well-prepared neutral expression that just concealed one of disapproval.

'If you'll just take a seat. I don't think they'll be long. If you'll leave the little boy with me when –'

'No, I'll take him in,' said Julie quickly. 'He's not used to being with strangers.'

'But –'

'I'm with him all the time, you see. He'll be as good as gold in there. Oh, and could I have the ten pounds for the fare now, please?'

'Oh, but –'

'It's money I can't do without. Every little item tells, when you've nothing to fall back on. And I don't want to feel under any pressure to tell the people in there what they want to hear.'

'Oh, but of *course* they only want to hear the truth –'

'I would like it now, please.'

Pursing her lips, the woman dived into a drawer and came up with a ten-pound note. With an access of kindliness, perhaps even a reluctant respect for the girl, she said: 'They won't try to trick you, you know, or make you say anything you don't want to say.'

'I hope *not*,' said Julie. 'I'm not going to tell them anything except what really happened.'

'If Miss Norris would come in now,' said a sandy little head appearing round the inner door. As Julie got up he slipped further into the office and held the door almost shut until she and Gary got to it, then opened it just enough to let them through. It was rather like going into a scary ride at a funfair. The sandy man ushered her almost apologetically to a seat, then scurried round to sit on the other side of the table, with two others. Once she had got accustomed to the dim amounts of daylight allowed into the room Julie sized up all three with an expert eye. Two priests, plus one ineffectual layman. She was used, in the Benefits Office, to summing up the officials behind the grilles and organizing things so she got the one she wanted, the one with the sympathetic face. This sometimes involved pinching Gary so that he yelled and she could let others go first while she quietened him. This time she chose the priest on the left, not the one in the centre who seemed to be the chairman, as the person she was going mostly to talk to. He was younger, less set in his expression.

'Thank you for coming, Julie,' said the more forbidding of the priests, trying to bend to her level. 'That's a fine little boy.'

'Yes, he is.'

'I think you know we're investigating allegations made about Father Pardoe?'

'Is that rumours?' He nodded, but looked none too pleased.

'Yes, it is. Could you tell us how long you've known him?'

Julie thought back carefully.

'It seems like all my life. He told me once he'd been at St Catherine's about eleven years, so I'd be eight when he came. I have a vague memory of another priest, an old bl—, an old man, but me mam and dad didn't go that often to church, so . . . I only knew Father Pardoe to raise my hand and say hello to all the time I was at school.'

'And when did you get to know him better?'

That was easy. She smiled with pleasure at the memory.

'Not long after this little fellow was born. He saw me wheeling him through the market, and stopped to talk. More than a lot of the congregation at St Cath's have done, I can tell you.'

She chucked her boy under the chin, as if to emphasize that she couldn't have cared less for herself, but she did like Gary to be admired.

'So you were . . . pleased when he stopped. Glad he took an interest?' asked the chairman.

'Yes. Yes, I was. You get to welcome any sort of contact, but he was really nice. He didn't preach or anything. It was all practical things – how much I got from the Social, whether the flat had everything I needed – that was a laugh! – whether I had any friends on the estate, that kind of thing. It was like he was taking a fatherly interest, which was more than my real father ever done.'

'I don't know your father so I can't comment,' said the chairman stiffly.

'But we do understand about families,' said the other, younger priest. 'We know they don't always function ideally. So tell us how your friendship with Father Pardoe developed.'

Julie took the opportunity to turn towards the more sympathetic priest and tell her story to him.

'Well, like I said, he asked about the estate, and whether I knew people there, and I said it got lonely sometimes, because I needed people to talk to – partly worries, being a new mother with no experience, but partly just needing other interests, something outside Gary and me and our needs. He understood that. He asked if it would help if he dropped round now and then, and I said it would . . . There was no harm in it. I knew that was what priests do.'

'Of course. So he came to see you, did he?'

'Oh yes. About a fortnight later. And we had a good chat. And he could see that – well – things were pretty basic in the flat, and there wasn't much likelihood of things getting better. You see, I told him that even if I could get a job, I didn't want one until Gary was two or three. I thought he needed me, not having a father. And like I told the woman outside, he's no good with strangers, because he's so used to me.'

'That's not such a bad thing, is it?'

'I don't think so,' said Julie stoutly. 'Though there may be problems when he goes to school. Anyway, Father Pardoe saw I'd got no washing-machine, and my stove was so old it was a fire hazard, and he said there was this fund –'

'The Father Riley Fund?'

'That's right. Left to the parish by some rich priest, to help members of the congregation in difficulties. He said there was a chance I might get some of the things that would make life easier from the Fund. And it was a great help. You wouldn't think my flat was much if you saw it, but you should have seen it before I got the basics. Anyway, that's really all there is. He became like a friend, an old family friend it felt like.'

'Did you become fond of him?' asked the chairman.

That Julie felt she was prepared for.

'Fond? Could you tell me what you mean by "fond"?'

'I'm sure you know what the word means.'

Julie thought.

'Yes, I do. But I also know that things people say can be twisted. If you mean did I like him, respect him, value his interest, find him warm and friendly, yes. But if you're trying to suggest –'

'I'm not trying to suggest anything. I accept that you were fond of him in the ways you've detailed.' But something in the older priest's voice suggested he had suffered a small defeat. 'Go on.'

'Well, he dropped round when he could, and I was always pleased to see him. He tried to get me to go to the Youth Club he'd started up, and I tried it once, but – they all seemed so *young*. Having Gary has cut me off from kids like that.'

'I think we understand,' said the younger priest.

'Julie, this is going to be difficult,' said the chairman, just as she was trying to turn away from him. She disliked him because he never lost his look of gravity, even of judgement. 'It's been reported to us that when Father Pardoe came round to visit you, very often the curtains in your bedroom would then be drawn.'

She looked him straight in the eye, her own eyes blazing.

'Well, who told you that, then? I bet I know. It has to be that old Mother Crabtree, down the back. You ought to be ashamed of yourselves, believing a foul-minded old gossip like her.'

'We don't necessarily *believe*, Julie, but we have to listen.'

'Do you? To every little scrap of nasty gossip that comes your way? When Father Pardoe has been a wonderful priest for years and years? I'd have thought he might have been given the benefit of the doubt, even by a priest. Would you like to know why the curtains were drawn?'

'We would, very much,' said the younger priest.

'Father Pardoe knew I preferred him to call when Gary had his afternoon nap. By the early afternoon I've had him since he's woken up, and he's tired and whiny and I'm in need of a breather – something to break the day up. So if he could juggle his other things, commitments I suppose you'd call them, that's when he'd come. I'd put Gary to sleep in the bedroom – there's just the one – and draw the curtains, and then we could settle for a talk in the other room or the kitchen. It made my day if we could chat about something other than nappies and baby food.'

'Well, you've certainly explained that well,' said the younger priest. However the older one in the chair was still looking at her in a judge-like manner that Julie found offensive. He obviously didn't believe her. She turned back to him.

'Look, it's pretty clear I need to spell it out. We never had sex. I'm not interested in older men. Perhaps I'd have fewer problems if I was, but I'm not. It never even occurred to me to think of him in that way. We never went to bed together, we never kissed, he never touched me like that – *nothing happened.* Is that clear?'

'And the child you're expecting?'

'Well, barring artificial insemination, it couldn't be his, could it, if you believe what I've just said. I go for boys of my own age. Most teenage girls do. As to who it was fathered this one –' she patted her belly – 'you can mind your own bloody business!'

She was on the verge of getting up, grabbing Gary, and

storming out when she realized she was supposed to be there helping Christopher. She swallowed.

'Sorry,' she muttered. 'That was rude.'

She looked into their eyes. The young priest looked admiring, seeming to believe her absolutely. The chairman, his mouth pursed, looked affronted and sceptical. The layman looked nondescript. At least, she thought, they know now I'm not a pushover.

Once he had made the decision Father Pardoe felt it almost beyond him to wait until Sunday. The urge to skulk, to hide, which a month since had dominated his every movement, had been succeeded by a determination to show that he existed, to show his friend – his one-time friend – the Bishop that the fact that someone had made vicious and untrue allegations against him did not mean that he instantly became a non-person. Mrs Knowsley, he knew, had brought about the sea change in his attitude, and as usual she offered intelligent support.

'Don't hide yourself away at the back,' she said, 'as if you'd done something wrong. And don't go to the front, like it was a challenge. Somewhere just forward of the middle would be ideal.'

It amused Father Pardoe that Margaret – or anyone – should be offering him advice on a matter like that. In one sense it could be seen as indicative of his fallen state – she behaved to him as if he was no longer a priest. On the other hand it showed her acting like a friend – and the sort of friend a priest rarely or never has among his own parishioners. He wondered, with a flash of insight, if that was what his life had always lacked. He wondered, too, if that was what he had been trying to find in Julie.

Again a vision of Julie's face came to him, this time as she had looked up at him one day in her shabby little flat when Gary started crying in the next room and she knew their little chat about this and that that liberated her from the drudgeries of everyday was at an end. He remembered her face, and he remembered his reaction too: he had been tempted to stretch over and kiss her. He was very glad now that he had not. But he should not deceive himself that in Julie he was just looking to find a friend.

On Saturday he went to St Joseph's in Pudsey to Confession. He had been to various churches in Stanningley, Bramley and Wortley over the last few weeks, out of an instinct not to make one church 'his'. He had 'his' church. On Sunday morning he had a light breakfast of coffee and toast, then decided to take the bus into the centre of Leeds, rather than use his car and have to find a parking space. Margaret was going to St Joseph's, as always. The question of her accompanying him had simply not come up.

The bus was on time, but was held up by an unappetizing-looking man who joined the queue at the last minute and, seeming not to know the Sunday fare, had to have a note changed. He came and sat in a seat two behind Father Pardoe. The bus was a 72, and went along the Headrow. Pardoe got off at the Library stop, walked up to St Anne's, and found himself a seat on the aisle a row or two forward from halfway back. He intended that the Bishop should see him.

It was ten minutes into Mass when he did. The Very Reverend Seamus O'Hare blinked, his mouth twisted involuntarily, then he continued with the Mass. Pardoe's face showed no emotion whatsoever. He was prepared. He took Eucharist from the Bishop, whose face this time was as innocent of any flicker of emotion as his own. Other people he knew were there of course, and he tried to acknowledge their acquaintanceship. Most of them, clerical or lay, responded, in some cases with a degree of embarrassment. As Mass drew to a close Christopher Pardoe felt a degree of peace and satisfaction he had not known for a long time. But he was also aware that the Bishop was not best pleased.

As the congregation trooped out, Pardoe encountered a former parishioner whose wife had been killed in a horrendous road accident on the motorway near Skipton. The man had moved into a small flat in The Calls to be near his place of work, but most of all out of an instinct to put his former happiness behind him. Now he was thinking he'd made a big mistake. He was eloquent on the loneliness of a big city, the cheerlessness of flats where business people perched rather than lived their lives, his nostalgia for the community at St Catherine's, where people really did *know* each other.

'Unlike *here*,' he said, nodding round the interior as they made their way through the main door and out into the street, 'where people just come on Sunday then scatter to the four winds.'

All the time, and still out in the warm fresh air, Pardoe listened sympathetically, as he was used to doing, but part of his brain was saying, 'He doesn't *know*,' and his eye was following the movements of the Bishop, greeting his flock on that pleasant Sunday, being the local pastor whom everyone was happy to have a word from. Pardoe was making his farewells to his friend when he sensed the robed figure coming up behind him.

'If I may have a word, Father.'

Pardoe turned. The tone of the Bishop's voice had been soft, and the set of his face was neutral but perfectly amiable.

'Of course, Bishop. It was a very fine service.'

An infinitesimal pause.

'I am not sure it was wise of you to come. Or considerate.'

Pardoe swallowed, but kept his voice similarly low.

'I've been going to Mass at a variety of places on Sundays. It seemed like an ideal opportunity.'

He got a tiny shake of the head in reply. Then:

'But nevertheless you would not deny that you had other motives in first sending me your letter then in coming *here*?'

Pardoe took a deep breath.

'No, I wouldn't deny that. I seem to be stuck in limbo in Pudsey. No one communicates with me, I get no whisper what is going on. A committee is investigating these foolish rumours: I have no idea who they are, what they are doing, how long they are likely to take. I have simply been stuck in this horrible position and left there.'

'What is there to tell you before the committee has reached a decision?'

'Quite a lot, I should have thought, as I've already suggested. And I would have liked the assurance that the committee will talk to me, that my side will be heard.'

'That is of course up to them.'

'If I were not heard it would be grossly unjust to me, and also to the congregation at St Catherine's.'

Thus far the interview had been conducted in low tones, with the utmost apparent amiability. Now the Bishop's expression twisted into hostility, and the low tones took on the character of a hiss.

'I should have thought that your congregation was already making doubly sure that their voice *was* heard.'

'I beg your pardon?'

'Don't tell me you are ignorant of this – this letter of support, what is in effect a petition.'

'I am totally in ignorance. I have, alas, had no connection whatever with any member of the congregation since I was suspended. I have wondered, in fact, if letters are being forwarded as they should be. I know nothing about any petition.'

'I should like to believe you, because this is emphatically not the way we do things in our Church.'

'Perhaps the way we do things is changing, Bishop. I hope you'd agree, in any case, that denying a man accused of serious misdemeanours the right to be heard is also not the way we should be doing things in our Church.'

The Bishop's head rose arrogantly.

'I have no doubt that the committee will consider the matter in the way that best serves the well-being and reputation of the Church. It is not my intention to interfere. You of course may make any representations to them that you choose. In the meanwhile,' he turned full on him a face that was no longer merely stern, but angry, 'I would ask you not to embarrass me or place me in a false position by coming to Mass or any other service here at St Anne's.'

'You are not suggesting I cease going to Mass, are you, Bishop? It is all right, I suppose, if I embarrass Father Connell at Christ the King, or Father Wishart at St Joseph's?'

'You are being impertinent and satirical. You are doing your cause no good at all. There are unpleasant rumours that the press is on to the story. I would strongly advise you –'

He pulled himself up, looked across Cookridge Street, and

something like a snarl came over his face. He had heard clicking, and now, feet away from him, he saw a photographer. Father Pardoe, following his gaze, saw the man too, and saw that beside him stood the unappetizing man whom he had noticed on the bus journey in. The cameraman was clicking for dear life, the camera shielding his face, but the other man was standing by with unconcealed relish in his eyes and the set of his mouth. The Bishop, signally failing to wipe the anger from his face turned on Pardoe.

'Your doing, I suppose? Your behaviour throughout this unfortunate matter has been absolutely deplorable. Whatever the outcome I shall hope never again to have you in a position of trust in this Diocese.'

CHAPTER 7

Black Monday

The *West Yorkshire Chronicle* hit the streets around midday on Monday. A story involving a Leeds United footballer brawling in one of the town's nightspots was the page one lead story, but Cosmo had got his piece nicely positioned on page 3.

THE PRIEST AND THE TEENAGE MUM

ran the headline. Mothers were always Mums to the *Chronicle*, even if they had murdered their children or were on the streets. Underneath the story began.

A Roman Catholic priest from Shipley is being quizzed by his Church over his relationship with a teenage mother on the notorious Kingsmill estate in the town.

Julie Norris, nineteen, in an interview with our reporter, said, 'He is my spiritual adviser.' However the Bishop of Leeds has set up a committee to look into the relationship between Father Pardoe, priest at St Catherine's Church, and Julie, who is pregnant with her second child. They will also investigate claims that money from the charitable bequest the Father Riley Fund, intended for parishioners going through difficult times, has been used to fund Julie Norris's lifestyle. Father Christopher Pardoe unexpectedly attended Mass at St Anne's Cathedral in Leeds yesterday, where a confrontation occurred between him and the Bishop in Cookridge Street.

Julie's parents, in an interview with this paper, said there was 'nothing new' about their daughter being in trouble, and that she had been 'on the slippery slope' since becoming pregnant at seventeen. They had thrown her out of the family home at that time, and now take the view that she has dug her own grave. Mr Simon Norris, manager of Shipley's smart Bettaclothes store, said, 'Anyone who says it's our fault doesn't know their — from their elbow.' His view was shared by his wife. A neighbour of Julie's . . .

And so it went on. The picture was masterly. It showed a snarling Bishop in close proximity to Father Pardoe's face. Anyone who didn't know Cosmo Horrocks might have thought he was trying to gain sympathy for the suspended priest.

'It's cunning,' said Terry Beale, sitting on Carol Barr's desk in the early afternoon, holding the early edition. 'You'd probably find it was true in its way, except for the description of Mr Norris's shop as "smart".'

'I didn't know you knew Shipley.'

'I don't. But if it was smart it wouldn't be called Bettaclothes.'

'But the rest you guess is true?'

'Trueish. I wonder exactly what Julie Norris's "lifestyle" is. But when a case like this comes up people tell all sorts of lies and let slip all sorts of things that incriminate them in a minor way, and all you have to do is quote them. Mind you, I'd guess that Julie's family are a pretty foul bunch, going by this.'

'Aren't you jumping through Cosmo's hoop – making exactly the judgements he wants you to make?'

'No, I don't think so,' said Terry, seeming stung. 'After all, they threw her out.'

'Maybe. On the other hand she could be the sort of slut no parent would want living at home.'

'Now who's jumping through Cosmo's hoop?'

Doris Crabtree gazed out of her sitting-room window across the neat but sparse expanse of her back garden to the rear view of Julie Norris's ground-floor flat. Nothing to see there these days. The view through the gap made by the demolition of the derelict council house opposite gave her no sight of Father Pardoe approaching on foot or by car down Kingsmill

Terrace, then turning into Kingsmill Rise, then, five minutes later, the curtains being drawn in the bedroom of the lower flat at number 5. It just never happened now. Doris Crabtree was a victim of her own success.

Doris had been christened sixty-five years before, among the last of the Dorises, in the Anglican faith, though that had subsequently meant less than nothing to her. The christening had been a gesture by her factory worker father that, in those years of Depression, he had kept his job while all around him were losing theirs. The next year he had lost his too, and never had regular work again until the war restored full employment. Though he was thereafter in work until he retired, he was an eternally embittered man, and Doris had grown up in an atmosphere of sour idleness, of pinched living and an air full of recrimination. It had proved to be her natural environment.

Doris had never loved in her life, nor been loved, though which was cause and which was effect would have needed a Solomon to decide. Her life for thirty-five years, since her husband had taken off with another woman who made him equally unhappy, had been as the gossip of the Kingsmill estate. No woman misbehaving with another woman's husband had had her errancy unnoticed or undisseminated by Doris. No man living beyond his income because he was fiddling the till receipts at work escaped speculation on 'how he did it on his pay packet'. In the old days she had stood at street corners or at her gate with others of her kind, often in apron and hair curlers, acting as the modern equivalent of a town crier. She had, in her way, enjoyed her life.

But she had been overtaken by late twentieth-century morality. The façades of life had broken down. Everyone seemed to be sleeping around, from dole recipients to government ministers and members of the royal family. If everyone was doing it, it was difficult to work up the outrage that was an essential ingredient of her brand of gossip. Departure from an accepted norm was interesting, conformity to it was not. She remained a chronicler, but her function as moralist had slipped away from her. The tabloid press faced the same sad falling-away.

That was why the story of Julie and Father Pardoe had been such a godsend to her, as it was to prove also to Cosmo Horrocks. Amid the wreck of sexual morality, when even Anglican vicars divorced and remarried and kept their parishes, the Catholic priesthood remained, in theory and by their vows, inviolately chaste. The Pope was extremely hot, if that was the word, on celibacy. The falls from grace of individual priests kept the power to shock.

It had pleased her in the last few days that Julie, whenever she had gone into the back garden to hang out washing, had seen her standing as she habitually did in her window and had raised two fingers in her direction. It was a sort of acknowledgement of her influence, and confirmed in her mind her conviction that Julie was a young woman of no morals, no shame.

'You're getting your come-uppance, my girl,' she had said to herself, with a satisfied smile.

It had been a story that she had realized from the beginning was too big for the estate. Talk there had been there – she had made sure of that, and had had some foul words shouted at her for her pains by some of the younger women housed there, girls of Julie's type. But the talk was a mere means to an end, and the end had been the letter – *signed*, for she knew from experience that anonymous letters were usually ignored – that she had written to the office of the Bishop, with dates and durations of the visits to Julie, the detail of the drawn curtains, and the fact of the second pregnancy. Writing the letter had been a matter of trial and error over a week, and had given her great satisfaction in a life not rich in such feelings.

On the Monday the story broke she heard the familiar sound of Mrs Mortlake's bang on the door. When she opened it on her avid face, Florrie pushed a paper into her hands.

'It's come out at last!'

Florrie was Doris Crabtree's Goebbels: the spreader of her word, her closest rival in the thirst for information, the one who most nearly approached her in understanding that knowledge is power.

'No! Already?' Doris said, appropriately delighted. 'What page?'

'Page 3.'

Doris pulled Florrie inside her kitchen, and they both sat at table while Doris folded the paper open, laid it on the table, then began a voracious read of the article, which was followed by a close scanning of the picture.

'Well, I never!'

She had sat back in her chair, looking in the direction of the ceiling.

'They've done you proud, Doris,' said her friend, who knew her friend needed her meed of worship.

'I never expected anything quite like this. Though the reporter did say it was a wonderful story.'

'It's a public service you've done, Doris. There'll be two people will be ashamed of themselves today, thanks to you.'

'If they've any shame left . . . You know, Florrie, I feel quite proud. Like it's my finest hour.'

'It is, Doris. Enjoy it now. You'll never do a better piece of work than you have with those two.'

Peter Frencham, headmaster of Bingley Road Comprehensive, walked through the playground to fetch the packet of sandwiches for his lunch that he'd left in the car, through the roar of the usual break-time rumpus. Out of habit he noticed all the pupils who were trouble, and any that were problems of a different sort. Ben Hayman, a new boy, might have been one of those, but obviously he wasn't. He was playing an improvised game of some sort with five or six of his classmates – making a great deal of noise, but causing no trouble. He had given him a 'minder' for his first few weeks of his new school – because it was usual to, not because Ben was black – but it obviously had not been necessary. Ben had made his own group right from the start, and Mark Leary, his minder, was nowhere to be seen.

Frencham still recalled with amusement his interview with Ben on the boy's first day. His parents had just moved to Shipley, and Ben was starting, without any obvious nervousness, three weeks into summer term.

'And what does your father do?' he had asked the boy.

'He's a drug pusher, sir, but I'm aiming at something a bit

more legit myself.' When his own jaw had dropped Ben had waited a second or two, then burst out laughing. 'Got you there, sir.'

Now, suddenly, there was Ben's cheerful face looking down at him from the great height of a very gangling fifteen-year-old.

'Sir. Could I ask you something?'

'Of course, Ben. Things going all right?'

'They're going fine, sir. It's a good school – I like it. I just wondered: have you heard of Andraol?'

'No, I don't think so. Should I have? Or is this another of your legpulls?'

'Would I do that, sir? Well, maybe I would, but it's not. Andraol is a performance drug used by sportsmen – banned by the AAA and all other sporting authorities. Not just because it's like cheating, but because of potential side effects.'

'I see. So why are you telling me about it?'

'Just thought you ought to know, sir.'

And Ben dashed off back to his unidentified game with his mates. Peter Frencham resumed his trudge back to his office. One more problem to add to his worries about Cassie Daltrey. And when his secretary came in with the just-arrived copy of the *Chronicle* folded to page 3, put it in front of him and tapped with her finger the name on the by-line, he realized as soon as he read it that she was not only pointing out that this was a story that centred on one of the school's ex-pupils; she was reminding him that one of the pieces in the Cassie Daltrey problem had a father who was a determined and ruthless muckraker.

On Monday morning Father Pardoe wrote once more to his Bishop. He decided to make this letter respectful but not obsequious, but as he worked at it he found that even respect was very hard to achieve. He had to tell himself that he respected the office, if not any longer the man. He tried, too, to stick to fact, and to put into the letter as little as possible of argument or pleading for himself.

I think if you ask yourself who has most to lose by the case becoming a *cause célèbre*, who will be most grievously hurt by newspaper publicity, you will see that your charges yesterday were unjust. All I was hoping to achieve by writing to you was two things: first that I be kept fully informed about what is going on in my case; and secondly that at some point in the Committee's deliberations my side of the story will be heard. I think these are modest and reasonable requests, and I beg that you will reconsider your position as a mere observer in this matter and try to ensure that they are met. I believe – it could hardly be otherwise – that we both have the reputation and well-being of the Church at heart, even if we may differ in minor details as to how that is best maintained and strengthened.

He was at this point in the letter when Margaret came in with the *West Yorkshire Chronicle*.

He had half expected it, had steeled himself against it, but yet the sight of himself on page 3, the teasing headline (not actually *saying* very much) and the tone of the report when he started to read seemed to him to spell a sort of death. How was he ever to be the simple parish priest of St Catherine's again? How was his name ever to come up without the identifying addition of 'You know, the priest there was all the publicity about' – or, worse, a wink or leer? He had been skewered, he was wriggling on a pin, and the pin was something that had never happened, something he had never done.

But he had wanted to.

He put the thought behind him. The fact that he had wanted to represented a victory, not a defeat. If he had not wanted to, the story would have no moral significance at all.

He read through to the end, went back to check one or two details, then threw the paper on his desk and turned to talk to Margaret.

'It's bad,' he said.

'Very,' she agreed. 'Quite horrible.'

'The question is, how we respond to it.'

Margaret did not blink at the word 'we', but stood beside him, considering.

'Could you issue some kind of statement?' she asked.

'Then you think there ought to be some kind of reply?'

'I don't see there's any alternative.'

'Not dignified silence?'

'How can you make sure the silence is seen to be dignified, and not taken as an admission of guilt?'

He thought about this, then sighed.

'You're right I suppose. I hate the thought of dancing to this man's tune. My instinct as a rule is to turn the other cheek. It's the most effective counter-measure I know, and hardly anybody ever tries it. But if it could be taken as an admission of guilt . . . There's another thing. I'm not the only one here to consider. There's Julie – the slur is on her as well. I wonder how they'll take it on the Kingsmill estate.'

'From what you've told me, I should think they'll take it very much in their stride,' said Margaret with a touch of grimness. 'They might turn her into some kind of local heroine.'

'You've got a point there. Quite rightly they might see her as a victim. But there are other people to consider too – her family, for example. I always found them antipathetic, but they are Catholics, and slightly more than nominal ones . . . But, so be it: some kind of reply will have to be made.' He happened to glance out of the window as he spoke. In the road outside, unusually, there were people loitering, watching the house. He made up his mind at once. 'Yes, definitely it will. I wonder if there is anyone sympathetic in local journalism I could arrange an interview with. And I could put him or her in touch with some of the more open-minded members of the St Catherine's congregation, if that would help, and not get them into trouble.'

It was the beginning of an hour of fairly hectic activity – a great relief after his weeks of passivity and waiting. By chance he knew Brian Marris, the very man Cosmo Horrocks had first consulted. He was a worshipper at the nearby Greengates church, but had been brought up in

Shipley. When he telephoned him as an ex-newspaper man who probably still had contacts he caught him already rather shamefaced, having discovered that the story he had been consulted about had broken. He told Pardoe of his minor role in Cosmo's news-gathering, and put him on to a probably sympathetic soul on the *Bradford Telegraph and Argus*.

'The fact that it's a woman probably won't do any harm,' he said. 'Look, would you like me to ring her and arrange it?'

'I'd be very grateful.'

'What time would suit?'

'Any time suits these days. I'm not going anywhere.'

While he waited for her he rang one or two of the St Catherine's congregation. He spoke in particular to Miss Preece-Dembleby, and after her to Mrs Jessel. He was glad to find both staunch supporters, but he said little about the case, and merely asked them if they would be willing to talk to a well-disposed reporter. That in itself would be sufficient to arouse the Bishop's ire. He impressed on both of them the need for caution and tact. 'We want the whole thing dampened down not stirred up further,' he said. 'I've no desire to start a war.'

The reporter who finally arrived was the sixth to ring the doorbell, not to mention attempts at telephone contact. She, of course, was the only one to be admitted. Her name was Jenny Snell, and she was thirtyish, attractive and forceful. She said she didn't want to take sides, thought her piece would be more effective if she didn't, but she was willing to put his side as cogently as possible. Pardoe sat with her for well over an hour, laying all the facts of his connection with Julie Norris before her, and keeping well away from his sense of grievance over the Bishop's handling of the case. At the end of the time Jenny Snell sat back in her chair in Mrs Knowsley's sunny sitting room and looked at her pad, considering the story in all its aspects.

'Money,' she said at last. 'The Father Riley Fund.'

'Yes. What about it?'

'Is that your Achilles' heel? Did you hand over vast sums to Julie Norris?'

'I handed over no sums at all. I bought her a second-hand

78

washing-machine, and a second-hand stove, and also several bits of furniture, usually from charity shops. It can't have come to more than two hundred pounds in all.'

'Why the fuss, then? Why does it come into the investigation?'

Father Pardoe shifted uneasily in his chair.

'Maybe because the Fund was used at all. I'd been under pressure over it for some time, because the use it was – is – put to is at my discretion. The Bishop wanted the Fund to be used for more general charitable projects, not to be channelled towards individuals, because he said that sort of need ought to be met by the Social Security system. "Ought to be, but isn't" was my reaction to that. But the Bishop got the two trustees on his side, and I thought it was politic to go along with it for a while.'

'So what sort of charitable project did the Fund get used for?'

Pardoe shifted uneasily once again.

'I simply don't know. Virtually nothing in the Shipley area, and it was in Shipley that the Fund was supposed to be used.'

'I see. Did you bring this up with the Bishop or the trustees?'

'Well, eventually I did . . . You probably think me slack, remiss, but the truth is the Fund didn't loom particularly large in my parish work. I had a little bit of money to play about with when there were cases of need, and then for a time I didn't – or didn't use it. There are other ways of relieving poverty and distress. But when I applied for a sum to buy equipment for the Youth Club and was knocked back, I started to get the feeling that the Fund had simply sunk into disuse.'

Jenny Snell frowned in bewilderment.

'But I thought you had sole say in the use of the Fund?'

'Under the will, yes. But when it was agreed that it should be used for more general charitable purposes, I could see that the sums involved might be large, and that it would be better if decisions were taken more formally, and higher up. The decisions were too big for one unsupervised man. And since I wasn't in sympathy with the new role for the Fund anyway, I said I would leave the decisions to the Bishop and the trustees.'

'I *see*,' said Jenny Snell.

'The Bishop is a man of unquestionable probity,' said Pardoe quickly. 'A mite authoritarian, but that's how things are in our Church. I think you must be *very* careful how you use this.'

'I will be. I'll write that section now if you like, so you can vet it. But how did you come to start using it again?'

'There was no problem. I'd never relinquished my rights under Father Riley's will. I simply wrote to the Bishop and the trustees saying there were two cases of distress in the parish of the kind the Fund was intended to relieve, and I would therefore be making use of it.'

'I see. Two. Who was the other one?'

'A very old woman in a very old council flat, terrified of running up high electricity bills, and therefore risking hypothermia much of the time by sitting there in coats and blankets but without heating. I bought her a modern, more efficient heater, and took over responsibility for the bills. She died a couple of months back, but at least in her last year or so she was warm.'

'That's all to the good, I think,' said Jenny Snell. She began scribbling in her pad, then handed over the result to Pardoe. It was a tactful and deadpan account of the Fund and his use of it, which managed not even to mention the Bishop.

'That's fine,' said Pardoe, handing it back. 'He won't like its being mentioned at all, but this man Horrocks has made it inevitable.'

'It's the sex angle the public is going to be interested in,' said Jenny. 'Will you be insulted if I ask you some categorical questions?'

'No.'

'Are you the father of the baby Julie is pregnant with?'

'No.'

'Do you know who is the father?'

'No. If we ever got near to the subject, I could sense Julie shying away. All she ever said was that she could expect no maintenance from him.'

'She might find herself under pressure from the Social Security people to give them his name,' commented Jenny. 'Have you ever had sex with Julie?'

'I have not.'

'And were the things that you bought for her from the Fund in any way payment for any other sort of favours?'

'They were not.'

Jenny snapped her notebook shut.

'I think that's all. We may have to meet again, or at least talk on the phone. You've got to face it: this could be a story that will run and run.'

'I do hope not.'

Jenny was sympathetic.

'I'm afraid you're caught either way. If you speak or if you stay silent. I'll try to see that your side is put with dignity.'

'There are worshippers at St Catherine's you could talk to.' He gave her the names of Miss Preece-Dembleby and Mrs Jessel. 'They said they wouldn't mind talking to you.'

'They're strong supporters?'

'Yes.'

'I may have to talk more generally to the congregation. See how strong support is, how strong the opposition.'

'That's perfectly fair. I've no objection. But I'd rather you held back for the moment, and only did it as a last resort.'

'Fair enough. Well – good luck.'

When she had gone, Father Pardoe felt drained. He went to his bottle of Irish whiskey, which he had now brought downstairs so that his occasional drink became a social one. He poured himself a modest slug, then called to Margaret in the kitchen. She knew what he would be asking her, and shouted through that she would like a gin and tonic. When she came in they sat together companionably and he gave her an account of his talk with Jenny Snell.

'She seemed a nice girl,' Margaret commented. 'But it could get you into more trouble with the Bishop.'

'I suppose so. Of course I have the well-being of the Church at heart, but I'm not sure lying down under injustice is the best way of promoting it. There are times when you have to kick up a rumpus.'

'Of course I see that. It's just that what I'd really like to see is you back at St Catherine's, doing what you've always done and what you do well. And I want that for your sake as soon as possible. Not that I won't miss you –'

'I hope you will.'

'But I've always hated to see power unused. And it's plain as plain that you've been a wonderful parish priest. I wish we had as good a one here.'

They had stood up, taking their empty glasses into the kitchen. When they had put them on the draining board Margaret turned round and smiled goodnight at Pardoe. On an impulse he put his arm around her and kissed her on the cheek.

'Thank you for what you just said.'

He felt her body so relaxed, in contrast to his own tensed up one, that he was about to clasp her more tightly in sheer gratitude, kiss her more tenderly, when she pushed him gently away.

'That's enough,' she said. 'We don't want to fall into anything, do we?'

Going up to bed he pondered on the possible significance of her words.

CHAPTER 8

Parish News

The public and sensational airing of the Father Pardoe story, anticipated though it had been by many, still bore most heavily on his supporters in the St Catherine's congregation, though it was also a cause of anger and disgust to the local Catholic hierarchy. The majority of the congregation did not take the *West Yorkshire Chronicle*, contenting themselves with the local free newspaper, but those who did were soon on the phone to their friends, and casual sales of the paper increased dramatically in the Shipley area. It was not prurience alone that impelled the faithful to go out and buy: they pored over the story because they knew at least one of the players in it, and they probably would have done the same if they had known someone involved in a spectacular road pile-up. When they had read it, got a handle on the ramifications of the story, they got on the phone to other friends, and either passed it on or chewed it over. It was something of a red-letter day for most of them, even if they shook their heads and said how shocking it all was.

Miss Preece-Dembleby – Edith to a very small circle of close friends – took the paper daily, and so was one of the first to learn that the story had broken. She read it through, then reread it carefully. It was part of her nature and her style of life to do nothing precipitately. Then she got up, opened a window, and lit one of her very rare cigarettes. Her mouth, when she was thinking a matter through, usually set in a hard, tense line, and when she had finished her cigarette she walked around the house for some minutes more, the muscles of her face more than usually tight. She was facing up to aspects of the situation that had not seemed to her hitherto to be of any importance. Now, apparently, judging by the newspaper coverage, they were very much part of the equation. She made a decision, then went in to the living room and took up the phone. She knew the number by heart.

'596371.'

'Hello Raymond.'

'Edith. I'm at the office.'

'I know you're at the office. That's where I rang.'

'I mean I'm busy.'

'But you haven't got a client.'

'How can you know that I haven't got a client?'

'Because you answer the phone differently.'

Miss Preece-Dembleby's tone in talking to her brother had altered significantly in the last few years. They had lived together from the time of their parents' death, she making a home for him in the house that had been left to her rather than to him because their parents had not seen her as a likely wage-earner, or wanted her to be one. Raymond at that time had worked in a bank, though later he had branched out to become a fairly high-powered independent accountant.

Things had changed four years before, when he had married. He was by then forty-six, and Edith Preece-Dembleby considered that if you had not married by then you could have no enthusiasm or aptitude for the state and would do very much better to let it alone. This feeling was not a selfish one. Though her brother's presence in her house was not an oppressive one – he was out from 8.30 to 5.30 every working day, and had things on most evenings – still, she preferred to live on her own. But when Raymond started paying court (in somewhat lugubrious fashion) to Nora Fitzgerald she thought that either he was making a fool of himself or he was lining his own nest. She had no other objections to the match. She liked Nora, who was a widow of an Irish farmer who had enjoyed the windfalls strewn on rural heads by the wise men in Brussels. Nora's children were grown up, she had no one to please but herself, and she welcomed the move to England and a rather more exciting social life. Edith had predicted the worst, and had a nagging sense of dissatisfaction that so far it had not happened.

'Raymond listen: the story has broken – the Father Pardoe story.'

'Oh, what a shame. What do you mean, "broken"?'

'It's in the *Chronicle*.'

'Oh Lord. Aren't journalists foul?'

'It's not a profession for gentlemen. There are a couple of paragraphs in the story about the Father Riley Fund.'

'*What?*' Edith remained silent, knowing he had heard, her forehead crinkled at the violence of his reaction. Oughtn't he to have expected it? 'Why on earth would they be interested in that, when there's all that stuff involving Julie Norris?'

'The stuff about Julie Norris seems to involve the Fund.'

'I mean all the sex stuff.'

'There is plenty about her too, and her parents. They come out very badly ... You're one of the trustees, Raymond, aren't you? I'm a bit puzzled because I thought Father Pardoe gave over control to you and the Bishop.'

'Only for a time. Look, Edith, don't worry your head about the Fund. It's really nobody's business.'

'How can you say that, Raymond? It's in the papers. Of course people are going to ask questions, and they'll do so whether you regard it as their business or not.'

She heard her brother groan.

'If journalists ask, that can be handled by the Bishop's office.'

'Parishioners are going to ask too. The money was left for their welfare.'

'Well, you can leave that to me.'

'Why did Father Pardoe resume control, Raymond?'

'I didn't quite say that. Look, Edith, this isn't women's business. I really can't answer questions on it.'

'There's no need to get pompous, Raymond.'

'I am not getting pompous.'

'Many people would find your attitude to what is women's business very old-fashioned.'

'I sincerely hope they would. You and I are not late twentieth-century people, Edith, let alone millennium people.'

'I think I can speak for myself about what sort of person I am.'

He sighed.

'All I meant to get across to you, Edith, was that this matter is confidential.'

'Well, that wasn't what you said, Raymond. I'm beginning to be rather glad that this matter, at least, is coming out into the open.'

She put the phone down, and resumed her thoughtful walk around the house. Her brother, having only his office, did not walk about, but sat slumped in his chair behind the desk. He was as thoughtful as his sister, but a great deal more unhappy.

Mary Leary collected the *West Yorkshire Chronicle* from the front doormat and skimmed through the stories on the front page. Normally she saved it for the evening and the boring bits of the television. She happened though to be waiting for her washing-machine to finish its current programme, and when she decided that the front-page lead was of no interest to her (for though she had married into a sporty family she had no interest in sport herself, and certainly not in footballers' drunken brawls), she opened to pages 2 and 3.

The word 'Priest' hit her at once. She had been fearing, expecting, waiting for the story to break. Always a strong admirer of Father Pardoe, she had known in her heart that if the story became a public matter the situation would change. The St Catherine's congregation would polarize, Father Pardoe's private business would become matters of comment and the subject of ribaldry: everything would be cheapened, vulgarized.

She removed the bed linen from the washing-machine and put in the shirts and the sports gear. She went about her business for the rest of the afternoon with a heavy heart. The Church had been the second centre of her life – not taking up as much time as her family, but coming to be almost as vital as an emotional centre. Because she clung to what she knew – something her husband had always counted on – the prospect of change always filled her with dread. The advent of Father Greenspan in Pardoe's place had confirmed all her fears. Now it seemed inevitable that – even if Pardoe was cleared, which she still believed passionately would be the outcome of the enquiry – people would feel that 'a fresh start' was needed, both for himself and for his old parish. She wanted nothing to do with fresh starts. She wanted to continue clinging to what she had always clung to. And part of that process meant not facing up to matters that remained dervishes, menacing but remote, shrieking unmentionable truths in the back of her mind.

She had tried to put from her mind the words she had over-heard two Sundays ago while coming out of St Catherine's. But she had not done so completely, and her fears for Father Pardoe were somehow mixed up with fear that, as the scandal snowballed, they would involve her husband, and hence herself and her family.

The phone rang in Simon Norris's glassed-in back office around half past two, and he slipped in there, whence he could keep an eye on his customers, to answer it. It was his wife, as it often was. She was terribly lacking in confidence, Simon was glad to say.

'Simon? The story's in today's *Chronicle*.'

'Is it? What does it say about us?'

'Well, not a lot. I'd like you to read it.'

'I'll slip out and get a copy.'

'No need to do that. Waste of money.'

'I'd like to have an extra copy, to send to Aunt Becky.'

Aunt Becky was Leonard's godmother, and the source of an expected legacy for the boy when she 'passed on' as the Norrises always put it. She was very independent-minded, though – 'wilful' was how Simon described her privately to his wife – and hence they made great efforts to keep in with her. She was currently away on some kind of retreat at Walsingham, though from her twice-weekly telephone reports it was a retreat as fraught and incident-packed as Napoleon's from Moscow. Aunt Becky was like that – peace was inimical to her.

'That's a good idea. She'll be chuffed . . . I think.'

Simon Norris waited until the shop was empty – they were

unusually busy for a Monday – then slipped two doors down to the newsagent's. He took the paper back to his office, opened it at page 3, then read the report in the intervals of customers who took up shirts then put them down again, or felt along the line of sports jackets to test the cloth. Norris could get quite tetchy with non-serious buyers.

On the whole he was satisfied with the report. By and large he thought Cosmo Horrocks had done a good job. He sniggered over the phrase 'Julie Norris's lifestyle' because he was pretty sure that if she had been living it up in luxury he would have heard of it. He liked the juxtapositioning of the committee of investigation with the information that Julie was again pregnant. He read the views of himself and his wife and felt satisfied that they had been correctly reported, even if he thought they could have been given more extended coverage. Aunt Becky would be interested, he thought. Aunt Becky had been persuaded to take the same view of Julie that they had, especially since she got pregnant. He sat thinking it over for a minute or two, then got back to his wife.

'No problem,' he said. 'I thought it was a good report.'

'Oh good. I just couldn't be sure.'

'Makes it pretty clear what kind of a girl our Julie is.'

'It does.'

'I liked the description of this place. "Smart". I liked that.'

'Yes. Can't do any harm, can it?'

More customers came into the shop, so Simon Norris rang off. As the afternoon wore on the number of people who came in was remarkable. His impression, though, confirmed by the till after closing time, was that few spent anything. Takings, in fact, were at the lower end of the acceptable for a Monday. From time to time, and increasingly, he got the impression that some of the shoppers were looking at the clothes as a cover for taking a quick peek at him. It dawned on him very gradually that his customers had read the paper and were coming to take a look at the most easily accessible player in Shipley's little scandal. He was becoming, in fact, something of a local celebrity. It didn't displease him. In fact, when he was alone in the shop at the end of the day he decided it was something he really rather enjoyed.

Simon Norris was decidedly short-sighted, and he had not noticed that most of the glances directed at him ranged from the incredulous to the hostile.

Terry Beale was out on an assignment at Elland Road when, in late afternoon, Cosmo rang the office of the Bishop of Leeds, so there was no chance of an extended linger by the coffee machine. It was in any case a ploy that he realized was wearing thin.

Cosmo was in high good humour. He had had a man outside Mrs Knowsley's Pudsey home when Jenny Snell arrived to be admitted, and had been informed of it. So the *Bradford Telegraph and Argus* was interested in the story. Probably then, so as to be different, they were giving Pardoe's side of the story. Great. It kept the whole thing on the boil. The *Globe* was already interested, and was pressuring him for more on the sex angle, and more on the financial angle too. Sex and money played well, whether separately or together. The *Globe's* interest provided Cosmo with an opportunity of the kind he relished: of going in where he knew he was not wanted.

'Bishop O'Hare's office.'

'Good afternoon,' said Cosmo genially. 'I hope it's not too late for you.'

'Too late?'

'In the working day. This is the *West Yorkshire Chronicle* here.'

'Oh.'

'Now don't be like that. I'm on your side.'

'What can I do for you?'

'I'd like to speak to someone about the Father Riley Fund.'

'So you are the man who . . . has the story in the paper today?'

'Yes. Cosmo Horrocks at your service. Now what I want to know –'

'The Bishop was most displeased.'

'I didn't expect him to be over the moon.'

'Then please don't pretend you are "on our side" as you call it.'

'Now, to business: I believe the Fund is for Shipley charities, left by a former priest at St Catherine's Church, is that right?'

'I really can't comment.'

'So, within reason, Father Pardoe was perfectly within his rights to siphon some of this money in the direction of an unmarried mother living in poverty, surely?'

'As I say I —'

'And was the Bishop involved in some changes to the running of the Fund and the use it was put to? I have heard a whisper that might be the case.'

'This is purely a matter for the Church.'

'Oh, is it? *Is it?* If a legacy is left for a certain purpose and that purpose is changed, then legal questions arise, don't you think? And apart from the legal aspect, there's the perfectly legitimate public interest as well, particularly in the Shipley area. Has the money been left idle, stacking up interest? That's not what charitable funds should be used for. Has it been diverted to other causes, in which case on whose authority? *What has happened to the money?* Has it simply evaporated? If it has, isn't it time the police were called in?'

Cosmo was enjoying himself. This was what he was best at: spreading the scope of the story wider, and in the process frightening someone or other, in this case a secretary who was used to having her word accepted as the Bishop's law. When, after a pause the woman spoke, she sounded unnerved.

'I think I shall have to talk to someone. Do you mind holding the line?'

'For as long as you like, darling,' said Cosmo.

He tucked the receiver between his shoulder and his neck and lounged back in his desk chair. He took from his pocket a pack of his foul cigars, found it was empty, crushed it and hurled it at the rubbish bin. His geniality undented, he lounged back still further and put his feet up on the table. Carol Barr, on a genuine trip to the coffee machine, thought she had never seen anything more repulsive than Cosmo in a good mood. It was the undertone of threat that was disgusting.

'Hello. Yes, I'm still here. Unfortunately, I hear you think . . . Ah, the Bishop will see me, will he? I think that's very wise of His Holiness. The sooner the better, I'd say. Can't make it before Thursday? Getting all the facts straight, I suppose. Well in that case Thursday it must be. Thanks for all your help, my darling, and I'll see you then.'

Having ensured that his reception at the Bishop's office, should he ever get there, would be as frosty as an antiquated deep-freeze, Cosmo put the phone down, and sat for some minutes in a state of blissful self-satisfaction.

Julie Norris found that she was out of milk and had to make a trip to the little parade of shops just off the estate. It was late afternoon, and she noticed nothing on the way there. However as she dawdled along the little row of half-hearted enterprises she got the idea that people were looking at her. She picked up her milk at the newsagent's instead of going further along to the corner shop, and from the counter as she handed over money she picked up the *Chronicle* as well. It was the first time in her life she had bought it. When she got out into the street again she scanned the front page then opened the paper up. Immediately her worst fears were confirmed. She saw the picture and the headline and knew that disaster had struck both Christopher and herself.

She felt a great wave of depression for his sake, but she decided to save the details to read at home, and tucked the paper in behind Gary in his pushchair. It was as she was setting off back home that a man passing her looked into her face to confirm a suspicion then shouted after her:

'You got yourself a good write-up today, love. I've often wondered what it takes for a middle-aged man to pull a gorgeous chick like you. Now I know.'

He was a man who Julie had caught leering at her before. The combination of her youth and her baby had made all too many assume that she was an easy lay. She looked straight ahead and walked on. She had not gone far when she knew for certain that people were looking at her. One woman – one of the legion of old-before-their-time working-class women who were a revived phenomenon of the age, though Julie did not know this, only feared it would happen to her – genially pointed to the bulge in her belly and shouted:

'Goin' to be born with a dog-collar on, is he?'

Because the woman was good-humoured and potentially friendly, Julie didn't ignore her.

'They got it wrong. He's not the father.'

'They gen'rally do get it wrong in t'papers,' the woman agreed. 'They just want a good headline.'

'He's just a friend – the best one I've had.'

'I've had times just like you when I needed a friend. Lucky you to have a good one.'

'Not so bloody lucky for him,' said Julie.

And as she trudged home, that was the overwhelming feeling she had. If it wasn't for her, Christopher wouldn't be in this mess. If it hadn't been for his kindly impulses, his instinct to provide not just material help but support as well, none of the gossip would have started. If it wasn't for me, Julie said over and over to herself. Me and that loathsome Cosmo Horrocks.

'Cassie?' said Samantha Horrocks. She spoke low, though her mother was out in the garden pulling up weeds, and her sister was upstairs doing her homework.

'Samantha! Any problems?'

'Not really. I just thought I'd tell you that the Mean Monster's story about the priest has broken in the paper tonight.'

'Oh really? All sorts of salacious innuendos, I suppose.'

'You bet. I thought I'd tell you so you can see the sort of thing he writes. Innuendos are the Mean Monster's stock-in-trade.'

'Still, if you're a priest you ask for it, in a way.'

'You're assuming it's all true. Knowing the M.M. the likelihood is that it's all a product of his imagination.'

'Probably. Though it didn't start with him, did it?'

'No. But I'd give the poor man the benefit of the doubt.'

'I suppose so. I'd want it if the horrible man got his claws into me.'

'Except –' Samantha changed her mind suddenly. 'Except

he'll be so busy with this story for the next few weeks I can't see him giving you a thought.'

Samantha had rung on an impulse and without preparing herself. She could tell that Cassie was not fooled by the sudden switch. Her voice was thoughtful for the rest of the call. But at least that meant she had got the message, however reluctant she had been to accept it. Samantha felt she had been rushed into something she was not ready for. And there could be no doubt that it was Cassie who was to blame.

When Janette Jessel, alerted by Miss Preece-Dembleby, had gone out to buy the *Chronicle* she had stuffed it into her bag as if it was pornography and gone straight home to read it in the privacy of her own front room. Her first reaction was of disgust: Father Pardoe deserved better, much better, than to be subjected to the sneering innuendos one associated with the tabloid press. She wondered at the mentality of people who followed with lascivious glee the supposed frailties of priests and clergymen. Her next reaction was one of anger. Father Pardoe had been shamefully treated: his years of brilliant service as priest at St Catherine's had been set at nought by the very men who should have been defending him – his superiors in the Church. He had been placed in a position where people assumed his guilt and sniggered about his sexual peccadillo before a word of the promised report had been read, or even written. She was aware, too, that Father Pardoe's support came by and large from the women of the parish. The men, openly or covertly, took the tabloid line: of course he was having it off. They all were, weren't they? Priests were only human, only like other men. *Così fan tutti.* Such a line was taken by the men because it made them feel better about themselves.

This thought must have remained in her mind when she rang Mary Leary to talk over what the publicity meant for the parish, and particularly for the campaign to support Father Pardoe.

'As long as there was just whispering about it around the parish, then we could be seen as making people's feelings known to the powers that be,' she said. 'But now that it's become a big local talking point –'

'National before very long, I wouldn't mind betting,' said Mary.

'Oh Lord, let's hope not. But that's what I'm afraid of. As soon as that happens you wonder where we can go with our little campaign. What can it do when he's got all the tabloids baying for his blood?'

'Well, we can use it to demonstrate that Father Pardoe has strong local support. We've played that down so far, so as not to annoy the Bishop.'

'Yes. I suppose it will last, will it? He will need local support more than ever now.'

'We've been very discreet, but perhaps too discreet. Now the whole thing has gone public, probably we should go public too.'

'It will make us very unpopular with the Bishop.'

There was a moment's thought at the other end.

'Do you care?'

'No.'

'I would have cared six months ago,' said Mary, 'but I don't now. I think the powers that be have been disgracefully unsupportive. You wouldn't expect them to act on pure tittle-tattle.'

'I think they've been running scared because of all those horrible cases in Ireland . . . And here . . . Boys usually.'

'It's always horrible when there's children involved, isn't it?' said Mary. 'That makes it so much more important that everyone realizes that the *women* are supporting him. We wouldn't be if there was any question of . . .of *that*.'

'It's a good job we do support him, because he doesn't get much in the way of support from the men.'

'Not a scrap,' said Mary, her voice sharpening. 'Basically they think a celibate priest is an unnatural thing.'

'They think it's an impossibility. They judge everyone by themselves. It makes me *mad* when Derek sneers and leers and tries to suggest that Father Pardoe is on his level.'

It was as if she had opened a floodgate.

'Oh, I'm so glad you said that. Con is exactly the same. He

wants to drag everyone down to his grubby moral standards. Someone like Father Pardoe makes him uneasy, so he jumps for joy if he thinks he's been exposed as a sham.'

'They're two of a kind, your husband and mine,' said Janette. 'That's probably why they're such buddy pals. They're both horribly self-satisfied, aren't they? Do you know I once heard Derek talking on the phone about one of his women, and when the person on the other end mentioned me he said I had a "good Catholic marriage". And then he laughed. They both did – you could tell.'

'It was probably Conal on the other end. That's exactly how he thinks. They've given us children – given us! – and once they've done that they can go off and do exactly as they please, while we have the privilege of bringing up the next generation to be exactly like them.'

'And like us. That's the really horrible part. Because we're to blame as much as they are. If they wipe their feet on us it's because we're natural doormats.'

'I know. And I saw it all at home, and yet I never thought for a moment it would be the same when I got married.'

'And yet it is. It's like we never escaped from the Victorian age.'

And so it went on, for more than half an hour. It was, especially for Mary Leary, a release, a transformation. They both realized that they had had this bond for years, but had never been brave enough to bring it out into the open. Now it was out, and they didn't only feel better for it: they felt they had to do something about it. Together, as friends. And as women.

Cora Horrocks was trying to wind down before her husband came home. It was always best to be in a relaxed mood, because he would almost certainly wind her up, and if he did that when she was already tense the strain could become intolerable.

Adelaide was upstairs preparing to go to bed, but Samantha was still out. Cora worried about Samantha. She had always been such a stable girl – whatever Cosmo might say or do. Yet there had been so many signs of pressure, of uncertainty, recently. She did hope Cosmo was not right about her and that teacher. In fact, Cora always hoped Cosmo was wrong, was always sad when his nastier conjectures proved right.

She had a lot to be grateful to him for, she knew that. He had in a sense rescued her. And if he seldom reminded her of that, it was always there between them – something unspoken because it did not need to be spoken. And her life with Alan was a memory so horrible that she needed no prompting to feel gratitude. For a long time after they had married she had even believed Cosmo to be a good man.

She hadn't believed that for a long while now. Nevertheless she still felt some tiny vestige of that old gratitude, and tried not to put into words her feeling of how much happier she and the girls would be without him.

She wondered if Samantha was with that teacher. She felt sure she went there much oftener than she actually told them about. Cora had always found Miss Daltrey very pleasant. Well, she would be pleasant to Samantha's parents if . . . She wondered what people like that *did*. She wondered if she and Samantha were doing it now. That was Cosmo, working his way into her mind. Taking her over. Not as Alan had taken her over. Less brutally, more insidiously.

She heard Cosmo's key in the door. Immediately her shoulders went tense. Please God he was tired, or dissatisfied with his day. When that happened he would most likely go straight off to bed. She stood up as he came in and gave him the usual peck on the cheek. Before the kiss had landed her heart sank, because she saw from his smirking expression that Cosmo was very satisfied indeed with his day's work.

It would probably have comforted Cora if she could have known that this was the last time she would ever have to welcome Cosmo home.

CHAPTER 9

Cosmo Solo

Cosmo left the offices of the *West Yorkshire Chronicle* late on Tuesday evening. It had been a day of hard, concentrated work, but a very satisfying one. The story was about to go national. This he was quite sure about. He had been faxed a mock-up of the next day's *Globe* with Father Pardoe on page 5 – not ideal, but good enough. His own name had been coupled in the by-line with the *Globe*'s principal smut reporter, Garry Higgs. A very satisfying sight. And it wasn't the end, not by a long chalk. Jenny Snell's article in the *Bradford Telegraph and Argus* had been interesting. His hunch about the Father Riley Fund had been right, and the Bishop would have a lot of explaining to do. The Fund would probably suffice as the next stage of the story, and it could be a stage much more sympathetic to Father Pardoe. Cosmo intended to proceed in the classic manner that tabloids always adopt with royals and other notables: you build 'em up, then you smash 'em down, then you build 'em up again, then you smash 'em down again.

Oh yes. This one was going to run and run.

The possibility that Father Pardoe was innocent of any financial wrong-doing led Cosmo to consider the possibility that he was equally innocent of breaking his vows with Julie. He considered this not out of any crusading desire for justice, still less for reasons of conscience concerning his own role in the story; he considered the possibility only in so far as it could be one further twist that prolonged it in the local and national media. A twist that could possibly be followed by the revelation of the real father of Julie's unborn child. Sex, followed by money, followed by sex again: a simple formula but an appealing one.

Cosmo frowned as he remembered an incident earlier in the day.

He had been looking over a story that Terry Beale had covered. Not an important one, naturally: it had been about a brawl at closing time in one of the central Leeds pubs between the discarded husband and the new lover of a woman from Armley. Cosmo had insisted on adding all the titbits and extras that the greenhorn reporter had left out: the fact that the woman was a 'mother of two', the fact that she had a long-ago conviction for soliciting. Eventually Terry had said:

'All women are whores to you.'

'It's called making a realistic assessment,' he had replied.

Thinking over the incident now, Cosmo decided young Terry was getting above himself. He had never been respectful, let alone admiring, but now he was barely attempting to hide his contempt. Something would have to be done about Terry Beale. He would have to be put in his place, then squashed down in it. Still, loathing the boy did not lessen his self-satisfaction at his own sharp reply to the boy's impertinence.

True to his agenda of sex, then money, then sex again, Cosmo's mind went back, as he turned off the Burley Road towards Armley, to Jenny Snell's article in defence of Father Pardoe. His, Cosmo's, hunch about the Fund had been based on the financial difficulties of the Catholic Leeds diocese. These went back a decade or more: they had overstretched themselves, and had found themselves in the position of having to sell whatever could be sold – unwanted nunneries, patches of land, even school playing fields. It had been that state of affairs, which was well known, that had led to Cosmo's guess. Not, of course, that he actually believed the Bishop had done anything criminal – though it might be amusing to throw an insinuation to that effect into Thursday's interview. He guessed he had taken over the running of it – the Bishop had to him the air of a control freak – so that he could siphon off the interest into the general fund to relieve the hard-pressed areas of expenditure. Or maybe he had gone further than that. Maybe the Fund had simply been swallowed up.

Oh, it was a lovely story, was the Father Pardoe one! He blessed the day he had overheard the talk in the train from London. He blessed the day he had had the phone call about Father Pardoe's whereabouts. As he drove down Bramley Town Street he ruminated on the matter, and actually smiled to himself. It had concluded so satisfactorily, that offer of information, though not quite in the way the seller had anticipated. And the information had been cheap at the price, no question of that. In fact, everything about this story had worked out brilliantly. He could see so much flowing from it. The parish people of St Catherine's were almost untapped as yet, at least as far as gossip and possible ramifications were concerned. In his experience stories led to stories led to stories. You uncovered one after another at St Catherine's, and then you started to refer to it as a 'troubled parish'. After that you could move from parish matters to private lives. Neither Christians in general nor Catholics in particular lived private lives of any greater purity or probity than sinners like himself, thought Cosmo. Not much, anyway.

That thought did not lead to any great introspection about his own standards. At least he wasn't a frustrated divorcee with nothing better to do than spy on her neighbours, he told himself contentedly. As he drove down the hill into Rodley he laughed at his second chat with Doris Crabtree, which had taken place that afternoon. What a wizened old witch the woman was! He had got out of her what little he could about Julie's 'other' man friend – not much more than a shape in the dark, really. In spite of the fact that it was so little, he had flattered the woman about its value and his interest in it, had given her his card, had said he was always ready to hear anything she had to offer about goings-on in the Kingsmill. When the story and its offshoots had died the natural death that was the inevitable fate in journalism even for the best of stories he would slap her down and tell her that grubby little stories about the grubby activities of grubby little people were of no interest outside their own grubby little patch. Build 'em up, smash 'em down: the twin imperatives of Cosmo's life – of life itself, he thought.

He came to the Wise Owl, then turned off left towards

home. His house, bought when he had moved to the North with Cora in the first year of his marriage, was a thin, high, terraced stone one, insulated for and from noise in a way none of your jerry-built modern houses were. No garage, of course, and Cosmo had had to rent a modern lock-up at the end of his cul-de-sac, a minute away from his front door. He liked to keep his car safe from the attentions of marauding yobs. He drove in to the end garage of the four, leant over and locked the passenger door, then got out and locked his own. Once the car door was shut he was in the dark, apart from a street light fifty yards down the road.

It was while he was pulling down the door that he heard a sound from the patch of waste ground beside and behind the lock-ups. He secured the door, then put his head round the side, intent on shouting at any courting couple.

The blow came with horrible force. He staggered, and croaked out a cry for help. He steeled himself for a further blow, but he felt himself gripped by the neck. He opened his eyes.

'You,' he said.

The only answer was a smile. Then he was dropped, and fell to the ground. He sensed his attacker raising his weapon, and he raised his hands, crying out, this time more strongly.

If only it was not so late. If only it was not so dark. But it was late, it was dark. Then the black shape of the thing that his attacker held fell on him again, then again, then again, and the terrible pain was succeeded by numbness, then by a complete loss of feeling. But though he did not know it, the blows continued.

CHAPTER 10

Police Pressure

The news of Horrocks's murder, coming only two days after his sensational story about Father Pardoe in the *Chronicle*, came as a double blow to the congregation of St Catherine's. Those who heard the news on Radio Leeds repressed the instinct to phone around to friends who might not have heard. That would be akin to admitting that the two things were connected. The more they sat down, over a strong coffee, to think about it, the more they decided that where the police would be looking first of all would be at the man's family. And in that they were right. But all of them had a sinking feeling in the pit of their stomachs that the police would quite soon be broadening out their enquiries. Where would that leave them? What was to be their line if suspicion began to be directed at them?

Cora was glad she hadn't woken the children the night before. It had been not long after midnight when the uniformed policeman had rung the doorbell. A neighbour putting his car away had seen the figure recumbent at the side of the garages. At first he had assumed it was a drunken rough-sleeper, but he had had the wit to take the torch he kept in his lock-up and investigate further. As soon as he had seen the blood, realized who it was, he had gone home and called the police.

The constable who had called had been very good, Cora thought: matter-of-fact and low-key, which suited the situation perfectly. Her identification would be better than any neighbour's could be, he said, and the best thing for her and everyone would be to get it over quickly. Cora was already in her nightdress, but she had slipped on a dressing-gown and gone out to the garages, heart thumping, at the policeman's side. When she saw the body, the state of the smashed skull, she had leant against the garages and retched, though nothing had come up. She hoped that for the policeman it had been a convincing substitute for grief.

Because when she had got back into the house and had sat for an hour and more over a strong cup of tea, she had realized that she had simply been reacting to the horror of the scene – the blood, the bone. She had felt no grief for Cosmo, no sense that his death was a blow to her. Surprise, yes, but nothing so personal or so strong as shock. Before long, she knew, she would be glad.

Later she had had a couple of hours of something that was nearly sleep. Then she had lain waiting for signs of life from the girls' bedrooms. When they had begun their daily fight for the bathroom she had gone out and told them that they would not be going to school that day.

'Why not?' asked Adelaide.

'I don't know how to . . .' She shook herself and looked at them both seriously. 'Your father was found dead last night.'

She could swear she had seen a flicker pass over Samantha's face.

'*Dad?*' said Adelaide.

'Yes. The police came to tell me after midnight. I'm afraid he's been murdered.'

She was looking at Samantha as she said that, and her face was perfectly impassive. It was Adelaide who surprised her.

'We won't have another daddy, will we?'

Cora flinched. Her middle-class decencies had been affronted.

'What – what do you mean?'

'You won't – like – marry again, so someone else is our daddy, will you? Can't we be on our own?'

Cora swallowed. How horribly quick the child was! And how exactly her thoughts chimed in with her own.

'Yes. I'll never marry again. We'll always be on our own.'

'But how shall we manage?' asked Samantha. 'I mean for money?'

'We'll manage somehow,' she said firmly.

Now, ranged around the sitting room, with the two police-

102

men in the armchairs, she wondered if Samantha had been awake last night, had heard the doorbell, heard her go out and come to a window to see. That would explain the flicker, her feeling that her news did not entirely surprise her. If she had talked to Adelaide, that would explain her quickness. The girls had been unusually noisy in the bathroom that morning, something that was sure to bring down Cosmo's wrath on them. Was that because –?

She dragged her attention back to the present, and to the two policemen sitting opposite her, looking at her intently but covertly. The middle-aged white one – Oddie he'd introduced himself as – was kindly-looking, but she wasn't so sure about the younger, black one: he looked big and formidable. Were they some kind of nice-guy – mean-guy double act?

'I know this will come as a terrible shock to you,' Oddie was saying, looking at the girls, 'but we do need to ask questions. Can you bear with me?' Both of the girls nodded. 'Chip in with anything you think relevant if your mother hasn't said it. Now –' turning to her – 'your husband was killed near his own home. This makes us wonder about people in the vicinity here. Were relations with the neighbours good?'

'Perfectly good. No quarrels with anyone.'

'He didn't really know them, except by name,' put in Samantha. 'He worked such odd hours that he was hardly ever at home when they were. We all know them, and get on all right.'

Cora nodded, but she felt worried. What Samantha had said was true and perfectly acceptable, but she was worried in case she was going to say too much, particularly about Cosmo as a father.

'Your husband was a reporter, I know. What was he working on at the moment?'

'It was a story about a priest, and his relationship with a young single mother.'

'Yes, actually I did know that. We saw the *Globe* this morning.'

'It would have been a big day for your husband, wouldn't it?' asked the young black sergeant. 'Seeing his name on a story in one of the big tabloids.'

'Yes, it would, though it wouldn't have been the first time. But yes, he'd certainly have been pleased.'

'You hadn't seen him to talk it over with him?'

'No, he went out early as usual, and didn't come back until –'

Cora had been cultivating an entirely neutral tone in all her replies, as if she was talking about the most distant acquaintance, but now a break was heard in the voice.

'Was there anything else he was working on?' Oddie asked.

'That story had taken him over,' put in Samantha quickly. 'He'd thought about nothing else for the last two weeks or more, and hardly talked about anything else either. All sorts of people rang him up with information and that. He was dead excited.'

'He may well have been working on something else as well,' said Cora, 'because reporters always are. But this was currently his big story.'

'So there could be a lot of fall-out from that,' said Oddie. 'The *Globe* report gave us the impression that this could be a story with a lot of angles.'

'I suppose it could. But he hasn't been walking about in fear of his life, or anything melodramatic like that.'

'He is a *priest*, this chap he was after,' said Samantha. 'Poor man.'

'My old mum says there's nothing more dangerous than a Christian who knows he's in the right,' said the black policeman genially. 'Because he's so convinced of that he believes he's justified in doing anything grubby or underhand.'

Cora sensed that Oddie was not happy at having to listen to his sergeant's mother's reflections on religion and its moral effects, but she smiled at the younger man.

'It's a long time since I went to church,' she said.

'Was your husband popular at work?' Oddie asked.

'I really wouldn't know . . . He specialized in rather sensational stories. And he wasn't a patient or a naturally friendly man. That may have made him enemies.'

'How long have you been married?'

'Twenty-one years.' Aware that she had paused before she

had said this Cora asked, 'Do you think the girls could be spared this? It's very distressing for them.'

As she said it she wished they looked more distressed. They were wide-eyed, bewildered, shocked, but not – not even Adelaide – distressed. However the senior policeman nodded. She thought he had probably registered the pause.

'Go to your room,' said their mother. 'I'll be up when I can . . . I didn't want them here,' she said, turning back to the policemen when they had slipped rather reluctantly out of the room. 'I think it's best if I tell you about Cosmo, and I can't be entirely honest if they're in the room.'

'Of course. We understand,' said Oddie.

'Not that I'd want to pretend we were a loving family. Cosmo needed a victim, and quite often it was one of his children. I'm trying to be as honest as I can, because I expect it's well known in their schools. And there was another side to Cosmo.'

'Yes?'

'I'll always be grateful to him. Before I met him I was in a relationship with a man . . .' She actually shivered at the memory – 'someone so dreadful, so vicious . . .'

'Where is this man now?'

'I don't know. I know he was given a long prison sentence about seven years ago, not before time. He could still be in, though they get out so early these days, don't they?'

'What was he jailed for?'

'Violence against a woman. Just like with me. He could be so charming, but when it came to it, what it always led up to was violence. He could be so savage, you wouldn't believe it. That's what Cosmo rescued me from.'

'In what way rescued?'

'He exposed him in the paper he was working on then. This man – Alan Russell his name was, or is – had a long history of it: women who wouldn't prosecute, women who went to the police but found they weren't interested, cases that went to court but he just got a fine or a suspended sentence because he was so plausible, so reasonable and charming. "IS THIS BIRMINGHAM'S MOST VIOLENT MAN?" was one of Cosmo's headlines. It didn't get any action from the police, but it kept him away from me, and when the climate of opinion about that sort of thing changed, the police knew their man.'

'And you and Mr Horrocks were married by then?'

'Yes, we married, and quite soon after we moved up to Yorkshire. I'll always be grateful to him.'

It was a statement that begged quite a lot of questions. And Oddie wondered how it fitted with her earlier one that Cosmo needed a victim.

Father Pardoe turned the radio off. It was John Humphrys interrupting people in the public interest on the *Today* programme. Not at all what he needed. He went on with the washing up that he was doing, after much protest from Margaret, because he knew she wanted to get off into town. A visit to Leeds was a big matter to her, and she liked to get in early and get back to Pudsey before the shops got crowded. He found washing up restful, almost therapeutic, and he could think through what his immediate course of action should be, as well as his long-term aims.

He found that the questions divided themselves up into two in his mind: what it would be politic to do, and what it would be morally right to do. The answers were usually diametrically opposed. For example, in the matter of the Bishop of Leeds's action in his case: the politic thing to do was to backtrack, apologize, defer; but since he was convinced that the Bishop had behaved unfairly as well as unwisely since the rumours first surfaced, the morally right thing to do was to question, oppose, press his case. On meditating things through, he came to the conclusion that he really didn't have any choice. He was too far down the second route to backtrack now. So far down, in fact, that the Bishop would require more in the way of backtracking, apology and deference than he could stomach giving.

At ten o'clock he switched on Radio Leeds for the local news. Keeping up with parish pump events was something he had always found it necessary to do when he was a functioning priest, and it was something he had resumed as soon as the shock of his suspension had worn off. He was, after all, still the priest of St Catherine's. He was pulled up short by the second item on the bulletin.

'The body of a man found battered to death last night on waste ground in Rodley has been identified as that of Cosmo Horrocks, a journalist on the *West Yorkshire Chronicle*. A spokesperson for Northern Newspapers who own the paper said: "We are devastated. It is difficult to take in. Cosmo Horrocks was a journalist to his fingertips. He will be much missed."'

Pardoe sat heavily down on the nearest kitchen chair, his mind blocking out the rest of the bulletin – blocking out, too, all his thoughts about his predicament. Was this Pelion heaped on Ossa? Was this something he would be involved in? It could be murder for the contents of the man's wallet, it could be domestic, or the result of some row or feud at work or in his neighbourhood. One of those, surely, was what it would prove to be. He remembered Cosmo Horrocks's face, standing there beside the photographer in Cookridge Street. A mean face – a face of petty grudges and low ambitions. The face of someone who had to have the whip hand. He could imagine him hated in his family, hated at work. Surely it was in the home or in the workplace that the culprit would be found. Probably it would be the sort of murder that solved itself practically at once. Please God it was so. Please God this would not be something that dragged him down with it, involved him in all the head-shaking that police questioning always led people to indulge in. People like his parishioners.

This led him to another thought: please God he didn't have to tell anyone what he was doing last night.

The doorbell rang. With a heavy heart and his feet also feeling like lead he dragged himself down the hall and opened the door on a middle-aged white man and a youngish black one, both of them brandishing cards in his face.

Simon Norris heard the news from a customer – or rather from one of those people who came into his shop ostensibly to buy but actually to get a look at him from behind the racks and shelves. Simon got on to his wife at once.

'Daphne? Have you heard the news?'

'No.'

'That Cosmo Horrocks, the one who wrote up the story. He's been murdered.'

'He hasn't!'

'Oh but he has. It was on the local news apparently. Customer just told me. By 'eck, Julie's landed herself in a pile of muck all right. The police'll be wanting to talk to her.'

'Will they? I don't know . . . Simon –?'

Something in her voice alerted him. It wasn't something he would normally have been sensitive to, but he did get the impression that she had been crying.

'Daphne, has something upset you?'

'Yes, it has rather,' his wife said. 'Nothing to do with this murder. I went to the butcher's about nine, and I thought he was a bit stiff like – reserved you could call it. But then this woman came in, someone I only know by sight, and she looked at me in a very sniffy way and I thought, "I don't know what *you've* got to be sniffy about." Then after a minute or two she came out with it. "You ought to be ashamed of yourselves," she said.'

'Ashamed of ourselves? What the 'ell have we got to be ashamed about?'

'She said: "Throwing out a daughter like that, just when she needed you most."'

'Well, our Julie should have thought of that first, shouldn't she?'

'"And then talking to the papers about her as if she was nothing but a slut," this woman said. "You must be some kind of monsters. I wouldn't wish parents like you on any young kid." I couldn't help it, Simon. I just burst into tears.'

'Daphne, you're not to take on. This woman's got to be wrong in the head.'

'I don't think she is, Simon. There were two others came in while she was speaking, and they both nodded. I think people got the wrong idea from that article. I wonder whether that Horrocks person didn't double-cross us – pretended to be putting our side of the story, but really . . .'

There was silence on both ends of the line for a moment. 'Well, if he did he's bloody paid for it,' said Simon Norris.

Father Greenspan was told the news by phone as soon as he got back to the Presbytery after the early morning service. It was the Bishop's secretary, and she said that the meeting set up for later that day for himself, the Bishop and the trustees of the Father Riley Fund could now be cancelled. Father Greenspan made an appropriate response to the news: he seems to have been a frightful fellow, was the burden of his remarks, but of course this was a shocking event. He took no pains, however, to make his voice anything other than perfectly calm and collected.

When he put the phone down he sat in the armchair by the phone and tried to order his thoughts. How would this affect his position, his hopes? Would this sensational twist to the Father Pardoe saga be the final blow to any hope the man still had of returning to St Catherine's? Would the police be connecting him to the murder, interviewing him, involving him in a third strand of shady or shameful transactions? Would the interest in the Father Riley Fund now cease, or would the national tabloids seize on the story with redoubled curiosity? The Bishop seemed to assume not, but Father Greenspan was less sure. He was perfectly confident in his world of ceremonial and parish matters of a straightforward nature, and especially so in the matters of prayers, retreats, observances of all kinds. In the world of human frailties, tabloid values and police investigations he felt himself quite at sea.

His mind was a chilly one, accustomed to setting out the ramifications of any matter in a manner that resembled a statement of accounts, with pluses and minuses and a balance at the end. In the matter of murder, and of publicity, he felt more at sea, more uncertain in his tottings up. When he had given it some prolonged thought, he decided that the press was certainly not going to lose interest in the matter, and that press coverage had done Father Pardoe hitherto no good at all, and was unlikely to do him anything but harm in the future.

When he got up from the chair he was smiling.

'I only saw him properly once,' said Father Pardoe, to the two serious men sitting opposite him. 'That was after Mass at St Anne's last Sunday. He had his photographer with him, taking pictures of me talking to the Bishop. You may have seen the picture in the local paper.'

'We did,' said the black detective. 'But at the time it wasn't a story we thought would be of any interest to us.'

'Maybe you were right.'

'Did you know in advance that the press were getting interested in your story?' asked the white one.

'I had a hint of it from the Bishop. But that was just before the photograph appeared.'

'How had he heard?'

'I've no idea. I am told nothing by that source. Word could have got around among the St Catherine's congregation that he'd been in the area talking to people. The way it was written up makes it obvious that he had – the Norrises, poor Julie, her neighbours.'

'But he hadn't talked to you.'

'No, he hadn't. He'd followed me to St Anne's on the bus last Sunday, and he was among the reporters waiting outside here on Monday. I suspected that approaching me and saying he wanted to put "my side" would be his next ploy. I pre-empted that by going to the girl from the *Bradford Telegraph and Argus*. I would certainly never have talked to Horrocks.'

'You feel strongly about him?' asked Peace.

Father Pardoe shifted in his chair.

'About the British press in general, to tell you the truth. Maybe I shouldn't say this, in the circumstances, but morally they're a sewer. They trade in human misery and degradation. The reporters and editors remind me of vultures, circling in the air looking for carrion. It's a national shame that people want to read that kind of thing.'

'Could you tell us what you were doing yesterday evening, Father?'

It was Peace, the black detective. The one with sharp

eyes. Father Pardoe tried very hard not to shift again in his chair.

'Yesterday evening? Well, I went for a walk. Normally I would do that in the afternoon, but there had been reporters outside all day, so I couldn't go for my usual constitutional. I realized about nine o'clock that they'd all gone – probably sloped off to one of the nearby pubs. When I got in –'

'How long were you out?' Oddie asked. Before he could reply Pardoe heard a key in the front door.

'About an hour or so.' He wondered whether to raise his voice for the next sentence, but decided his interviewers were not stupid, so he kept it at its usual low tone. 'After I got in Mrs Knowsley and I were discussing things – the newspaper stories, the Bishop's reaction and so on – until quite late.'

At this point Margaret came into the sitting room. The men got up and the visitors were introduced. The moment they all sat down Oddie put the same question to her.

'Could you tell me when Father Pardoe came back from his walk, and what you did afterwards?'

'Oh yes. He got back somewhere around a quarter past ten. And then we sat up talking about the case – his suspension, that is. I've got very partisan since Father Pardoe came as my lodger. It was around 11.45 when I went to bed, and I heard him come up about ten minutes later.'

Pardoe realized with a shock that he felt glad that she had told the lie that he had been careful not to tell.

Doris Crabtree was so flabbergasted by the news as relayed by *Look North* on the television at eleven o'clock that she trailed all the way along Kingsmill Close, Kingsmill Rise, Kingsmill Crescent, and then the whole length of Kingsmill Grove to Florrie Mortlake's little first-floor flat, to sit in her kitchen and give expression to her shock. Over and over again.

'I can't get over it,' she said. 'There was him, just yesterday, sitting in my front room large as life and nice as pie, and now today, *gone*. He was that friendly, you wouldn't believe, said how useful what I'd told him had been, and how he'd be interested in anything I might happen to hear in the future. It hits you, doesn't it, something like this. "In the midst of life we are in death." Well, *this* drives that home, doesn't it? There's no justice about it either. Because a nicer chap you couldn't hope to meet . . .'

Thus Doris Crabtree, at inordinate length, illustrating the truth that anyone who has ever studied the media must learn: that the carrier of news is often the worst possible interpreter of it.

The editor being busy at a summit meeting with the newspaper's proprietors, it was Marcia Moore who received the two detectives when, at her suggestion, they called at the *Chronicle*'s offices when the last edition had been put to bed.

'I have more to do with the newsroom than the editor,' she said, as they marched, Marcia leading the way, from her office in its direction. 'So I can probably tell you more.'

'Good,' said Oddie. 'Now, we haven't got a time for the murder. He was found just after midnight, but he could have been lying there a fair while. We shan't get the result of the autopsy until tomorrow, if then, so it would help us if we could know when he left here last night.'

'Yes, I realized that,' she said. 'Though of course he didn't necessarily go straight home.' She had a newsperson's instinct to teach her grandmother to suck eggs. 'I've asked the night security man. He's a dozy individual. He didn't see Cosmo go out, but he thinks there was still someone in the newsroom when he came on duty at nine.'

'Not too helpful,' said Oddie. 'So we could try to find out if any of these were still around at that time,' he said, as they walked into the newsroom.

'You can try. There's not usually many by late evening. They have to come on duty early in the morning. If Cosmo was around so late he was probably stewing over his priest-and-bimbo story.'

They were standing by the door, and the black policeman's eyelid twitched. She looked at him boldly.

'You didn't like him?' he asked.

'Couldn't stand him. In fact, I'm glad to have seen the last of his leering face, glad I shan't have to smell his foul little cigars, glad I shan't have to have any more rows with him about his bogus expenses claims. I'm not alone. You won't find much grief for him here. Correction: *any* grief.'

And no grief was what they got when they separated out and went around the newsroom. Cosmo was not loved, that everyone made clear, and would not have wanted to be loved. The adjectives used varied, but they were mostly within the range used by tabloids for our contemporary monsters. They didn't get much either on when Cosmo had left the office.

'He wasn't here – at least not in the newsroom – when I slipped in and out at ten fifteen because I'd left my house keys in a drawer,' said Carol Barr to Charlie Peace, as he perched on the side of her desk in the little bit not occupied by her computer. 'He could have been in the loo, of course, or in the library, or anywhere else in the building. I didn't notice that his screen was showing anything, but that's probably not significant. Cosmo was basically a notebook-and-pencil man.'

'And there was nobody else here?'

'No. I thought Terry Beale might be, but he wasn't.'

'Why?'

'One of the arts team was off, and Terry was covering an Opera North first night. He felt a bit unsure of his territory, thought he might need the library if he wasn't to make a fool of himself. Probably the opera wasn't over by then.'

'But they could, say, both have been in the library?'

'Oh yes. But if Terry killed him it would have been on impulse, there and then. You'd have found the body in the stacks, or by his desk there. He wouldn't have followed him home and done it.'

'Terry didn't like him?'

'Terry loathed him. We all did.' She paused as if wondering whether to say what was in her mind, but after a second she did. 'With Terry it was very strong, almost personal. We could never see why it should be.'

'Is Terry here now?' asked Peace, looking round the newsroom.

'No. India's playing Pakistan in the World Cup at Headingley, and they're expecting crowd trouble. I think he's probably covering that, because I haven't seen him all day.'

She hadn't meant to, but as the big policeman got off her desk, nodded, and moved away, she realized that she had really landed Terry in it.

By mid-morning the news was beginning to get around the parishioners of St Catherine's. Miss Preece-Dembleby heard it on Aire Waves, the commercial station that had a nostalgia hour from eleven to twelve with regular news updates. She rang Janette Jessel first, being careful to switch the radio off, because she would have died rather than admit to listening to old Vera Lynn and Ann Shelton records to opera-loving Janette. When she had retailed the gossip in a thoroughly efficient and genteel manner to her, she got on to Mary Leary and did the same. Then she sat down and wondered whether she should ring her brother.

After the call and a pause for coffee Mrs Leary continued to iron Monday's wash, but she was thinking hard. She still had the conviction that the parish activists were getting – no, *had got* – into things deeper, murkier, than they understood. She tried to tell herself she was being stupid. A priest is suspended, a journalist gets on to the story, the journalist is murdered. It seemed like a simple progression of events, and if it *was* that simple it had the appearance of implicating Father Pardoe or his parishioners at St Catherine's. But that was absurd: the dead man presumably had a private life, a professional life. Both spheres could probably produce a better motive than the Father Pardoe story could. And then, he apparently had been battered to death. This suggested some kind of mugging. People these days got killed just for the contents of their purses or wallets. Our streets held the equivalent of the eighteenth-century footpads. That was probably the most likely explanation of all.

But in spite of deciding that, in spite of telling herself that she had not been *regretting* getting involved in the movement of support for Father Pardoe, there still niggled at the back of her mind a feeling that they had sailed into uncharted waters, and that those waters had turned out to be much choppier and murkier than they had banked on.

She put the last of the ironing, Mark's cricketing and gym

gear, down on one of the several piles that sat on the kitchen table beside the ironing-board. Suddenly she felt a rare need: someone to talk to, someone to swap conjectures with. She rejected Miss Preece-Dembleby as too prim and buttoned-up, and got on the phone to Janette Jessel.

'Janette? You've heard of course.'

'Yes. Edith Preece-Dembleby rang. Isn't it *horrible*?'

'I find it – I don't know – bewildering. I wondered if we could meet for tea and cakes. Have a talk.'

'Love to. I feel the need to, to tell you the truth.'

'Me too. Where?'

'The Fir Tree? Not much option really.'

'Not really. I resent paying to eat cakes so much nastier than any I would ever make myself.'

'True. But that's not really the point, is it?'

'No, of course it's not. See you – when? Four o'clock?'

'See you then.'

Mary Leary collected up her washing, and began going round the various rooms upstairs distributing it – first Donna's untidy bedroom, then Mark's much more organized one, then the marital bedroom, from her wardrobe to Conal's, then to the chest of drawers that had drawers for both of them. It was a routine, a dance she did every week, where any variation in the steps would irritate.

Then she went down to the basement and the games room there. Its big cupboard was where Conal and Mark insisted on keeping all their sporting stuff, including the gear they were both rather particular about. She put Conal's golfing shirt on a pile of similar ones, then put Mark's cricketing shirt and his gym shorts and vest on their appropriate piles. She was about to shut the door when something struck her.

There was something wrong, something different about the cupboard. Something that was not there. She stepped back to survey it, and then realized what it was. But why –? What use –?

It hit her like an exploding grenade.

She shut the door and leaned the back of her head against it. She wished with all her heart that she had not arranged to have tea and cakes with Janette Jessel. How on earth was she going to seem natural? How on earth could she manage to put up any sort of convincing pretence? How could she think of anything except what that space signified?

CHAPTER 11

Feminine Unease

Miss Preece-Dembleby set out from her home on Thursday morning with the intention of calling on her brother at his office. The nagging anxiety she had that he was *involved* in something had only grown since their conversation on the telephone, and it had coalesced with her general uneasiness about the parish that she loved, the priest she respected, and the priest she did not respect, adding up to a general feeling that somehow things were out of joint. Miss Preece-Dembleby was essentially a watcher, a cataloguer of life's ills and follies, but there were times when she felt imperatively the need for action, and at such times she could be decisive.

Halfway to her brother's office, however, she changed her mind. Walking had clarified her thinking, as it often did. If she visited Raymond, and even if he was unencumbered with a client, she would be subjected to exactly the same line as he had taken on the telephone: this was not her business, not women's business at all, it was a parish matter, confidential to the two trustees and the Bishop, and he wasn't willing to say one syllable more. She was perfectly capable of dealing with her brother on a personal, domestic, psychological level, and would quite often have the better of any disagreement of that sort. On the professional, work level of his life she was at a disadvantage, having no education or training beyond her sixteenth year, and in any case liable to be wrong-footed, as anyone would be, by the plea of confidentiality.

She determined instead to visit her brother's home, an imposing late Victorian dwelling, not unlike the one she had shared with him for years, just over the borderline between Shipley and Saltaire. He had bought it as a bargain when he

117

was married, pleased to stick with the sort of house he knew, and had then spent a fortune bringing it up to his standards of comfort and suitable middle-class elegance. She shook her head, in fact, at the amounts he had spent on central heating, decorating, and overplush furnishings. She did the four-minute walk briskly, her mental clock ticking away the whole time. When she arrived there the door of the house in Elmtree Lane was opened by her newish sister-in-law, her smile expressing genuine pleasure.

'Edith – this is a surprise.'

'Hello Nora. Do you have a minute?'

'Of course. I've got coffee on. Come in.'

'This isn't really a social call, but –'

Nora waved any protest aside, and in a matter of minutes they were in the living room, with its bulky and convention-ally handsome furniture, and Edith was ushered down into one of the cretonne-covered chairs, while Nora bustled back to the kitchen to fetch a tray of coffee with Marie biscuits on a delicate silver stand. Nora was, on the surface, as conventional a person as her second husband, but Edith felt she had never got to know her well enough to judge whether this was anything more than a façade.

'Was it the June bazaar?' she asked now, herself settling back into the embrace of her armchair.

'No, it was – well – more personal than that,' Edith said, feeling something close to a flush rising to her cheeks. 'It's very difficult to put it into words but it's something that has been troubling me very much. Nora, have you had the feeling that Raymond has been worried recently?'

Nora frowned.

'He's seemed a bit harassed – put upon, you might say. I haven't thought too much about it. I don't generally ask about his work, and sure with that kind of thing you're bound to have problems and uncertainties now and then, aren't you? It's a difficult time, everyone says so. My own money isn't earning half the interest it was a few years ago.'

'How long have you sensed he's been worried?'

'I suppose it's been coming on gradually. Let me think: two or three months maybe?'

'And you thought it was the general economic climate, or perhaps problems with one of his clients?'

'Well, it's not personal. And I've never had any sense that his business is falling off.'

'No. That doesn't leave very much . . . Does he ever mention the Father Riley Fund?'

Nora looked at her sharply and again creased her still handsome brow.

'I think I've heard of it from him – maybe when he's off to a meeting or something. He's certainly not mentioned it recently. But I have *heard* of it recently. Now where –?'

'In the papers maybe.'

'Oh, of course,' she said, her face closing. 'Poor Father Pardoe. Now that's a nasty business, don't you agree?'

'I do.'

'And do you know I can't get Raymond to agree with me,' her sister-in-law said, not greatly to Edith's surprise. 'In fact, I can't get so much as a whisper out of him on the subject.'

'They're saying that Father Pardoe misused the Fund for this poor creature the daughter of those odious Norrises,' said Edith, abandoning any pretence of neutrality. 'Now I talked to Mrs O'Keefe who lives on the Kingsmill estate at church last Sunday. She says the girl is living in pretty abject poverty. He can't have misused much, can he?'

'Surely he can't.'

'And it sounds like exactly the sort of case the Fund is meant to be used for.'

'It does.' She thought, and then added: 'Though Father Riley, whoever he was, was maybe not as used to Catholic girls being unmarried mothers as we are.'

Edith leant forward in her chair.

'The fact is, Nora, I was under the impression that the Fund had been taken over by the Bishop and the trustees.'

'I know nothing about that.'

'I suppose if Raymond had been really worried he would have discussed it with you.'

Nora shook her head vigorously.

'That he would not. We never talk about such things because I've no interest in them whatsoever. I'm a farmer's wife, or widow – I took a keen interest in the farm, the animals, even the crops, and I could cope with the ups and downs of prices and what the livestock market was doing. But the sort of high finance Raymond's work involves him in, that means less than nothing to me.'

A sudden, uncomfortable thought struck Edith, prompted by something Nora had said earlier. It was a thought difficult to put into words.

'Nora, you said your money wasn't making what it used to. You do still keep control of it, don't you?'

She was heartened when she saw her sister-in-law looking at her pityingly.

'Edith, we're not living in the nineteenth century, you know. I have heard of the Married Women's Property Act, and I do know the sort of thing that makes for friction in a marriage. Handing over control of money would come pretty near the top of the list.'

Edith felt rebuked for her lack of experience in marital matters, yet elated too.

'So Raymond never suggested that he might manage your investments?'

'He may have hinted he could give me advice. If he did I took no notice. I'm not so green as I'm cabbage-looking. For better or worse I decide where my money goes, so the blame rests with me if it does less than brilliantly. And if I decided I wanted advice, I'd go to someone else. We have a perfectly satisfactory marriage, Edith, but sometimes my greater experience has to rescue Raymond from his ignorance of the state. Rest assured: I'm a woman who manages her own affairs.'

Walking home, Edith felt a wave of gratitude flood through her that there was no question of Raymond appropriating and misusing his wife's money. The drama of that, if it ever came out, or if it even was suspected, would have been hard to bear. Yet when she thought about it, the fact that she could even consider the possibility of that happening said something about Raymond's character, or her view of it: he was weak, easily led, fell into things because he had no clear or strong system of morality built into his make-up.

And that thought left the worry about the Father Riley Fund very strong in her mind. Had he misappropriated funds, perhaps in cahoots with his fellow trustee? That was Gerald Sooter, from Bingley. A picture of him – long, gangly, runny-eyed – came into her mind. He was only an occasional communicant at St Catherine's, and Edith had exchanged words with him on barely more than one or two occasions, but she had heard someone describe him as a 'genetically modified twerp'. Edith liked the phrase, and thought it fitted. Though she would never herself use language like that, she rather relished it when other people did. Now the memory of the description added enormously to her disquiet. Why on earth had a man like that been made a trustee?

The home of Janette Jessel was only two minutes away. Edith considered whether she ought to drop in on her: she liked her, and she had been to her house more than once on parish business, but they were not on terms where she would consider herself justified in calling without some sort of specific business. Though Edith lived her life by a pattern of rules, many of them antiquated, some of them ridiculous, she had never regarded any of them as totally binding: circumstances altered cases, she was well aware, and exceptional situations called for bold behaviour. She decided to go out of her way and call.

The Jessels' house was a recent one, part of a small estate built on the playground of a Victorian primary school that had outlived its usefulness in an era of declining births. This was not a jerry-built estate of homes where everyone peered over the tiny apron of back garden that their neighbours had, and heard the television programmes and love-makings indulged in next door as clearly as if they were in the next room. These were rather more substantial, with three bedrooms, and looking out in a row on to an older street. Even so Edith did not regard them with favour. The newer the house the worse built, she believed, and the new estates of the last twenty or thirty years were the slums of the early twenty-first century. She had no doubt that buying this house was Derek Jessel's decision.

121

In fact she suspected that most decisions in the household were his.

When Janette opened the door the expression on her face was surprised but welcoming.

'Miss Preece-Dembleby! Come in. Tea, or coffee?'

'Neither thank you. I've just had coffee with Nora, Raymond's wife. Are you alone?'

'Of course,' said Janette, ushering her through to the rather cramped sitting room. 'With Bill at university and Jack at college in Leeds all day and most of the evening, I usually am.'

'You're not looking forward to your brood flying the nest, then?' Edith asked, sitting down nearly in an armchair.

'It's as if they've flown already. Maybe it would have been different if we'd had a daughter . . .'

'Daughters fly the nest too, you know,' said Edith. 'Though I never did.'

'Perhaps you were the wise one,' said Janette.

Edith felt that, judging by the expression on Janette's face, they were getting into painful waters, so she came right out with her preoccupation.

'It's the murder.'

'I thought it must be. It's terrible. I feel so *bewildered*. If only one knew it had nothing to do with –'

'But we don't – not yet at least. And of course one worries. It sounds silly to suggest that anything we did in support of Father Pardoe could have led to that dreadful smut merchant who was hounding him being killed, but . . . Oh Janette, I've been getting such upsetting ideas and fancies!'

'I know. I'm the same. And Edith – may I call you that?'

'Of course, my dear.'

'I've had a phone call from Roger Malley – do you remember him? His wife was killed in a car accident, and he moved to Leeds to be nearer his work.'

'I remember. Quite tragic. I never knew him well.'

'We did, and I was very close to his wife. He was at St Anne's last Sunday,' explained Janette, 'and spoke to Father Pardoe on the way out, not knowing anything about the trouble he's in. Anyway, he was still close to Father and the Bishop when they were, well, having the set-to that the photographer got the picture of. He says that the Bishop was accusing Father of organizing what was virtually a petition from the congregation, and he was clearly very angry.'

Edith looked worried. She had always been so strong in her support of those in authority in the past.

'The Bishop was? Oh dear. We seem to have done more harm than good.'

'Yes,' agreed Janette. Then she thought. 'Though we've no reason to think Father Pardoe is annoyed about it . . . If only we could speak to him.'

Edith considered this slowly.

'The place where he's staying hasn't actually been named in any of the newspapers, has it? Anyway, we might compound the harm we've done if we try to do that. The thing that was in the back of my mind as a possibility was getting in contact with the police investigating the case.'

Janette Jessel's face showed her surprise.

'Oh? But wouldn't that be practically asking them to make a connection?'

Edith shook her head, but not entirely confidently.

'Not necessarily, I don't think. You see, Janette, the thing I dread most is opening my front door and finding the police there, flashing their little cards. It would make me feel so guilty. Then they'd demand to come in, and they'd be questioning me on *their* terms. If we were to contact them, say that we'd done this and that, and that we were worried that quite inadvertently we might have contributed to a situation that conceivably had led to murder, then if they decided it was worth talking to us they'd be doing it on *our* terms.'

'Ye-e-es,' conceded Janette, rather reluctantly. 'I suppose so. But wouldn't we be focusing their minds on Father Pardoe, when really it should be on something else – the awful man's domestic situation, for example, or his colleagues on the *Chronicle*?'

'I don't think so,' said Edith more firmly. 'With the story breaking and being in the national gutter press as well as the local paper, it's something they're bound to have very much on their minds. Let's try thinking this through, shall we? The

123

story, as the press has got hold of it, is a two-pronged one. On the one hand there are the allegations about Father Pardoe and Julie Norris.'

'That's the part of the story that gives it its popular appeal,' said Janette. 'Aren't the English dreadful sometimes?'

'Mostly, in my opinion.' Something struck Edith, and she let it distract her for a moment. 'That poor girl. You know, I feel there must be something *to* her, for Father to take all that trouble with her. Maybe some of us should try to do something for her.'

Janette looked sceptical.

'I think most of the support will come from her own generation.'

'I hope so. *Girls* of her generation, I would guess. But she may still need money, some kind of material help. I'm sure the girl feels hurt and betrayed by the newspaper interest, but one can't, luckily, see a pregnant woman with a toddler lying in wait for this reptile and bashing his head in. The Norrises seem to have co-operated quite disgracefully with him, which rather rules them out unfortunately. And of course Father Pardoe is out of the question. That leaves the other part of the newspaper interest: the Father Riley Fund.'

'Yes,' agreed Janette. 'You know, somehow I've never been able to take that seriously. I just can't see him handing over large sums of money to the girl so she could go out and live it up. Not Father Pardoe.'

'Nor did he do anything of the sort, I'm quite sure. Apparently she lives on the breadline, like most of these too-young mothers, and the most he did for her was get a few basic comforts and appliances, all of them second-hand.'

'Of course you'd know, your brother being a trustee.'

'Raymond has told me nothing – less than nothing,' said Edith Preece-Dembleby, with something of a judge's sternness. 'He's clammed up on the subject. I learnt what I've just told you from Mrs O'Keefe, on the Kingsmill. Now, of course there's a possibility that this was just an example of what was in fact a more widespread misuse of the Fund, but it's a possibility I personally would ignore.'

'Of course,' agreed Janette. 'Anyway, from what I've heard Father had given up control of the Fund to the Bishop and the trustees.' She pulled herself up. 'That brings it back rather close to home for you, doesn't it?'

'Don't be embarrassed, my dear. Yes it does. You know, I've just been talking about it to Nora, my sister-in-law, and I got the awful idea that Raymond could have been squandering or misusing her money.'

'Edith!' said Janette, shocked. 'What gave you that idea?'

'I don't know . . . Something *furtive* about Raymond when I raise the matter of the Father Riley Fund. I thought he might have got into financial difficulties.'

'I've never heard of his firm having problems. Derek says he's got loads of clients.'

'But Raymond's always been one for a flutter at the races, and on the Stock Exchange too . . . Oh, it was just a silly thought, and quite wrong, because Nora's in full control of her own little fortune, so she says. But the question of what Raymond may have been doing with the Riley Fund remains. The problem is what we do next.'

Janette took her time over that. She hadn't taken kindly to the idea of going to the police, though thinking it over she had to admit there was a kind of sense to it.

'You know, if we did go to the police, or for that matter if they came to see us, it would make sense to edge them in the direction of the Father Riley Fund.'

Edith's face expressed distaste.

'I couldn't do it myself, not with Raymond being one of the ones involved.'

'No. But I could.'

'I shrink from it. I'm old-fashioned, and I do shrink from any scandal coming close to my family. I can talk about it to you, but –'

'You must realize that, even if Raymond is involved, the person responsible is almost certainly the Bishop.'

Edith looked even more anguished.

'Oh dear. Such a masterful man. And what you say would not be true if there was any . . . private peculation.'

'In any case,' said Janette, 'the police won't need any

direction to look at the Fund. It was a prominent part of the original story, and in the version in the *Globe*.'

'Oh dear yes. Of course it will be in their minds anyway.'

'Hadn't we better consult Mary about this?' Janette said after a moment's thought. 'She was at least as active as either of us in deciding to write to the Bishop.'

'Good idea. Why don't you ring her?'

Janette stood up, turned towards Edith, seemingly about to tell her something, then changed her mind and went to the telephone.

'Mary? Janette here. I've got Edith Preece-Dembleby here . . . Yes, we've been talking over what we should do in the light of the murder of that awful journalist . . . Well, actually Edith thought we *should* do something, because if it turns out to have something to do with our appeal to the Bishop, it will look better if we have approached the police first . . . Oh . . . Yes . . . Yes . . . Of course I see your point . . . Yes . . . Yes . . . I'll talk it over with Edith.'

When she had put the phone down she came back to the little group of easy chairs and sat down, very pensive.

'I suppose you got the gist of that, Edith?'

'She was against it.'

'Yes. And not just that – quite shocked and disturbed by the idea. I think "agitated" is the best word to describe it.'

Edith chewed the matter over in her mind, then said: 'You were going to tell or ask me something before you went to ring her, then decided not to.'

'You're very sharp. Yes . . . This will probably sound silly. I phoned Mary on Monday, after the story broke in the *Chronicle*. I wondered where that left our little campaign in support of Father Pardoe. One thing led to another in our talk – which was almost our first *real*, open conversation. It became – I don't know – a sort of meeting of minds, an overflowing of emotions.'

'What about, my dear?'

'Basically marriage. Our marriages. The position of Catholic women, and the sort of marriage most of us find ourselves in.'

'I see. I think I can guess the drift of what you were saying.

I'm not quite the dried-out stick some people see me as, and I have my eyes and ears in good working order still. I sometimes wonder whether I've been – not wise, but at least lucky, in not falling into that sort of marriage, as you said earlier. I do value my independence.'

'I can see you understand. It seemed like we were saying things we'd wanted to say to each other for years, because our husbands are so similar, and are friends, but hadn't said them out of some sort of misplaced loyalty to them. Anyway, she rang me yesterday and suggested we ought to talk. I was quite happy with that, and we agreed to meet for tea and horrid buns at the Fir Tree. As I say, she had sounded quite normal, eager to have a chat . . . But then –'

'Yes?'

'When she got there she was preoccupied. Sort of shut down. We went through the motions of talking about the things we'd talked about on Monday, but . . . there was nothing there.'

'Her heart wasn't in it any more?'

'More than that. She was not just preoccupied, I thought, but eaten up with worry. She could hardly think of anything else, and when she talked about marriage, or Father Pardoe or whatever, she was always saying the wrong word – you know, a word close in sound, but not the one she wanted, like elderly people do. She was just going through the motions of having a conversation.'

'Something had happened between her ringing you up, and her actually getting to the Fir Tree to meet you, you think?'

'I think it must have.'

'You didn't ask her what it was?'

'No. I didn't like to pry. I hate it when people try to press me about Derek and his . . . habits. But more than that: I had the feeling that what had happened, or what she had discovered, was so terrible, or dangerous, or distressing, that it was something she *couldn't* tell me.'

They chewed over the matter for a half-hour or more, but in the end they decided there could be no question of going to the police when Mary Leary was so decidedly against it.

Their discussion, however, turned out to be quite academic, because when Edith Preece-Dembleby arrived home she found two policemen on her doorstep flashing their ID cards in her face.

CHAPTER 12

Roots

When Mike Oddie and Charlie Peace got back to their car after talking to Miss Preece-Dembleby, Charlie sat slumped for a moment in the driver's seat, apparently on another planet. He had been brooding since he'd clocked in that morning. Eventually Oddie recalled him to business by asking 'How did she strike you?'

'Just thoughtful. Not depressed, but as if something was on her mind.' Then he jumped. 'Christ! Sorry! You meant the old biddy in there.'

'Whereas you were talking about Felicity. What do you think is on her mind?'

'I'm afraid her father is proposing to come and live with us or near us, and use Felicity as a doormat again.'

Charlie's partner Felicity had a father who wrote mediocre novels that unerringly failed to ring the bell with readers. He was recently widowed, and with a nice line in self-pity had written letters regretting that his daughter was not available to act as his housekeeper.

'Felicity is long past the doormat stage,' said Oddie firmly, 'thanks partly to you but mostly to herself. When you get home tonight why don't you sit down and ask her? Now, if you gave any part of your mind to it, what did you think of Miss Preece-Dembleby?'

Charlie dragged his mind back to the job in hand.

'At first the whole thing struck me as a bit of a comedy act,' he admitted. 'I mean, this prim and proper old biddy sitting there with her hands in her lap and saying things like, "It seemed as if the women of the parish were waking up." It made me want to laugh.'

'An unlikely Germaine Greer?'

129

'Way over the top,' agreed Charlie. 'Miss Marple leads the feminist revolution – thirty years after the event. But if you shut your eyes and listened to what was being *said*, it was very sharp. And if you looked at the face – the eyes, the mouth – you saw that she was noticing everything. She was talking about the parish, her brother, Father Pardoe and so on, but all the time she was noticing *us*.'

'We probably were a bit outside her experience.'

'Way outside. Still, she was coping. Registering differences in age, background, wondering how we got on, wondering whether we formed some kind of double act, which she'd probably heard of, registering as soon as I opened my mouth that I was a Londoner, wondering what I was doing up here. All in all I'd say she is a very sharp lady.'

'So we take notice of what she said?'

'Absolutely. Father Pardoe is innocent, the victim of smears and perhaps a plot, possibly the designated fall guy for someone else's financial misdeeds. And the women of the parish are on the warpath, sensing they're still victims of a very old-fashioned sort of male chauvinism. And somehow these two things are connected, but I'm not sure I understand how.'

'No . . . Leave that for a moment. I'd go along with everything you say. But I do wonder how the feminine awakening in the St Catherine's parish is our affair. At the moment I can't see that it is, though the Fund certainly bears looking into.'

'There is one other thing,' said Charlie.

'What's that?'

'In one respect she seemed muddled, and I don't think she's a muddled lady. She was willing to talk about the Father Riley Fund, but whenever she talked about her brother she tended to get more reserved, bottled-up.'

'We had to screw out of her the brother's connection with the Fund.'

'Yes . . . I think she'd like it to be the Bishop who's been playing hanky-panky with the capital, but she's not sure, and she's instinctively trying to protect the brother without having any great confidence in his honesty.'

'Fair enough. I expect I'd be muddled in that sort of

130

circumstance. What next, then? Maybe we should get on to Headquarters and see what's been happening back there.'

But when they got back on to Sergeant Coppin at Millgarth, who was co-ordinating the murder enquiry, they found he'd hit a snag.

'This young chap you want to talk to.'

'Terry Beale?'

'Yes, him. Not at the *Chronicle* offices today, wasn't in yesterday either, and no call in to explain his absence. He's not at his digs at Kirkstall either, and he didn't sleep in his bed last night. No explanation given to his landlady.'

'Not necessarily an unusual thing for a young chap.'

'But it is for him, she says.'

'He's not from round here, is he?'

'No – from the Midlands. Place called Harborne – suburb of Birmingham, apparently. We've got a home address from his landlady, and confirmed it with the *Chronicle* offices. He's with them on a one-year placement for aspiring journalists. He's a graduate of Warwick University. That's one of the things that irked Horrocks apparently. He couldn't stand graduates – they got up his nose.'

'Sounds like the police. Right. Many thanks. We're going to have to consider sending someone down there, though there's no guarantee that's where he's gone. Would you get on to the *Chronicle* and his landlady and tell them we need to know if he has any contact with either of them.'

Oddie turned to Charlie in the seat beside him and looked at him speculatively.

'What do you think?'

'Is it sensible to go all that way with so little to go on? The only thing to connect him to the murder is the fact that the two disliked each other. On the other hand, Horrocks's former job was down there. That mate of yours that sent you the cutting – where was he from?'

'Coventry. The cutting was from the *Coventry Evening News* and they were cock-a-hoop (though they tried to pretend they were grieving). One of their former reporters had been murdered! Read all about it! It's a funny old world.'

'The lack of grief is unanimous.'

'Even among his family. I suppose that means that Cosmo's gallant rescue of Cora Horrocks from the abuser took place in the Coventry area.'

'Presumably. You think that should be looked into?'

'Of course. That's one known violent criminal in Cosmo's history. Add to that that Cora herself had every chance to wait for her husband and bash his brains in. She had the advantage over most of the suspects in that she knew his habits and was on the spot.'

'Looks to me like I'm being selected for a trip to the Midlands.'

'You are. I'll get them at Millgarth to ring the *Evening News* there and find someone for you to talk to who was there in Cosmo's time and knows all the dirt on him.'

'What will you do?'

'I'll dig deeper in the parish. I have a fancy to start with the stand-in priest.'

'Miss Preece-Dembleby gave the impression she had a very jaundiced opinion of that one, didn't she. Do you know where he lives?'

'There's a presbytery close to the church. Father Pardoe's home, of course. If he hasn't moved in or isn't there, there'll be someone who knows where he is.'

'Right you are. I'll drive you there and then be on my way.'

So it was that, three and a half hours later, Charlie was ensconced in the late afternoon, at a time when ten years before most pubs would be closed, in The Blackbird, a journalists' waterhole a few hundred yards from the offices of the *Coventry Evening News*, opposite Len Foxley, an elderly journalist, currently editing the readers' letters page, a man in his fifties with an on-going thirst problem and a surprisingly sharp memory, considering the alcoholic haze through which his professional life must have been lived. Charlie, a sharp dresser, averted his eyes from the threadbare tweed sports jacket that looked as if it had been made for an ill-co-ordinated hippopotamus and from sports trousers that looked due for a dry clean the year Thatcher came to power.

He concentrated on his notebook and his glass, which was being emptied at about a tenth the speed of Len Foxley's.

'He was a keen beggar, give him his due,' Len Foxley was saying, the due-giving being obviously a preparation to putting the boot in. 'Went after stories like a terrier after a rotten bone. Dead eager to make his mark, because he'd set his sights on London and one of the big tabloids. That narked a lot of people on the paper, but most of us knew he'd never make it, so we just laughed about it behind his back.'

'He wasn't liked?' suggested Charlie.

'Liked? You're joking! You haven't got far in your investigations if you can even suggest that he might have been.' He downed the second third of his second pint. 'Listen, young feller. You'll get nowhere if you don't take on board the fact that Horrocks was the pits. Standards of probity and fair play may not be very high in the world of journalism, but even by those standards Horrocks was a rat. There was nothing he wouldn't do to get a story, and no story so unappetizing or depraved that he wouldn't go after it and revel in every sordid detail. He was mighty good at the tut-tutting too – the "It pains me to have to tell you this" stuff that tries to make readers feel better about enjoying that sort of muck-raking.'

'Sounds to me as if he ought to have made it on to the tabloids,' commented Charlie.

'Going just by his stories and his presentation you'd be right. The reason he didn't was that he was no good at brown-nosing people. You've got to arse-lick the editors, the owner, all the powers-that-be on a paper if you're to get a regular job on what used to be called Fleet Street papers. Give Cosmo his due, he tried it. But he was so convinced he was cleverer than anybody else in sight that the insincerity was blatant. You could see it even in the little world of the *Evening News*. While he was telling the editor what a brilliant journalist he was, his face and voice showed he knew the man was nothing but a second-rate provincial hack, because nothing but a hack would be hired to edit a paper like the *Coventry Evening News*.'

'But that's what Cosmo always was too.'

'Always. We laughed when he got the job in Leeds. It was

a step up all right, but not a very big one, and not the one he craved. And that's where he stopped for the rest of his life.'

He downed the final third and handed his glass to Charlie. It looked as if it was going to be an expensive session.

'His present wife – did you ever meet her?' Charlie asked, coming back with the refill.

'Not that I remember. Married her just before or just after he left here. She was one of his stories, you know.'

'Yes, she told us.'

'And it was a genuine story – not like some of his. The man this woman was with – what's her name, now –?'

'Cora.'

'That's it. The man she was shacking up with was a monster. He got his kicks from – well, from kicks. And punches, wounding – you name it. And plausible as you wouldn't believe. Up before the magistrate or a judge he would make them believe he was a much-wronged man, put upon for years, who suddenly snapped when it all got too much for him. Had juries eating out of his hand. Of course police were different then.'

'So the old hands tell me.'

'None of . . . your sort in the force, or not so you'd notice.'

Charlie directed one of his ferocious looks at him, but he was hidden behind his beer mug. 'More to the point, they were mostly working-class chaps who took a bit of domestic violence in their stride. Grew up with it, and not averse to a bit of it themselves from time to time. So it took a while – and it took a string of articles by Cosmo – for the penny to drop: this man was way out of the league of men who occasionally punched their wives. In actual fact the violence wasn't just against Cora: there was a string of women – occasional partners, one-night stands, former girl-friends. Cosmo really went at it, tracked them all down, went to court records, discovered aliases. He should have been a private detective or a policeman.'

'No thank you,' said Charlie.

'Anyway, he built up a dossier on this bloke such as you wouldn't believe. Names, dates, places, court hearings, the lot. And incidentally it was pretty damning as far as others were concerned: police, social workers, probation officers, judges. When it broke it made one of the longest-running stories I can remember.'

'When he was doing all this digging, was Cora living with the man – what was his name?'

'Alan Russell. Oh, I don't think so. Out of the question, I should have thought, because she'd have been dead meat if he'd got so much as a whiff. Quite early on, if my memory serves me, Cosmo got her away and into hiding. I suppose things were building up between her and him, though he had a partner – a gorgeous redhead we saw him with now and then – and a new baby.'

Charlie considered this.

'You mean he was having it off with the two of them?'

'Wouldn't know. None of us knew. No one at the *News* got more than a toehold in his private life. The mind boggles, frankly. All we know is that about the time he left for Leeds – the Alan Russell story having netted him the job there – he and Cora were an item. I believe he had a kid or kids by her later. Poor little buggers. Cosmo and kids just don't go together. You'd have thought he'd have insisted it be exposed on some bleak Scottish mountain. Anyway that's what happened. Look lad, my glass has been empty more than three minutes.'

Charlie chewed over this new information while he collected a fresh pint. His doubts found expression as he sat down again.

'It never struck me, looking at the body, that Horrocks was likely to be a ladies' man.'

'Being a bit looks-ist, to coin a phrase, aren't you?' said Len Foxley roguishly. 'It's not the handsome hunks always pull in the birds. For all I know Casanova was an ugly little runt.'

'It's often power pulls them in,' conceded Charlie. 'Politicians use that.'

'Well,' said Foxley, 'journalists have a sort of power.'

'Or influence, as much as power,' went on Charlie. 'Sleeping with the boss beats taking a course in management any day.'

135

'And you're forgetting gratitude. I'd be grateful to any man, even if he was an ugly dwarf, if he'd rescued me from Alan Russell.'

'True enough. But we've shifted round to seeing it from Cora Horrocks's point of view. Cosmo may have been as randy as a cock sparrow, but if he *wasn't*, then there was presumably something about Cora that drew him.'

Len Foxley shrugged.

'Who can get to the bottom of that kind of thing? I have my ideas . . .'

'And what are they?'

'There was this notion around at the time – one of the things people were talking about, arguing over – that women who were abused by men asked for it, wanted it, went unconsciously after the men likely to do it. So the woman's no sooner escaped from one relationship where the man has beaten her up than she gets into another with the same sort of man. It was some woman who ran a hostel for abused women who started the idea.'

'The notion's still around,' said Charlie. 'But I haven't any impression of Horrocks as a man who was violent towards women.'

'I wasn't really thinking of that,' said Foxley. 'There's different ways of skinning a cat, you know. Cosmo's forte was verbal skinning. He was a sadist with the tongue, using words to humiliate, torment, rob people of their confidence and their self-respect. Come to think of it, it's a damned good job he never became a schoolmaster. You could drive a kid to suicide with a tongue like his.'

'What you're saying is that he saw Cora as a natural victim, and took her on as someone it would be a pleasure to victimize, in particular when her expectations must have been of someone benevolent who had acted as her deliverer?'

'Something like that. Worms turn, though, don't they?'

'It's taken this worm an awfully long time to turn,' commented Charlie.

'There's always the final straw,' returned Len, who wielded a powerful journalistic cliché. 'Anyway, I wasn't only thinking of her. There's the child too, isn't there?'

'Two of them.'

'That household could have been a hell-hole of resentment and rebellion. Were the kids of an age to strike back?'

'One of them was,' said Charlie thoughtfully. And in truth he had given Charlie plenty to think about. The next time he went up for a refill he got one for himself as well.

Three-quarters of an hour and a lot of journalistic gossip later, Charlie was in his car and on the way northwards to Birmingham, still chewing over the information that Len Foxley, at a liquid price, had provided him with.

It was suggestive, that was for sure. Charlie had had recent experience of how bitterness could destroy. He had talked to the black mother, still young, of a young man who had died in police custody. The boy had been a schizophrenic, there was no doubt he had killed himself, but equally no doubt that he had been handled insensitively, and with massive ignorance of the problem. He had every sympathy for the mother, but he could see with dreadful clarity how her immense, corrosive bitterness, two years after the death, was destroying her life and poisoning her personality.

Could gratitude do the same? Or at any rate gratitude that is gradually undermined, shown to be misplaced, corroded by being directed at a nature that gradually shows itself wholly unworthy of it?

Say Cora had married Horrocks out of genuine gratitude, and to give herself a home and a protector. The gratitude was quite natural: he had led a campaign against the man who had made her life a hell of fear. Then say she had found out, over the years, that the basis of her marriage was a sham: the man she regarded as her protector had merely regarded her plight as a ploy in one of his usual pieces of self-serving muckraking, and had married her because, like Alan Russell, he had seen her as ideal victim material. And if, as her children grew up, he began to mould them similarly into potential victims, would she not, at some point, snap? Seize any chance of ridding herself of the man and starting again?

Charlie pulled himself up. He had looked into the eyes of

the elder daughter of Cosmo Horrocks and he had not seen a willing victim there. They had been troubled eyes, but they had been aggressive ones too.

He sent his mind back towards Cora. The fading of gratitude could be a gradual thing, and a final snap could therefore be explicable. At some point Cosmo could have done something that finally destroyed the last dregs of that gratitude and driven his wife to that most usual of crimes, a domestic: a spouse killing a spouse. What might it have been in this case? The younger one, Adelaide, it would most likely be. The one least able to defend herself. Because the elder one could certainly have done that – and not just defended herself, but hit back. She was at an age that is the borderline of childhood and adulthood – the age of passionate loves and hatreds, joys and tragedies. She certainly would have had the strength. He could well imagine she would have had the passion. Or could the mother have got in first, because she saw the way things were going?

When he got to the outskirts of Birmingham he pulled up outside a newsagent's and bought an *A to Z*. He was expert these days in finding his way around strange cities, but Birmingham he found stranger than most. When, in early evening light, he found himself in Harborne, he stopped again to identify Terry Beale's home address: 10 Thornbush Farm Lane. Ho-ho, he thought. Fat chance of any remnants of a farm in this suburb. When he got there he found a stubby street, with two late Victorian terraces separated by a scruffy piece of waste land from a similar smaller terrace. It was at the farthest end of the little street, the last of this group, that number 10 was to be found. Charlie left his car, however, halfway along and walked towards the three-storey, dingy, redbrick house. The whole had an air of low expectations – an air he was used to in the immigrant areas of London and Leeds.

He heard the noise from fifty yards away. It was a woman's voice, singing: a fruity voice, no longer young, but carrying. It was a pop song she was singing, a long-ago one, but Charlie recognized it because it was a Beatles number:

'We all live in a yellow shubmarine, a yellow shubmarine,

a –' He was nearing the house now, and the obvious was unavoidable: the woman was drunk, and the noise came from number 10. She stopped in mid-tune and shouted:

'Rejoice and be exceeding glad.'

A man's voice shouted: 'Mother!'

'What's the matter with you? I'll rejoice if I want to. I've got plenty to rejoice about. Raise high the fucking roof-beams, carpenter. "I'm just a puppet, a puppet, a puppet on a string."'

The man's voice came again, and again it irritated her.

'Fuck off. I'll do what I frigging like. I'm shelebrating. Not every day I have shomething good happen to me.'

Charlie turned into the little scrap of front garden, up a couple of steps to the front door, and rang the bell.

'I'll get it. I said I'll get it. My fucking house. What do I care what people *think*. They can think what they fucking *like*.'

The door opened.

Charlie saw first a glass, half full of brown liquid, then he saw the hand holding it, then his eye went up the arm to the crimson, blotchy face, crowned by a magnificent head of red hair.

'Who are you? Oh, don't bother to tell me. I won't remember. Come in and join the party. Come in and shelebrate that bastard's death.'

CHAPTER 13

Awakening Women

Oddie wondered what it was about Father Greenspan that was so instantly dislikeable.

With his customary coolness and sense of justice he mentally withdrew that last word and substituted 'off-putting'. Then he wondered whether the kernel of the matter was that the man did not arouse trust. This was something to do with his plumpness, the shininess of his black hair, the curving smile of his self-satisfied mouth. Somehow around this sort of priest the word 'sleek' seemed to cling as the inevitable adjective.

'About the Father Pardoe matter I can make no comment,' he was saying, smiling ingratiatingly. 'I'm sure you will understand. I earnestly hope he will be found to have acted with complete propriety in both the matters that are the subject of the investigation, but of course I can't prejudge that. The enquiry is being conducted by a completely impartial committee of three. I can't see, to be quite truthful, why you think there might be any connection between those matters and this shocking murder.'

'It's merely a possibility,' said Oddie, stretching relaxedly in his rather hard chair and trying to convey the impression that priesthood cut no ice with *him*. 'The story of Father Pardoe's suspension breaks, the story is taken up by the national tabloids, the man who broke the story is murdered. Could be coincidence. Could be cause and effect.'

'Yes . . . Yes, I suppose so. If there is a connection, I'm not sure that I can be of any help in your investigation. I'm simply the stand-in.'

'I realize that, but events *since* the suspension are of particular interest to us. I did wonder for example how far the

140

truth – I mean that he is under investigation, and not at a retreat – had got around the parish.'

Father Greenspan donned an expression of concern and compassion.

'Well, I'm afraid it *has* – little by little. It's been quite a while now, and priests very rarely go on a retreat of such duration. He's been seen in Pudsey. Yes, it has got around.'

'And I gather there has been some kind of appeal to the Bishop.'

'Ah yes – the ladies, bless their hearts. Not always wise, but we'd love them less if they were, wouldn't we?'

Yuck, thought Oddie.

'So you thought it was unwise,' he said. 'Was that because they assumed Father Pardoe was innocent?'

'Not *exactly*, though one should hardly prejudge an enquiry's conclusions, as I've already suggested. No, what was unwise, in my view, was that the letter cast doubt on the procedure, on whether he would get a fair hearing, implied the whole thing was based on gossip. Now that last really was unwise! The Bishop is impeccably fair in all his dealings. That letter got up his nose, I can tell you!'

'You talk of "ladies" in connection with the letter –'

'That was because it was some ladies in the parish who were the moving spirits. They got some men to sign as well. It would have looked very odd if they hadn't.'

The man's smile and his smoothness were so cat-like that Oddie wondered if he wasn't purring.

'Why do you think the Bishop was annoyed?'

The priest frowned.

'I thought I'd made that clear. The letter seemed to challenge his authority.'

'I should have thought a petition to him *acknowledged* him as the ultimate authority.'

But Father Greenspan did not seem to understand.

'It cast serious doubt on his judgement,' he said, the smile becoming strained. 'We're old-fashioned in the Catholic Church: the Bishop's word goes.'

'I see. Were you aware of this letter before it was sent?'

'Certainly not! I would have moved heaven and earth – so

141

to speak – to stop it if I had been.'

'But you know now who were the moving spirits?'

'Oh yes. Mrs Jessel, Mrs Leary and Miss Preece-Dembleby.'

'Did you learn that from parish talk?'

'From the Bishop himself. He has his sources of information. I came in for a tiny portion of his wrath. Luckily I was able to assure him that I was quite ignorant of what was going on. He's a very fair man.'

That was not quite how he was beginning to seem to Oddie.

'And it was Father Pardoe who came in for the lion's share of his wrath?'

'Is that surprising? To go to Mass at St Anne's, knowing the Bishop would be officiating. I can't think of anything more unwise.'

'Miss Preece-Dembleby tells me that Father Pardoe knew nothing of the petition.'

'Then we must hope that is true. But it was unwise whether he knew of it or not. While the investigation was going on it was out of order to embarrass the Bishop by appearing at Mass in the Cathedral.'

'But he would need to go to Mass, would he not?'

'Of course. There are more than thirty churches in the Leeds area he could have gone to. It was a dreadful lapse of judgement and taste.'

Walking back to his car, Oddie decided that Father Greenspan was stronger on taste than on judgement. He certainly wouldn't want to be in a position in which that young jar of holy oil was his spiritual adviser. He wondered, even, whether the truth about Father Pardoe's suspension hadn't been helped on its way around the parish by his stand-in.

There was something else that rather puzzled him about his talk with Greenspan (he was reluctant any longer to 'Father' him in his own mind). To him the letter to the Bishop had been an unwise (how often had he used the word?) attempt to pre-empt the findings of the investigating committee and question the Bishop's decision to set it up at all on such a very flimsy basis. He thought it was probably both of these things, but he had had the impression from Edith Preece-Dembleby that it was something else as well – a sort of generalized protest that embraced a multitude of grievances that had somehow been brought to a head by the persecution (as they saw it) of Father Pardoe. But on reflection he decided that it was perhaps not surprising if these grievances had passed over Greenspan's head, as a new man in the parish. And as a man whose idea of wisdom was very much of this world.

He put the point to Janette Jessel, sitting in her conventional, overstuffed drawing room – a setting that seemed to him at odds with her intelligent, sensitive personality, as if its decor had been chosen without reference to her own tastes. They went through the ostensible reasons for the petition, and finally Oddie said:

'I get a feeling –'

'Yes?' He thought she tensed up.

'– of something more. Perhaps something Father Greenspan didn't grasp. As if somehow the petition brought to the surface a whole rag-bag of grievances and discontents.'

'Oh, it did!' The moment she had said this, she made an effort to put her rational, sensible self back in the driving seat. 'Though it's not altogether easy to put into words what they were . . . It seems odd talking about them to a policeman.'

'Pretend I'm your priest,' said Oddie, with a grin.

'It would be easier to pretend you're a woman,' said Janette, reciprocating the grin. 'We found it – after initial hesitations – easier to talk about this with each other. It was as if the feminist revolution had come and passed everywhere else in the Western world, but had somehow slipped around us. Of course that's not entirely true. Catholic practice as far as for example contraception is concerned has changed enormously in the last twenty or thirty years, absolutely in defiance of the hierarchy and of Rome. But I get the nasty feeling that it hasn't changed because women objected to being baby-factories, constantly on the conveyor-belt, but because a large family hits the husband's pocket.'

'The whole family's pocket,' Oddie pointed out.

'Yes. But I don't want to pin it down to an issue. The protest was really about the fact that all the decisions seem to be taken by men. And not just mainly, but exclusively.

The woman's role is still a matter of flowers for the church, cakes for the bring-and-buy sale, brewing tea and buttering scones.'

'I understand. But why should that come to a head in connection with Father Pardoe?'

'Oh, sheer accident, I suppose. A matter of timing.' She frowned, trying to decide if there was anything more. 'But it is typical: the Bishop gets wind of gossip. *He* decides to set up a committee, on that committee he puts only males, and they pontificate on a matter in which the other main player is a young woman. It all seems so archaic.'

There still seemed one factor in the equation missing, and Oddie chanced his arm.

'Were there personal dissatisfactions behind this as well? Domestic ones, perhaps?'

Janette thought, or hesitated before she replied.

'Yes. I don't want to go into them, because they can't be relevant to your investigation, and because I wouldn't want you to think I was speaking for anyone other than myself. My husband – Derek – is not a bad man. But like most of the St Catherine's husbands, his ideas are stuck in a time warp. It's the domestic equivalent of the Church situation. The woman stays home, she makes life comfortable for the man, she supports him in his decisions. Leaving him to do the interesting things, him to have the freedoms, him to be *less* involved in all the family matters, and yet boss.'

'And you think religion's a factor in this.'

'I'm sure it is. It provides the ideology and the practice that the husbands find so convenient. In other respects they leave it to the women to *do* religion for the family, while they're busy having the fun.'

Oddie decided against asking what she meant by 'fun', and simply said:

'I suppose Miss Preece-Dembleby was a bit outside this part of the protest. You and Mrs Leary must have felt most strongly about it.'

He immediately got the feeling of her tensing up again.

'I really wouldn't like to say anything about that. Those are personal things, aren't they – at least in part. I think you should talk to her about them, if you think it worth while. To be honest, I don't see how the Father Pardoe matter, or our letter, could have anything to do with that awful reporter's death, but you won't want me telling you your business.'

'If it's not relevant, we'll soon be on to other things – in fact we already are. In any police enquiry, elimination is the main task in the early stages. Meanwhile I'm grateful for your help. You've given me a lot to think about.'

But when he got back to his car he found that the elimination of the Father Pardoe strand in the investigation was not immediately on the cards. That became clear when he got on his mobile and talked to Headquarters.

'Coppin? I've just finished talking to Janette Jessel, and I'm on my way to talk to Mary Leary.'

'Right boss. But before you do, I think there's something you ought to know. We've just got Horrocks's notebook from Forensics.'

'And?'

'It has the name Leary in it.'

'Really? Male or female Leary?'

'No indicator. From a quick look at it I'd say it has the Father Pardoe story in note form right from the beginning. Want to come and take a look at it?'

'Very much. But I'd also like to talk to Mary Leary while I'm over here. Do you think you could fax a copy of the relevant pages to the Shipley station?'

'No problem.'

Oddie was developing a close and pleasant relationship with the Shipley uniformed policemen. Co-operation was his watchword, and he was not the type to pull rank or superior savvy. He was presented with four pages of fax as he came through the door, and five minutes later he was sitting in the station canteen stewing over a photocopy of scrawled but legible handwriting.

The fish is off, and so is the chicken.
Now she tells me she's getting off at Grantham.

PRIEST – SCANDAL.
Leary. Father Pardoe.
Derek, Julie Norris, Mary.

That was all quite interesting to be going on with. Oddie
cast his eye over the other two pages. An address for the
Norrises. *Father Riley Fund.* Father Pardoe's address in Pudsey.
What is the Bishop up to? Later on, when the notes were
becoming more sketchy, probably because he had got the
story firmly in his mind, there was *Who are the trustees? Who
are the committee?* Interesting questions, thought Oddie. He
might have conceived a grudging respect for Horrocks, if it
weren't so abundantly clear that he had a mean little, dirty
little mind.

He felt, when he rang on Mary Leary's front door in
early-evening sunlight, that he was much better equipped
than he had expected. The front door was solid, the sort of
wood that resists a modern saw, and the house was large,
stone, a genuinely imposing Victorian residence. Someone
had done pretty well for himself, Oddie thought. Or had had
it done for him by an earlier generation.

'Yes?'

'Detective Superintendent Oddie.' He pushed his ID under
her nose, but she barely glanced at it.

'Oh . . . Well, you'd better come in.'

The voice attempted normality, but did not achieve it. He
noticed she did not ask if it was she he wanted to talk to. She
either assumed it or hoped that it was. Why should she do
that, though? Because she thought she could conceal, gloss
over or put the best front on some inconvenient fact she was
afraid might come up?

When he sat down in the handsome armchair, amid furniture that, though old, made a clear statement, either a class
one or a financial one, he said, to make conversation:

'Nice house.'

'The family one. Con's family,' Mary said neutrally.

She sat down, and Oddie stole a look at Mary in the sun-lit
room. He was in fact more interested in the woman than in
her surroundings. She was a healthy, bonny-looking woman,

but the lines of the face were drawn and the eyes haunted. Sleeplessness and fear, Oddie diagnosed.

When he got on to the subject of the petition he sensed relief, and made a note to get off it as soon as possible.

'We all felt so sorry for Father Pardoe,' explained Mrs Leary. 'We felt there had been an undue haste, and that perhaps the Bishop had acted on parish tittle-tattle. Maybe we went a bit far.'

'Surely writing a letter hoping the matter was cleared up as soon as possible – I gather you didn't say much more than that – was hardly going far.'

But Mary Leary was not backing down.

'We got a dozen or more signatures, making it look too much like a petition. The Bishop likes to be firmly in control. He doesn't like anything that seems to question his judgement or limit his powers.'

'A control freak?'

'I'm not sure I know what that means, but something of that, I suppose. The picture of the two of them in the paper was rather unpleasant.'

'I take it that you have had second thoughts about what all of you had been doing.'

'I suppose I have. Not that I waver one iota in my support of Father Pardoe. I'm quite sure he is innocent of the charges. It's just a question of method.'

'Was your husband against this petition – let's call it that.'

She shook her head.

'No, not particularly. He rather leaves that sort of thing to me. I don't think he has views one way or another. Men are very cynical, though. They do tend to believe sexual allegations against priests.'

'What is your husband's connection with Cosmo Horrocks?'

Fear flushed through her eyes, then vanished.

'Connection? None that I know of.'

'Or your own?'

'None. I've never seen or spoken to him in my life.'

Oddie raised his eyebrows.

'The name Leary appears in his notebooks.'

'It's a common name.'

'True. But it appears in the section when he first gets wind of the Father Pardoe story. Does your husband know Janette Jessel's husband?'

'Oh yes. They're quite friendly.' An unpleasant thought struck her. 'You're surely not saying that Con and Derek gave him the story. I couldn't bear that. And if Con did he'd have come out more against our petition.'

'I'm not saying they gave him the story. Might your husband and Mr Jessel travel together?'

A shadow flitted through her eyes.

'They do sometimes. They both have business in London now and then, and they try to arrange it at the same time. They might have a meal together, or do a show, and maybe travel home together.'

Her mouth was tight, her voice under strict control. She suspects they go to strip joints or brothels together, thought Oddie. That thought was interrupted by the sound of the front door, and through the sitting room door he saw a tall teenager dashing through the hall and hurrying down to the cellar. There was the sound of a cupboard door being opened, then the footsteps dashing back up again.

'You're home early, Mark,' his mother shouted, unable to hide the tension in her voice.

'Teacher's ill. I'm off to do some hurdles practice.'

The front door banged shut.

'Sport, sport, all the time,' complained his mother.

'Back to your husband,' said Oddie.

'Shouldn't you be talking to Con?'

'I will if necessary. Let me make myself clear: I'm not accusing your husband of anything, Mrs Leary.'

'No, of course not.'

'I just want to get events straight in my mind. Has he been to London recently?'

'Not long ago. Maybe a fortnight or so ago.'

'Did he travel there or back with Derek Jessel, do you know?'

'I've no idea. It's not the sort of thing he'd mention.'

'Why on earth not?'

'He knows I'm not particularly fond of Derek.'

'Can you imagine them talking over the Father Pardoe affair, perhaps over lunch?'

'Yes. Yes, I can.'

'Why do you say it like that?'

'It's the sort of thing men like talking about . . . I'm sorry: I shouldn't say that to you.'

'Not at all. You interest me. You mean a subject like a priest having sex with a teenager?'

'Yes. They sort of gloat . . . leer.'

'Your husband and Derek Jessel?'

'Men.'

'And never women?'

'The women in the congregation were much more sceptical, and more understanding too.'

But it was a woman who had dobbed Pardoe in it, as one of Horrocks's reports in the *Chronicle* had made clear. Oddie edged his way forward, preparing to leave.

'So it could be – it's hardly a vital point – that overhearing your husband and Jessel on a train was the starting point for Horrocks's interest in this –'

'You can hardly blame them for that.'

'I don't. But beyond that your husband has no interest in the Father Pardoe story, except perhaps a salacious one, and no connection with Cosmo Horrocks?'

'None at all.'

'That you know of.'

'That I know of.'

'And your interest is just in the petition, which you now think may have been unwise.'

'Just that. Nothing more.'

Then why are you having to strain every muscle to stop your hands working together nervously, and why is there a nerve in your left cheek that refuses to bow to your will and twitches away at any question that seems to come close to the matter you are nervous about, Oddie wondered. You saw the petition as a protest against male domination, yet you are straining every nerve to protect your man. Was that just the Tammy Wynette syndrome?

You are frightened, my lady, he thought, and riddled with doubts and fears.

And yet, he decided, on the way back to his car, she hadn't bothered to hide her scorn for some of her husband's attitudes. And she had taken his questions, which were simply designed to establish how Cosmo had cottoned on to the story in the first place, as implying some guilty connection between her husband and the reporter, or between her husband and the Father Pardoe business.

But he shook himself. Face anyone with a policeman asking questions and they immediately think they or someone close to them is being accused of something. It's a perfectly natural jump to conclusions.

But she was nervous because she was already accusing him in her own mind, he thought. She was already sick with worry when she opened the door.

He sat in his car for a few minutes. At some stage he was going to have to talk to Leary and Jessel. But he couldn't see that it was urgent, couldn't see them as anything but catalysts. Julie Norris was more pressing, though she was quite possibly a catalyst too – for the whole investigation of Father Pardoe. He himself could speak to her parents, and in a grisly way he rather looked forward to that, but he had no doubt that Charlie was the one who ought to speak to Julie. More her age, presumably more her outlook on life.

How was Charlie going? he wondered, and reached for his mobile phone. At first he thought the reception was more than usually terrible, then he managed to distinguish the sound of singing – a woman singing – and broken glass.

'Charlie!' he shouted. 'Where are you? What are you doing?'

'Don't panic, boss,' came the answer, dimly through the racket. 'Just getting things under control.'

CHAPTER 14

Fallen Woman

Charlie made his way down the hall, registering the heavy sway of the woman in front of him, then through to the living room, which was a chaos of glasses, newspapers, computer print-outs and discarded clothes, which a young man was vainly trying to put into some order since hearing the doorbell. The woman stumbled across the room and sank into an armchair. She gestured towards two outsize bottles, one of red wine and one of white, and then seemed to feel her social obligations had been fulfilled: her eyes glazed over, and she lost interest altogether in her guest, seeming to have been set off on to some impenetrable reminiscence by something on the tape in the background, which Charlie guessed to be crap music from around the 'seventies.

'Terry Beale, I presume,' he said to the back and backside of the young man who was still scrabbling round among the scattered paper and newsprint on the floor. He hurriedly got to his feet and peered at the identification that Charlie had pushed under his eyes.

'Yes. Oh, police. I was half expecting you.'

Like his mother he made a jerky movement, this time in the direction of a chair. Charlie ignored it.

'Is there anywhere we can talk?'

'We danced to this at the old Cellar Club, Harvey and I,' suddenly announced the woman. 'Before I set eyes on that heap of cow dung. Thank God someone has done the decent thing at last. I wonder what took them so long.'

Terry Beale stepped forward and made some kind of shushing motion to persuade her to shut up. Then he stepped back again, acknowledging the futility of it.

His mother had not noticed him. Something in the music

on the tape, which had changed to a song Charlie recognized, had caught her notice or tickled her fancy. 'These boots are made for walking,' she spat out, as Charlie's mobile phone bleeped without her registering, 'and that's just what they'll do. One of these days these boots are gonna walk all over you.'

She hurled her glass at the wall.

'Too late!' she howled. 'Too bloody late!'

'Just getting the situation under control,' muttered Charlie into his phone.

'Her sister's coming,' whispered Terry Beale in his ear. 'She should be here any minute now. She's the only one who can handle her when she's like this.'

Charlie shouted, 'Get back to you,' into his mobile, then turned to the young man.

'What are you going to do when she gets here?'

'Get a bus to the station, then a train back to Leeds. But you can drive me to the station if you want.'

'I can drive you back to Leeds if that's where you're going.'

As Terry nodded, there was a ring at the doorbell. While he was out of the room the woman stirred to life again.

'This should be the happiest day of my life,' she said, looking bewildered. 'So why do I feel so rotten?'

Charlie was about to suggest that it was because she had drunk herself sodden when she made a lunge towards the kitchen and he heard retching sounds. The sensible-looking middle-aged woman who now came in with Terry raised her eyebrows and went through to the kitchen.

'There,' Charlie heard her say. 'You'll feel better in a minute. No, you don't want another. No, you don't. I'm going to make some coffee now . . .'

'So what do we do?' asked Charlie, turning to Terry.

'I get my bag and we slope off.'

'Will it take long? Shall I wait in the car?'

'It just needs fetching. I never had a chance to unpack.'

He dashed up the stairs, and Charlie heard from the kitchen a couple of 'Just one more's and firm responses to them before Terry scurried down again and they went out into the road, both with a great sense of relief.

'Aunt Fran will cope,' said Terry, as if Charlie was blaming him for skiving off. 'She's the only one who can. I somehow get it wrong – always have.'

'I take it this is an occasional thing, rather than a habitual one?'

Terry nodded, his hands nervously clasping and unclasping themselves.

'It is now. I believe it was once a constant problem, and I was taken into care – when I was too young to remember. It was the shock of that that brought her out of it. We had some pretty rough patches when I was growing up, but on the whole it's just at crisis points that she gets tipped over the edge. To tell you the truth, I sometimes think she welcomes the crises – as excuses. But that's mean of me. She hasn't been a bad mother – there's many worse.'

Charlie got into the car and leant over to open the passenger-seat door. He pressed buttons on his mobile, then gave Oddie the message that he was on the way back to Leeds with Terry Beale. Then he pushed his key into the ignition.

'Do I take it you came down to try and prevent this?' he asked, as they started away.

'That was the idea. I should know better, but I never do. I heard the news on Wednesday morning – that's yesterday, isn't it? – on Radio Leeds, about seven o'clock. I stuffed some things into my holdall and got a bus to the station. There wasn't a train to Birmingham until nine forty, so I was kicking my heels for an hour or more, and I made the mistake of ringing Mum to tell her I was on my way. She smelt a rat, and wheedled out of me what had happened. So by the time I got to Birmingham she was soaking it up and in what I call the first stage, which is being maudlin. Not about Cosmo's murder, but about What Might Have Been, if he hadn't come along. I rang Aunt Fran, but she was on a quick visit to my gran's in Plymouth. The rest has been just coping with her, getting a few hours' sleep, then coping all over again.'

'Let's get this straight, just for the record. Harvey is What Might Have Been; Cosmo is what actually happened; and you are the result, after which he ditched you both.'

'Spot on,' said Terry becoming more cheerful. 'You can forget about Harvey, though. He's a bit of Mum's private mythology. The boyfriend before Cosmo, and probably no better or worse than most of the men she's taken up with. She's not a tart, but when she does take up with a man she always gets hurt – never seems to learn.'

'What does she do for a living? Anything?'

'She's a freelance journalist. That probably sounds like nothing, but actually she's pretty good, she gets commissions, she gets good ideas of her own, and usually what she writes gets into print. She earns a living, and she has done since she climbed halfway up on to the wagon.'

'Well, that's something she owes to Horrocks, I suppose,' said Charlie. Terry Beale grimaced. The hands resumed the convulsive claspings.

'Cosmo was an all-right journalist by his own murky lights, but he wasn't interested in teaching anybody. The teaching process was just a way of putting people down, for him. I found that out the hard way, by being put down in my turn.'

'You'd better tell me about Cosmo and his relationship to you and your mother – the whole caboodle, right from the beginning.'

'I don't know the whole caboodle. I was part of it from early on, but not really of an age to take notice. He left Birmingham when I was four months old. He'd more or less shaken Mum off a couple of months before that, so anything I know about those times I learned from Mum, who is hardly an impartial witness.'

'I'll make allowances for that.'

'According to Mum she took up with him after meeting him in a pub or bar. She was a stringer on one of the local free sheets at the time. According to her the agreement was that he'd get her on to the *Coventry Evening News*, or at least one of the OK papers in the region. Probably he didn't put it into so many words. Or maybe he did. He was a lying toad. Anyway she got more and more demanding and aggrieved – you've seen her, not at her best, but you can guess – but when she got pregnant he had the ideal excuse for not doing anything about it. Probably he didn't have the power anyway. He was a tolerated, not an influential figure, or so I'd guess. By the time I was born Cosmo was one hundred per cent taken up with a new story about a serial abuser of women. He dumped Mum and went off with one of the women in the story – went off literally, because he got the job in Leeds.'

They were speeding towards Derbyshire, and Charlie shifted in his seat, feeling they'd jumped the first hurdle.

'Right. That's got the outline. It backs up what I was told by a journalist in Coventry. I hardly need to ask you about your mother's feelings for Cosmo.'

'No. Vitriolic. The most cherished hatred of her life.' He shot a quick look at Charlie. 'That doesn't mean she killed him. In fact, I suspect she will be lost without him.'

'You say she's had a series of men in her life since. You'd think Cosmo would have been replaced at some point as the cherished hatred of her life.'

'Would you? I think the first big betrayal always rankles the most. Anyway, why should she have replaced him? None of the later ones registered anywhere near Cosmo on the Richter scale of human awfulness.'

'We are getting the feeling that he was a man without a friend, or even an ally,' Charlie admitted.

'He was. And that was how he preferred to be. The phrase Mum always uses about him is "He made me feel so small". That makes it sound very trivial –'

'Not necessarily. Not sustained over a long period.'

'No, I suppose not. I pity the man's family. I realize now he was incapable of a relationship of equals. He had to put you down, rob you of confidence or self-esteem, humiliate you as publicly as possible. I've known people who are incapable of praising anyone. This was something else: a need to degrade and hurt.'

'I'm surprised you didn't get some inkling of this from your mother's bitterness – something that might have warned you against making contact with him. Because that is what you did, isn't it? It could hardly be merely coincidence.'

'Oh, that's what I did all right. The only coincidence was the *Chronicle* offering a scheme to train rookie journalists.

When I saw that I shoved in my application pronto . . . Yes, I suppose I should have realized, not just from what Mum said about him, but from the fact that contact between us and him was zero. But children don't, do they? They always seem to dream of meeting up with their absent parent.'

'Not in my case,' said Charlie. 'My absent parent is a blank in the chronicles of my mother's bedmates. I don't think she has the first idea herself who he was, or rather which one it was.'

'I suppose that simplifies matters,' said Beale.

'Maybe,' said Charlie. 'I think it hurt when I got into my teens and started wondering.'

'That's how it was with me. Wondering whether my mum was really telling the truth.'

'One consequence of seeing my mother's emotional messes has been I've tended to stick with girlfriends. I've been with my present partner six years.'

'An eternity by present-day standards,' said Terry. 'Anyway, I got one of the jobs, got a bed-sit in Leeds, and when I started I angled to get Cosmo as my minder. That wasn't too difficult. The others had registered he was the one to avoid. I'd registered that myself.'

'I've been given the idea that things didn't go too smoothly.'

'We loathed each other. Maybe that's not as disastrous as it seemed to me at first. Plenty of people loathe their parents. But in my mind the personal dislike took on another dimension, and he came to embody for me all that is wrong with British journalism: the tone of jeering, of raucous disbelief in any notion of probity or idealism, the conviction that everyone's on the make or the fiddle, that everyone's having it off with someone on the side, that anyone with beliefs and ideals has to have feet of clay.'

'The great tabloid culture, in fact,' said Charlie. 'I gather Horrocks had ambitions to get on a national tabloid, but wasn't good enough at the arse-licking.'

'That figures. If you denigrate everyone you come into contact with, you need to be a very good actor if you start sucking up to anyone.'

'It's ironic that Cosmo got into the tabloids the day after he died.'

'Isn't it? Good enough to make you believe in God. I gather he had had stories in the nationals before, but this was big time. I'd had inklings of this story when I passed his desk and he was on the phone. I knew it was something big, something juicy with pus . . . Boy, I hope this priest he was gunning for is innocent. I'd hate Cosmo to be proved right in his last big story.'

'You sound as if you may be disillusioned with journalism.'

Terry Beale thought.

'I'm not sure I had illusions. I grew up with newspapers and magazines and journalists around me, so I knew what I was getting into. I'm not interested in moulding readers' opinions to suit myself, nor in entertaining them with prominent people's sex lives. But I am very much concerned about informing them. I think there's a culture of keeping people in ignorance of things, and I think it's very much a matter of "us" who are fit to know of such things, and "them" who aren't. We keep people uneducated, breed up *Sun* readers, so as to have an ample supply of "them" to feel superior to. If I find there's a place for someone who just wants people to be given all the facts, then I'll stay in journalism. If there isn't any more, then I'll find something else to do.'

They drove on for some time in silence, then Charlie said: 'Horrocks never suspected who you were, did he?'

'Never. One of the unsatisfactory men Mum took up with actually married her, and we both took his surname. Three months later he was gone. I suspect if you'd asked Cosmo what his son's Christian name was, he'd have been pushed to remember.'

'So you were never tempted to blow your own gaff and have it out with him.'

'No. What would be the point? He would never have felt guilt, shame, any emotion like that. In fact it would just have given him yet another weapon to use against me. By the time he died all I wanted was to have as little as possible to do with him, and pass on to another job somewhere else – nowhere near him, and not too near my mum. I think it's time, don't you, that I took my conception for granted and stood on my own two feet.'

'Emotionally as well as financially?'

'Exactly.'

'I think you're right. You seem to get less and less nervous the more the miles separate you from your mother.'

'Hmm.' Terry Beale shot him a glance of admiration at his sharpness. Charlie thought they were getting rather too young-men-together.

'What were you doing on Tuesday night?'

'The night of the murder? I was at the Grand Theatre, covering Opera North's *Arabella*. I was expert reviewer for the occasion, having seen all of five operas in my life before that one.'

'Did you go back to the *Chronicle*'s offices later?'

'No, I went back to my digs. What is this? It said on the news that Cosmo was killed near his home.'

'You could have followed him there. They suggested in the offices at the *Chronicle* that you might need to do research there to write your review.'

'I did it before I went. I photocopied bits of Kobbé and *The Viking Book of Opera*. And during the interval I hovered round the real critics picking up little bits and pieces. They all go into the small stalls bar at the interval to avoid mingling with the hoi poloi and hearing what they think.'

'What time did the opera finish?'

'About half past ten, I think. I was home by eleven.'

'Did your landlady see you?'

'No. I've got a key. She would be in bed by then.'

'What did you do?'

'Cobbled together a review then faxed it to the office.'

'Your landlady has a fax machine?'

'I have my own.'

'Do you have a car?'

'No, but I've a licence. When I need to I have a car from the *Chronicle*'s pool.'

'But you didn't have one on Tuesday night?'

'No. I got a bus back to Kirkstall. There are plenty, even at that hour.'

That would probably not be true if he had wanted to get out to Rodley, Charlie suspected. But he could have borrowed a car, or taken a taxi. Dangerous but . . .

'And on Wednesday morning you took off for the station early on, and rang your mother from there. So presumably she was at home.'

'Of course she was at home. It was about eight thirty.'

'And you wouldn't know what she was doing on Tuesday evening?'

'You'll have to ask her when she sobers up – if she remembers. I do know she went round to my aunt Fran's to leave something for her to take to Gran – a birthday present. Beyond that –'

Charlie registered that to 'leave' something didn't mean that the two sisters necessarily saw each other. In fact both mother and son were still very much possible suspects. Terry Beale looked at him as they sped past Sheffield and the Meadowhall Centre, and he read his thoughts accurately.

'Mum didn't know Horrocks still lived in Leeds, and certainly didn't know his address.'

'You hadn't told her anything about your relationship with him?'

'I may be young and a bit green, but I'm not stupid. She commented when I applied for the job on the *Chronicle* and when I got up here I told her he no longer worked on the paper – I said I thought he'd gone to Glasgow.'

Charlie nodded and drove on. He tried to make his face totally impassive. Because he had realized, as no doubt Terry had too, that she could have had advance notice of the story in the *Globe* from some contact in the newspaper world. Someone who knew of her past involvement with Cosmo, someone who knew, even, that her son by him was currently working for the *West Yorkshire Chronicle*, someone who shared her rage at his past behaviour, or someone who just enjoyed making trouble. She could then have found out his address quite easily from the telephone directories in the local reference library. Then she would have known her son had been lying to her.

Come to that, could much of what he had just been told be a lie? Could mother and son have been working together to kill the household's great hate figure?

Charlie dropped Terry off at Kirkstall, then rang Mike Oddie to get an update on events. Then he went home for the night. His speculations on the Beales were brought to an abrupt end soon after, because his partner Felicity told him she was going to have a baby.

CHAPTER 15

Dilemmas

Father Pardoe sat hunched in the easy chair of his bed-sitting room upstairs in Mrs Knowsley's. It was not despair he now felt, as it had been in his first weeks there; it was uncertainty, almost bewilderment. And it was complicated by the fact that he didn't want Margaret to know he was sitting alone pondering, not for too long, anyway. It would worry her, make her feel guilty, seem to her, perhaps, as if he were betraying her with his doubts.

This is almost like being married, he thought.

Analysing the nights since they had fallen into – into *sin* he had to think of it as – there had been two nights when they had had sex together and he had gone back to his own bed, one which he had spent entirely in his own bed, and two when he had spent the night with her. It was clear how he ought, as a priest, to regard these nights. The one spent on his own was the only one in which he had been faithful to his vows, and the others were terrible lapses from them.

Only somehow, suddenly, he was unable to see them like that. To him those other nights seemed right – not necessarily right as a way of life, right always for him in the future, but right for him and for her in the particular circumstances they were in at this particular time. He had always tried to regard the sins of his flock with – not tolerance, perhaps, but with understanding. Was it wrong of him to exercise the same understanding on his own backsliding?

He was aware that in the past, at any time before the last five years or so, he would have agonized about any fall from chastity – agonized before, agonized afterwards. Somehow the terrible cases of the last few years – many in his own Ireland, all trumpeted in the loathsome media – had changed things. There had been terrible cases, involving children: they had been *crimes*, not just sins. And they had been covered up by the hierarchy, the perpetrators moved on to do the same elsewhere.

If the Church would do that for such wrong-doers, how much did they wink the eye at more ordinary sexual lapses? He began to look at his fellow priests and wonder how many of them had strictly followed the vows of chastity they had made. Such vows had never been part of the early Church's rules. How many would bet that in a hundred years' time it would still be enforced? Indeed, it would surely be unenforceable.

With Julie it would have been downright wrong, a betrayal of what she clung to him for. With Margaret . . .

The bearing his new relationship had on his suspension he tried not to put in the forefront of his mind. Obviously denying, truthfully, any impropriety with Julie Norris lost some of its force if at the same time he was having an affair – a love affair, a sexual relationship, whatever words were used – with Margaret. The cases were very different of course, worlds apart, but in the eyes of the Church they were practically identical. The sin he was committing was the same as the one he was unjustly accused of. But that was not what he should be thinking of now. He should be trying to understand in what light he viewed the relationship, in what light Margaret must view it. Did she see it as the beginning of a permanent relationship, one involving, presumably, his leaving the priesthood? Did he himself see that as his future? And if it was not that, was it not simply casual sex?

He pulled himself up. What Margaret might or might not think was pure speculation. Best to start with himself. Then at least there was some chance of reaching the safe shore of certainty.

How *did* he regard it? Did his fall mean he could never again consider himself as a true priest?

No, on reflection, he did not regard it as that. He got up and walked around the room, then sat down again, conscious that Margaret might be listening downstairs. He said to himself: ignore my feeling that this was *right*. Say I admit to myself that it was a lapse. Should I see it as quite different in kind from, say, a lapse in charity, or a lapse of truthfulness? Any priest has such lapses; certainly he had had them himself, and many of them, since he dealt more than most men with a wide range of people who at times sorely tried his charity, and who needed to be handled in ways that sometimes stretched his devotion to the absolute truth.

When he had decided that probably many, even most, priests failed in their vows, he wasn't thinking mainly about men who turned out to have a regular mistress and illegitimate children going way back, like the Scottish bishop recently hounded by the tabloids. He was thinking about men who effected a compromise with their sexuality by occasionally giving way to it. To adapt St Augustine, they said: 'Oh Lord, make me chaste, but not entirely.' Presumably they thought like him: this was not a special falling, but a sin like any other sin.

He shook himself. He had begun the process of sorting this out in his own mind, but there remained the imponderable of Margaret. His instinct was to try not to thrash things through with her until the current crisis – the crises of the enquiry and now the murder – were over. The danger was that they distorted everything. Crises, whether national or domestic and personal, always did distort things, so that one only saw clearly when one had come through them.

He thought back to the crucial night. It was Sunday, and they had been going over the shocking events of the day: the Bishop's anger, the hideous public humiliation of the press photographer and reporter, the fact that now things were inevitably out into the open. He had become more and more distressed, his disillusion with the Bishop becoming a sort of code for his anger at his treatment, his doubts about how his Church organized itself and conducted itself in difficult situations. Then, as they prepared for bed, the kiss – the kiss that could no longer be put down to friendship, gratitude, other feelings. Then the walk up the stairs to Margaret's bedroom, a journey when somehow each seemed to be supporting the other.

He looked at the events for a clue to Margaret's feelings, her attitude. He had to admit he did not know. Would it be best to ask her, bring it out into the open? He shrank from that, and told himself that Margaret had given no sign of wanting it.

However, when he went downstairs and took his raincoat off the hook for a walk to the newsagent's for a paper, Margaret came to the kitchen door and looked at him, trying hard to erase any suggestion of worry from her face.

'You do realize, don't you Christopher, that the last thing I'd ever want is to put pressure on you? All I want, truly, is for you to be back at St Catherine's and a parish priest again.'

He walked over and kissed her.

'That's in the lap of the gods, Margaret, if you'll pardon a paganism.'

'I feel so bloody guilty,' said Charlie, as he and Oddie got into the car and began the drive towards Shipley.

'I don't see why,' said Oddie. 'Beyond the obvious fact that you dunnit.'

Charlie was uncharacteristically roundabout in his reply.

'Abortion is different when you've been partners for several years, isn't it?' he said. 'It's not like some poor teenager who's been ignorant and unlucky. I'd have been pretty unhappy if Felicity had wanted that, but of course she doesn't.'

'So?'

'She says she's not going to apply for this lectureship she'd have had a good chance of getting by all accounts. Says the most she'll do is the occasional teaching hour, or marking. She's decided for the first years she's going to be a full-time mother.'

'Unfashionable, or it would have been ten or twenty years ago,' commented Oddie. 'Now it's not so much unfashionable as uneconomic.'

'She doesn't say so, but I can't help feeling that if I had a different job, a nine to five one, she wouldn't have decided to make this sacrifice – because that's what it is.'

'At least with you becoming Sergeant the financial pressures won't be as great.'

164

Charlie cast him a look.

'You're joking,' he said sourly. 'And there's another thing: she wants a church wedding.'

'You were intending to get married anyway.'

'I wasn't thinking of a church wedding.'

'So what did you want? An underwater one in the West Indies? A blessing on Haworth moors?'

'Don't be sarky. I'm old-fashioned. I don't see what's wrong with a registry office.'

'And she wants the white caboodle, with bridesmaids?'

'I think she's thinking in terms of pale blue . . . The trouble is my mother will back her up to the hilt.'

'I don't think the mother of the bridegroom has much clout in all this.'

Charlie shot him another look.

'You've *met* my mother.'

'True. Still, look on the bright side. It'll be a day to remember. And you'll make a handsome couple.'

Charlie brightened a fraction.

'Yes, we will,' he said complacently. 'So what's the order of the day, boss?'

'It's sorting out and weeding out. By the way, one we can weed out is Alan Russell. He might have been eligible for parole by now, but three years ago the woman who ran the educational programme in his nick was won over by his highly deceptive charms. She planned an escape for him that was to end up with the pair of them making a new life in Spain. Which in Russell's case would have been pretty much like his old life in Britain, I'd guess. Anyway the result is he's still got eighteen months to do.'

'Good. Well that's him knocked off the suspect list. How do we share out the others? Do I start off with Julie Norris?'

'I think so. More of her age, more of her mindset, probably. Hey – you've got more common ground still: a baby on the way.' Charlie grunted. 'I suspect you'll do better without an oldie.'

'What will you do?'

'I was going to go and see the parents, but I think I'd rather have you with me. I get a whiff of an unusual and complicated situation there. How else explain their behaviour to their own daughter?'

'It's not as unusual as you make out,' protested Charlie. 'A lot of parents are just itching to get rid of their children, but they just sit tight, on and on, because they're allowed to do anything they want to do at home.'

'Julie was only seventeen.'

'Well, yes, that's a bit young. Anyway, I'd certainly like to get a look at them.'

'So if you let me off on the Kingsmill estate before you get to Julie's des. res., I'm going to look around to see if Julie and the priest were a subject of scandal over a long period, and what and who could have triggered off the investigation of the man.'

So when Charlie banged on Julie Norris's door, trying to be heard over the squeaks of the Teletubbies, he was on his own, and glad to be. When the door opened, Julie was bent over clutching a paw of a child of about two, and it was only when she straightened to look at his ID that Charlie saw how pretty and appealing she was.

'Is it about that creep from the *Chronicle*?' Julie asked. 'I thought your lot might come. Don't expect me to express any grief.'

'You'd be out on your own if you did,' said Charlie cheerfully, following her through to the dark and messy living room. 'I don't think journalists set much store by being popular. Not his kind of journalist, anyway.'

The Teletubbies were ending, and Julie switched the set off.

'He really gave me the creeps,' she said, without waiting for a question. 'It wasn't *just* that he was pushing his way into my private life, though that was bad enough. It was – well, you can see I'm practically shivering at the thought of him, can't you?' Charlie nodded, though shuddering was more the word. 'He stood at the window there, looking in here after I'd shut the door in his face, and he just leered at Gary and me. You could see his horrible mind working, thinking how he'd describe how grotty this place is. His kind are like rats at a garbage tip.'

'Was that the last you saw of him?'

'Yes, thank God. Though I heard he paid a visit later on to Doris Crabtree out the back, her who landed poor Father Pardoe in it and started the whole business.' She jerked a thumb towards the back window and the house to be seen through it. Charlie filed the name in his mind in case Oddie didn't get on to her.

'We've wondered a bit how it all started,' he said. 'Why should she do that?'

'Because she's a nosy old cow,' said Julie promptly. 'Anything going on, she knows it, spreads it, and makes trouble if she can. If they'd known anything about this estate they'd have binned her letter the moment they got it and thought no more about it.'

'Who's they?'

'The people in the Bishop's office. That's who she wrote to. She saw I was getting visits from a priest, and she saw the best way to make trouble about it. You wouldn't think they'd take a mucky letter like that seriously, would you?'

Charlie had to agree in his mind that he wouldn't.

'Maybe it's the fact that you're pregnant again,' he suggested. 'She could have said that Father Pardoe was the father.'

'I wouldn't put it past her, lying cow. And in case you're interested, he's not. And he's not Gary's father either. He – the one I think is his father – was working in a bar in Toronto last I heard of him, which is nearly two years ago. We've had no contact since I moved out of his parents' house and came here.'

'I didn't mean to pry. It's no business of ours chasing errant fathers. I'm interested because I heard last night that I'm going to be a father.'

She immediately relaxed, and smiled.

'Oh, that's nice. If it's wanted.'

'Oh, it's that. A bit unexpected, but definitely wanted.'

'I only seem to be able to pick blokes who don't want to know. The father of this one –' she patted her stomach – 'is nothing to do with all this, and I haven't seen him since half an hour after I told him I was pregnant. They asked

167

me who it was at the enquiry, and I told them to mind their own business.'

'Was that the Bishop's enquiry?'

'Yes.'

'So far you're the only person we've interviewed who's talked to them.'

'A lot of good it did me, or Father. There were three of them. They were kind enough, I suppose . . . Do you want my opinion?'

'Very much.'

'There were two stooges, and one who might be a bit more independent. He was the young priest.'

'And who were the others?'

'An older priest. He was a pretty strong-minded type, stern almost, but he'd be a Bishop's man. Believes in authority. Then an anonymous-looking chap, not a priest, who hardly said a word. If you were looking for a weak link, he'd be the one.'

'Someone who could be bullied, you mean?'

She smiled, knowingly. 'Yes.'

'You're very sharp. You should be using that brain.'

'I am. I'm bringing up a kid.'

Charlie sighed silently. He foresaw months of arguments with Felicity along the same lines. Arguments he would lose, as he just had. Julie saw she'd landed a blow under the belt.

'Sorry. I didn't mean anything personal. I'm not saying what I'm doing is what I've always dreamt of doing. But you have to make do with what you've got, don't you?'

A bleak thought in a bleak room, Charlie decided.

Oddie got on to Doris Crabtree almost immediately. She had been cited but not named in the article in the *Globe*. He stopped and talked to a group of young women with toddlers and they turned out to be friends of Julie Norris, and immediately identified the 'old cow' who had 'landed her in it.' He was round knocking on her door within ten minutes of having been dropped off by Charlie.

'I've never been so shocked in all my life,' she announced,

leading him through to the kitchen and pouring him a cup of heavily stewed and lukewarm tea. 'One minute he's sitting there just like you now and talking to me nice as pie and really interested, encouraging me to tell him everything I know, the next I hear he's on the local news, murdered!' There was a relish, but also more than a touch of regret in her tone.

'So you'd talked to him about Julie Norris, had you?' Oddie asked.

'O' course we talked. That's what he come for. He found out it were me wrote to alert the Bishop about what was going on. It was my duty, and I've always done that, whatever the cost. And there's been young sluts around here shouting after me and calling me names, I can tell you.'

'And what was going on, do you think?'

'I don't need to spell it out, do I? He'd arrive down Kingsmill Rise, he'd ring the doorbell and go in, and then the curtains would be drawn in the bedroom. And the few times they weren't, they'd be in the kitchen where I couldn't see 'em.'

Oddie refrained from saying that she'd brought him into her kitchen, and it was a perfectly natural place for a chat.

'So you suggested he might be the father of the child that's on the way?'

She sniffed.

'I mentioned that fact, and let them draw their own conclusions.'

'And the Fund that he'd been using apparently for her benefit?'

'Don't know owt about that. I'd seen her showing him the telly set once, and I wondered if he'd got it for her, but I couldn't be sure, so I kept quiet. No, it was just the other I told them about, and that was enough. Makes me sick, that . . .'

'What does?'

'Him giving her money from this Fund. Her having televisions and washing-machines and anything she asks for. I grew up when folk were lucky to be in work, and my dad weren't one of the lucky ones. We lived off bread and dripping half the time.'

The words should have made her a more sympathetic figure, but the sour expression, the obvious jealousy of one who, whatever the rise in national expectations since this woman's childhood, was still near the bottom of the pile, nauseated Oddie. He suppressed a sigh.

'So you think Father Pardoe may be the father of Julie's forthcoming child.'

'I'm not accusing him. But it seems pretty likely, doesn't it?'

'There've been no other men visiting her?'

'Oh, I never said that! That'd be pretty surprising, young women being what they are today. A man's only got to ask her and she pulls up her skirts.'

Oddie suppressed another sigh, and put on an expression more alert than he thought this woman's information justified.

'Let me get this right, because it could be important: are you accusing Julie of being a prostitute, or a part-time one?'

She pursed up her lips and thought before replying.

'No, I'm not. Not at her house here, any road.'

'But you have seen men going there.'

'Oh yes. A man, anyway.'

'One man?'

'Aye. One man went there several times.'

'What was he like?'

'It were last winter. I couldn't see what he was like. Lighting's dismal round here, because the kids throw bricks at the bulbs and the council doesn't bother to replace them. He were taller than Father Pardoe – not so bulky. I could only see the outline of him as he come down the street.'

'Last winter. How far gone is Julie's pregnancy?'

'Happen four or five months. You're trying to say he's the father of her child, aren't you?'

'It's a possibility.'

'You middle-aged men stick together, don't you?' It was Oddie's turn to feel he'd had a hit scored against him.

Father Pardoe felt a certain awkwardness that day in sitting down to lunch with Margaret, and he needed all his social arts to hide it. He told her about his walk, and the man in the post office who had come up to him and wished him luck because he always supported people who were being turned over by muckrakers.

'That was brave of him. Did he know the man had been murdered?'

'He did. Said it made "not a ha'porth of difference". And of course it doesn't. I'm quite convinced his murder had nothing to do with my suspension and the story he made out of it . . . There's a bit of good news, by the way.'

'Good news?'

'I think it's good. I got a letter today, asking me to meet the committee of enquiry. I think that's a polite way of asking me to appear before it.'

'That's wonderful! Just what you've been wanting.'

'Yes, it is . . . Odd how this business has made me suspicious, though. Once I got over the euphoria, I started wondering whether they would have heard my side of the matter at all if it hadn't been for Horrocks's murder.'

Margaret considered this.

'You mean the spotlight is now on them, in a way it wasn't before, and they're being careful to be meticulously fair.'

'Yes. Or to seem to be.'

'That's being doubly cynical!' said Margaret. 'But take heart: if they are still bent on being unfair, it will be much more difficult with everyone's eyes on them. I suppose that's what made the Bishop so angry.'

Pardoe pulled himself up.

'We mustn't find the Bishop guilty without his being tried. Forget what I said, and assume I will get, and always would have got, a fair hearing.'

'It's what you've been pressing for, and what you should have had weeks ago . . . Christopher, you do realize, don't you, that no one will ever know about – about what's happened between us.'

Pardoe looked at her and nodded.

'Yes, I do. I've never trusted anyone more absolutely than I do you, Margaret. I've wrestled with it – but perhaps I don't need to go into that. You will have guessed all that. I can't see that it's anything more than a sin like any other. I've been guilty – all priests have been guilty – of plenty of sins, and I hope I've been conscious of them, tried to face up to them. But since I came here, you've been a life-line, been the most wonderful help and support in every way. I shall never forget what you've been to me.'

'That's all right then,' said Margaret, smiling and getting up to go to the kitchen.

But Christopher Pardoe, registering the warmth and friendliness of the smile, wished he had not discerned, intermingled with them, a brief shaft of pain.

CHAPTER 16

Dysfunctional

Charlie was saying goodbye to Julie Norris on her doorstep when he saw Oddie come round the corner and go in the direction of the police car. He raised his hand to him and turned back to Julie.

'I'm grateful to you for your help,' he said. 'I hope all goes well with you and the new baby.'

'Yours too. It must be wonderful to look forward to a birth.'

Charlie looked around him, taking in the garbage tip on the vacant lot opposite.

'Why don't you try and get the council to find you something better than this –'

'Dump. Say it. What's the point? I've got me mates around here now. Anyway, you could say it's coming home. It's where I was born.'

Charlie raised his eyebrows.

'I didn't realize that.'

'Nor did I. It's on my birth certificate as parents' address. I insisted on having it when I moved my things out. Thought I might need it, dealing with the benefits people and that. When I commented on it to my mother she just said: "You started life in a slum, and you'll be there for the rest of your life."'

'She sounds a real charmer.'

Julie shrugged, refusing to be cast down.

'I've had to find friends to replace my parents. Not just since Gary came along, but always. My aunt Becky was always nicer to me than they were. And Father Pardoe was the best of them. OK, it's pretty depressing here, but one thing I'm never going to do is take it out on the babies. It's not their fault if their mother's been a bit of a slut, is it?'

'You're not a slut, Julie. Don't think like that.'

She smiled wanly.

'Bring Father Pardoe back for me, will you?'

'You know I can't do that. I'm not the Catholic Church.'

'What I really mean is: bring him safely through all this. Get justice for him. He's a good man, one of the best. And I didn't do him much good, I'm afraid.'

'We'll do our best. Keep fighting.'

Back at the car he said to Oddie: 'That was an interesting titbit.'

'What was?'

'Julie was born on the Kingsmill.'

Oddie's eyebrows went through the roof.

'Really? I suspect that's not something the Norrises go around telling people.'

'No. Might give us an interesting topic for small talk when we go visiting them in Beckham Road.'

'Which I think we should do now.'

Modest though Beckham Road was, they both recognized the decisive step up the Norrises had made when they moved from the Kingsmill. The house seemed dead, though, where the Kingsmill was alive, if depressingly so – teeming with dubious life bent on the struggle for survival. It took some time for the door to be answered to their ring, but Oddie had observed a shape in an upstairs window and told Charlie to keep on ringing. When the door was opened, Mrs Norris ushered them inside with not a glance at the identification. Oddie and Charlie had long realized that they looked like a police team, and were thought to 'look bad' in neighbours' eyes. It was something they could live with. It certainly got you inside houses and business premises quickly.

'I'm sorry to keep you waiting,' said Mrs Norris almost ingratiatingly. She was watery-eyed, and her voice had a grizzling quality that Charlie in particular found unsympathetic. 'Come through. You've come at the right time. Simon will be home for his lunch in five minutes. He's found that in the places he usually goes to he's getting funny looks at the moment. That's what being in the news does for you, doesn't it?'

She seemed not to have made up her mind whether this was ungenteel or rather exciting.

'Sometimes,' said Oddie genially, letting the armchair embrace him like an elderly lover. 'It's not always nice to be looked at. Those articles by Cosmo Horrocks didn't do you any service.'

'Oh, I don't know about that,' said Daphne Norris quickly. 'He was very fair, we thought. He just wanted to make sure our side of things was put. We were grateful to him.'

Both men repressed the sceptical jeer they felt.

'I see,' said Oddie. 'As far as you were concerned he was perfectly fair in his reporting.'

'Oh yes. We'd no complaints at all. What can you say when your daughter's been having an affair with a priest and is expecting his child?'

'Julie categorically denies both these things,' put in Charlie. He received a sour look for his pains.

'Well, she would, wouldn't she? What I say is, you reap what you sow in this world, God sees to that. And Julie's reward is to be stuck in that hell-hole of an estate, with two screaming kids. She'll not get any sympathy from me.'

Mrs Norris had not learnt anything about the art of getting the listener on her side since she had been interviewed by Cosmo Horrocks, Oddie thought. He said:

'I'd have thought you might have been sympathetic. After all, you'd been in a similar position yourself, hadn't you?'

She looked at him in venomous outrage.

'What's she been saying? You don't know what you're talking about. I was a married woman. Simon and I were newly wed, and we hadn't the funds for anything better. We soon got out of the Kingsmill, I can tell you . . . There's Simon now.'

She scurried out into the hall, and they could hear a whispered but intense confabulation at the front door before Simon Norris came in. Oddie knew his type at once. He'd had an inspector when he first joined CID who had that neat-moustached and spitfire-delivery approach. He had had to take decidedly early retirement.

'I hear you've been talking to our Julie –'

'She's not "our Julie",' put in his wife. 'Never was.'

'She'll say anything to bring the family down. No pride, no pride at all. Yes, we had a brief spell on the Kingsmill. We were just married then, and had to take what we could get. Fortunately a relative helped us to buy this place. That was the happiest day of our lives, when we could wipe the dust of that place off our shoes.'

They seemed more upset by the slur on their social standing than by any attempt to involve them in the Horrocks murder. Oddie decided to back-pedal and get back to the real matter in hand.

'Well, well, that wasn't what I came here to talk about,' he said, resuming his geniality. 'Can I ask you what you were doing on Tuesday evening?'

Both the foxy faces became suspicious.

'That's the night Mr Horrocks was killed, wasn't it?' Simon Norris asked.

'Yes.'

'I don't know what you think you're –'

'Just answer please.'

They looked at each other.

'Well, we were here.'

'Alone? Anyone to vouch for you?'

'Well, Lennie. He was here too. And we talked to Aunt Becky later on.'

'How later on?'

'Oh, well after ten.'

'Who rang who?'

'She rang us here. What is –?'

'And did she talk to both of you?'

'Yes.' The tone of the replies had sunk into a sullen hostility.

'Can we have her number please?'

'My God! We're really suspects!' It was a reaction Oddie and Charlie were used to. From feeling slightly uneasy at being questioned at all the interviewee gradually accumulated a monstrous grievance: they, respectable they, were being treated as possible criminals! Didn't the police recognize sterling citizens when they saw them?

'A lot of people are in the frame,' he explained patiently. 'It's a very large frame. A reporter is a man with many aspects, and he usually has many irons in the fire. That Father Pardoe story was only the most sensational at the time he was killed.'

'But why pick on us? We had no quarrel with him. He let us put our point of view very fairly.'

Oddie raised his eyebrows quite theatrically in his direction.

'And did you get no feeling that people in general would consider that you came out of that article rather badly? That Horrocks's intention was to let you condemn yourselves by your own words?'

They looked at each other, but neither would back down. Simon looked back at Oddie, belligerently.

'No! . . . Well, Daphne did come in for a little unpleasantness at the butcher's the other day. But that's just people's ignorance. They don't know what it's like, having a daughter pregnant at seventeen.'

'It's something quite a lot of people experience these days. Now the phone number of your aunt.'

Oddie passed across to Simon Norris a sheet of his notepad, and reluctantly he took a pen from his pocket and began writing, talking, nagging at his grievance the whole time.

'Seems to me you're going at this in a right arse-over-tip manner. Who'd kill a man because of a newspaper story he wrote? Make more sense if he was killed about a story he still hadn't published. But it stands to reason what you should be looking at is his family. Isn't it true that most murders are domestics?'

'A lot of them are,' said Oddie, holding out his hand for the slip.

'There you are, then.'

'And do you know a lot about Horrocks's family?' asked Oddie, handing the slip to Charlie. Expecting a confession of total ignorance, he was surprised by the reply.

'I know his daughter is having it off with her history teacher.' Norris all but spat. '*Female* history teacher. Doesn't it make you sick? If Lennie knows about it, the whole school probably knows about it. And nobody does a thing. If it was a male teacher and a girl pupil, he'd be out on his ear, and quite right too. But with perverts they use kid bloody gloves!'

Charlie paused at the door to raise an eyebrow in Oddie's direction, then went out into the kitchen, taking out his mobile as he went.

'Have you seen your daughter since she moved out?' asked Oddie conversationally.

'We have *not*, not beyond her coming back to collect her things. She wouldn't be welcome here.'

'I've seen her in the distance in Shipley,' said Daphne Norris, 'and gone the other way.'

'And if you think that's heartless, we don't give a stuff,' said her husband. 'A girl who's pregnant at seventeen and can't with certainty name the father isn't fit to live in a respectable family home. I wouldn't have her near our Lennie, and that's a fact.'

'But that wasn't when things went wrong between you, was it?'

'What do you mean?'

'I'm just guessing, but from the way you talk you'd always regarded your daughter as a problem.'

'That's because she's always bloody well been a problem.'

'Right from the time she was born,' put in Daphne Norris, the whinge in her voice becoming more pronounced. 'That birth was the most horrendous experience of my life. The labour went on and on, the most appalling pain you could imagine. Then to have to take her home to the Kingsmill – sitting in that miserable hole of a flat day after day, listening to her crying – she never stopped. I began to hate the sight of her.'

'Sounds to me like post-natal depression,' said Oddie.

Norris's mouth twisted into a sneer.

'Oh, they give everything high-sounding names these days,' he said. 'Keeps the trick-cyclists in business.'

'Did you talk about it with your doctor?'

''Course not,' said his wife. 'What could he do about our living on the Kingsmill?'

'Post-natal depression is a clinical condition. Something can be done about it.'

'We cured that by moving,' she said complacently. 'Aunt Becky helped us with the down payment on this place – all paid back by now. It was like finding ourselves in heaven after a year in hell.'

'When was this?'

'Oh, Julie would have been about six months old. We'd had a year or more in that place, like I said. Never been back there – wouldn't set foot in it.'

'But after you moved, you didn't get on much better with your daughter?'

Neither took his question as implying criticism.

'Not much,' Simon Norris said. 'And then, when Lennie came – we waited until we were really well established before we had him – when Julie was six, she was such a cow about him, resented him to that extent, that we just knew we'd had a bit of bad luck with the one kid and a bit of good luck with the other. It never does any harm to face the facts, does it?'

Oddie stirred uneasily in his chair. He felt he was entering uncharted, rather frightening psychological territory.

Charlie, in the kitchen, was talking to Aunt Becky.

'So you phoned them on Tuesday, when you got home.'

'Oh yes. I knew they'd be waiting for the call, so I had to ring, though it was late.'

The voice was cheery, fruity, outgoing. Charlie could imagine Julie preferring her aunt to her parents.

'How late, in actual fact, was it?'

'Maybe half ten, maybe a quarter to eleven. Something like that. I'd rung them several times while I was on the retreat, gave them all the gossip, but they'd want to know that I was safely home.'

'Of course. And you spoke to both of them?'

'Simon answered, then he put me on to Daphne.' She'd been talking away happily, but now she paused. 'What *exactly* is this all about?'

'We're investigating the death of Cosmo Horrocks.'

'Who's he when he's at – Oh! That was the journalist who published all that stuff about Julie and the priest.'

'That's right.'

'Simon and Daphne sent me the story. Well! So you're investigating them! They won't be best pleased. That's another mess that girl has landed them in.'

'It may well be there's nothing in the story at all. You can't believe all you read in the papers.'

'No. Still . . . Mind you, I always liked Julie.'

'I've just been talking to her. I liked her very much indeed.'

'You'll think I'm old-fashioned but I'm afraid when I heard she didn't know for certain who the father of her child was, I washed my hands of her. Maybe I was unfair. It could be how it was told me. I know she's had a raw deal in the past, with her parents so taken up with Lennie as if he's God's gift, but I felt there were limits.'

'I don't think it would have been put to you so that Julie showed to the best advantage, do you?' Charlie strayed from his brief and said persuasively: 'I think she could do with a friend now. My impression is that Father Pardoe became a sort of parent to her, gave her help and advice, but of course now she's lost him too.'

'Hmmm. I don't know. Simon and Daphne would be furious. And this about the priest . . .'

'I don't think there's anything in that.'

'I should hope *not* . . . What's *your* motive in this, young man? I can hear you *are* young. Why should a policeman bother his head about whether Julie has any friends or not?'

'I'm not talking as a policeman,' said Charlie, coming clean. 'I've just heard I'm going to become a father. That's frightening enough. To hear you're going to become a mother, on your own, with another kid to look after, and not yet twenty – if I was in her shoes I'd be terrified.'

There was a silence, then an ungrudging admission.

'Yes. I see that.'

'I can give you her address.'

'I've got her address. I send her a card at Christmas.'

'You said you'd washed your hands of her.'

'Yes . . . Well, I suppose in the back of my mind there's always been the feeling that I'd only heard Simon and Daphne's side of the story. And they've never had a good word to say about Julie. Never.'

When Charlie slipped back into the Norrises' sitting room, Oddie was back on the subject that interested him.

'You mentioned Horrocks's daughter – Samantha I presume. Is your son a friend of hers?'

'Oh, I don't think so,' said Daphne quickly. 'She'd be quite a lot older than Lennie.'

'How did the subject of her come up, then?'

'It came up when the story came out – Monday, was it? Lennie saw the story, saw the reporter's name for the first time, and said his daughter was at his school.'

'And that she was . . . involved with her history mistress.'

'Yes. No, I think it was the next day he told us that. The story was all round the school by then, the story of Julie and the priest, I mean, because of course Julie had been a pupil there not so long ago, and the older kids would remember her. We so hoped that wouldn't become common gossip, for Lennie's sake: he's terribly sensitive. Anyway, Lennie had been talking about the story and how he met the reporter with one of the older boys, and that's how he found out. There's a lot of whispering about that teacher in the upper forms. Of course when Simon heard about it he went spare.'

'Do you bloody wonder?' Simon put in.

'What I wonder is whether her father had heard this rumour,' Oddie mused.

'If he had, he wouldn't be very happy about it, would he?' exploded Norris again. 'It's what I said: you're looking in the wrong places. You don't get murdered for writing newspaper stories. Look closer to home. That's where you'll find a motive strong enough for murder.'

Later, walking back to their car, Charlie muttered: 'I should bear it in mind: there are worse parents than my mother.'

'Not many better, if you ask me,' said Oddie. 'She kept you on the straight and narrow.'

'Yeah, even if she never stayed there herself,' said Charlie. 'What's the betting Mrs Norris was in the family way, as they used to say, when they got married and set up home on the Kingsmill?'

'I thought that. The whole situation somehow works better that way. Then the post-natal depression after the birth, the failure to recognize it or treat it, combined with the virulent hatred of where they were living.'

'Aunt Becky, who got them out of there, sounds a much cheerier soul,' said Charlie. 'She confirms their story, by the way.'

Oddie sighed.

'Pity. They'd make lovely culprits – people it would be a pleasure to arrest. But of course what he said about looking closer to Cosmo's home, though it was pure self-interest on his part, trying to turn us away from him and Daphne, was quite right. It's time we started looking at the family – and friends too, if there are any.'

'Actually, that's what I've been looking at already,' Charlie pointed out. 'His wrong-side-of-the-blanket family.'

'Well, let's turn our attention to the right side. Nothing I've heard about Horrocks suggests he would have a benign tolerance of the sexual minorities.'

'Everything I've heard suggests he would use anything that came his way to cause trouble and unpleasantness and make life miserable for people. That applies to his newspaper stories, and it probably applies to his private life as well. He loved to show who was boss, who was cracking the whip. So in a way his attitude to lesbianism or whatever is irrelevant. Maybe he didn't even have one. But he'd assume one to make his daughter's life a hell. Maybe he even had plans to make that his next story.'

Oddie pondered.

'Interesting thought. Maybe we should get on to the school's headmaster, see if he's available for a chat.'

'What about the areas we've still got to look at?' asked Charlie. 'The St Catherine's menfolk, the Bishop and his commission?'

'We'll go back to the Shipley station and set those up

182

afterwards. This is new, and may just be a bundle of nasty rumours, but it's close to home for Horrocks, and I'd like to establish whether there's any basis of truth in it. I'll get on to the headmaster now.'

CHAPTER 17

Regardless of their Doom

'I'm Peter Frencham,' said the man waiting for them at the school gate, shaking them both by the hand. 'I thought I'd come out and guide you through this mêlée.'

Both Oddie and Charlie decided that they liked what they saw. He was in his early forties probably, but with grey beginning to show in his temples and worry lines already forming around his eyes and across his forehead. Par for the course, most likely. The main thing was that he looked capable and dependable: if one didn't always agree with his decisions one would know they had been taken after careful thought, and he would explain them in a way that could be understood.

'Lunchtime chaos, I suppose,' said Charlie. 'I remember it well.'

They were about to set off through the mob for the school buildings when something caught his eye. Two boys a hundred yards or so away had spotted them, and had turned with military precision and begun to walk away. Charlie touched Peter Frencham's arm.

'Who are those two boys?' he asked. The words were no sooner out of his mouth than the smaller of the two turned round to try and catch a furtive glimpse of the school's visitors. 'Oh, I think I could guess one of them.'

'Yes, he's very like his father.' The headmaster lowered his tone. 'Unfortunate for the boy, you might say.'

'Very. So, that's Lennie, is it? How would they know who we are?'

'It's all round the school – probably all round Shipley – that the Horrocks murder is being investigated by a police duo, one middle-aged and white, the other young and black.

It's a bit too much like a TV crime series pairing not to cause comment. It gives them a delicious sense of watching something on the box come to life.'

'Who would be spreading this? I've been off in the Midlands, so Mike was on his own most of yesterday.'

'Samantha Horrocks only had one day off when her father was killed.'

'Of course.'

'I gather she's not pretending to be grief-stricken. I've been rather wondering whether it was Samantha that you wanted to talk to me about.'

They were at the door of the main building, and he pushed it open and led them down corridors, some of them containing excited children who stopped their shouting when they saw them. Eventually they arrived at a quieter area, where Peter Frencham opened a door.

'Before we get on to what we've come about,' said Charlie when the door had shut behind them, 'could I ask who that boy was with Lennie Norris?'

'Ah, that was Mark Leary. The Leary family's prominent in the St Catherine's congregation, I believe.'

'I've talked briefly with his mother,' put in Oddie. 'The boy dashed in and out to get some sports gear, but I only caught a glimpse of him.'

'It's a very sporty family – the men anyway. The father played football for Shipley years ago, and he was following in *his* father's footsteps. Took over the family firm – electrical goods – as well. They're pretty substantial people in a Shipley context. The daughter's just come to us, and her teachers speak well of her – keen brain, with a touch of rebelliousness that doesn't go amiss. The mother's a very sensible woman.'

'Yes,' said Oddie cautiously. 'Seemed rather nervous when I spoke to her.'

'Really? Maybe it's the Church being thought to be involved in the Horrocks case.' He seemed about to say something, but then changed his mind. 'Was it Samantha Horrocks you wanted to talk about?'

'Yes, it was,' said Oddie. 'Of course we've been interested in his family, as we were bound to be, but somehow the coincidence of the Pardoe story and the killing meant that we've concentrated on that so far. Now something's come up.'

'I think I can guess what it is.'

'It concerns a history teacher.'

'Yes . . . Superintendent, I'm quite happy to fetch Cassie Daltrey so you can have a talk with her, but do you mind if I fill you in with a bit of background first?'

'I'd welcome it.'

The policemen made themselves as comfortable as possible in upright chairs. Peter Frencham perched on his desk.

'First, the girl herself: Samantha lives a bit outside our normal catchment area, but she got a transfer here from Rodley because she's very keen on history. It's a subject that's being downgraded in schools these days, more's the pity, so it's important when there is someone who wants to specialize that they get the best teaching. Cassie Daltrey's one of the best, and her reputation reached young Samantha. I talked to the girl and her mother – her father never came into it – organized the transfer here, and on the whole it's all gone very well.'

'Right. But people have been talking, have they?'

'Yes. I should say it's happened before – talk I mean. And the truth is that it may be there's talk *now* because there's been talk *before*. Do you take my point?'

'It mushrooms,' said Oddie. 'There were allegations about Miss Daltrey and a pupil in the past –'

'Three years ago.'

'So people are just waiting for something similar to happen again.'

'That's exactly it. I sometimes wonder whether something rather similar hasn't happened to Father Pardoe.'

'Talk begets talk. But in fact I think things have happened rather differently in his case. And we haven't heard of any serious sexual allegations about him in the past.'

'Right. I think what I really meant was that the spate of sexual allegations here and in Ireland against priests and nuns means people look closely and sceptically at the conduct of all the Catholic hierarchy. Just one more point. I knew there was

186

talk going round in the upper forms, the odd smutty joke too, as you can imagine. I was about to have a quiet word with Cassie, suggest that any special tuition would have to take place here in school, not at her flat. How she'd have taken that I don't know. But another business came up, and like a coward I put Cassie and Samantha on the back burner. I'm afraid I was glad to. That's about it, really.'

'Thank you for being so frank.'

'I'll fetch her now and leave you both alone with her.'

The staff room was further down the corridor, and it was less than a couple of minutes before Frencham was ushering in a quietly smart, brisk but decidedly pleasant woman probably, Charlie thought, in her early thirties. Oddie took the desk, she and Charlie the two chairs that the headmaster's study boasted. Cassie Daltrey was on the surface completely cool and in control.

'I gather it's about Samantha,' she said at once.

'That's right.'

'I thought it might be. She told me her father was making what you might call tabloid noises. I wonder, could I tell it to you in my own words – rather as if you were the headmaster? I'd expected to be called in for a little chat with him before too long.'

'Please, go ahead. We might interrupt to take up points as you go along.'

Both men, however, registered in their minds that she had been preparing for a chat with the headmaster, so her account was likely to be, if not untrue, then pre-packaged with her own slant.

'First, yes: I'm a lesbian. I have my own circle, here and in the towns around, and in Leeds. I'm discreet about it, and I don't resent having to be discreet. If there was a heterosexual teacher in the school who had a fair range of partners I would expect him or her to be discreet too. You could say I'm old-fashioned like that.'

'And if one of your pupils were to ask you about it?' Oddie put in.

She paused for a moment or two to think.

'Yes, that's a question, isn't it? It's probably only a matter of time before one does. I'd probably say my private life is my own affair. And provided I am discreet about it, I think that is the case. If I flaunted my sexuality then I'd have to expect questions, discussion, jokes and public scandal even.'

'Fair enough.'

'Right. Now – getting a star pupil in history these days is a bonus. If you downgrade a subject it loses prestige and most of the bright kids start thinking in terms of doing something else. *Except* the ones who really have a talent for it, a feel, an instinct – call it what you like. I mean the ones for whom nothing else will do. I had it three years ago, when I first came here, with a girl called Nicola Barnes. She could have sailed into Oxbridge, but that option doesn't have the prestige with the young it once had. She opted for Leeds, and living at home, which I think of as a shame, and second best, but the economic pressure to do that is very strong these days.'

She paused. Oddie seemed about to fill in the gap, then decided not to.

'There were no rumours, no talk while she was here. Quite rightly. Nothing went on. I gave her special tuition, if necessary at my home, but nothing happened, and I made sure nothing did. Since then she has become part of the lesbian scene in Leeds. And so –'

'Talk started here, you mean?'

She shrugged.

'Yes. I still don't know for certain how it got around, but I suspect worried parents. Mrs Barnes started wondering about the friends her daughter was bringing home. And then people cast their minds back and started asking questions about her and me. The talk never got going until six months after she'd left here. What it did mean was that when I got another potential star pupil, and it was a girl, the talk was ready made. I was exceptionally careful, but there was always going to be jokes, name-calling, that sort of thing. I suppose I should be grateful: students are more sophisticated, and a bit more tolerant too, these days. Twenty years ago things might have got really nasty.'

'So you gave up the private tuition classes at home?'

Cassie Daltrey shook her head.

'There I didn't have any option. I need a break at the end of the day before teaching at Samantha's level, and the school doesn't stay open all evening – budgets don't allow that. So we've had the odd tuition session at my flat, and I've been as discreet about that as possible, and made sure she has been too.'

'And Samantha herself?'

Was there a slight tightening of the body?

'What about Samantha?'

'I imagine she's heard the rumours, maybe come in for some smutty jokes.'

'Both. Samantha's the one student I couldn't fob off with the line that my private life is my own business. I told her about it over coffee the first time she came to my flat. But Samantha needs the tuition if she's to get to Oxford. She has to make up for lost time, as far as the teaching at her old school is concerned. And Oxford is what she wants, and no substitute. No, that's not true: she'd have settled in the end for anywhere away from home while her appalling father was alive, but Oxford she has a yen for. I tease her and say it's watching videos of *Brideshead Revisited*, but I think it's just as likely to be Oxford's first-rate reputation for history. She's a girl who knows where she's going. She also, like Nicola, has a *sense* for history. That's vital.'

'And that is all there's been?'

'That, Superintendent, is all there's been.'

'But there's been trouble for her at home, has there?'

'Trouble with her father. Really you ought to talk to Samantha about that. She just alludes to it with me, and shrugs it off. Says she's learnt to cope with his kind of beastliness. I think she doesn't want to upset me, though she wouldn't. She'll talk about her father generally – or would, before he died. A terrible father: an emotional sadist, someone with a real taste for humiliation. But please do remember that Samantha was about to get away from him. I really believe that: if all this hasn't upset her she should get to Oxford, and with a bit of luck go up in October. And I can assure you, Samantha is not a murderess. She has the strongest possible sense of right and wrong. That's why she passionately hated all the things her father did in his professional life, particularly his thirst for destroying people.'

'She felt morally outraged by his journalistic standards?'

'Yes. I think that puts it pretty well . . . And by the way, Superintendent, my guess – it's no more – is that Samantha is definitely heterosexual. I've never seen anything to suggest otherwise. So when he made allegations about her and me, she could test his standards of proof and honesty for herself, in her own life.'

And that, essentially was all they got out of her. They probed, asked her to amplify and explain, but five minutes later she was on her way back to the staff room to collect the headmaster. She paused for a moment in the empty corridor to collect herself. A litany was running through her head: 'If only that were true. If only that was all. If only just for once in my life I had been wise. If I'd just let it emerge, what she wanted – not tried to pressure her my way. But I didn't, and I lost her. What a fool I am. And I never learn. It will happen again. And one day I'll be ruined.'

In the headmaster's study the two policemen were doing an expert appraisal of her performance.

'The sanitized version,' said Oddie.

'Probably,' said Charlie. 'But very well done.'

'She was prepared.'

'I suspect someone in her position, with her tastes, is always prepared.'

'Good point. And if there *is* anything more –' Oddie shrugged – 'the girl is about to go to Oxford, it seems.'

'Where anything goes, you mean?'

'That wasn't *quite* what I meant,' protested Oddie. 'But at least she'll be away from this particular influence, and she'll be prepared for anything. I wasn't quite convinced by the lady's protestations that she'd been super-careful: they didn't gel with being unable to avoid special tutorials at home.'

They were interrupted by the headmaster coming back into his study. He was keeping his face studiedly neutral, being the complete professional.

'Got all you want?'

'For the moment,' said Oddie, collecting his things together and getting up. 'It's not over till someone's in handcuffs.'

'May that be soon. I'm thinking of his daughter. She needs to settle down if she's to get the grades she needs for Oxford.'

Oddie nodded.

'Yes, so Miss Daltrey said. Just one small thing before we go: when we were talking about your taking this matter up with Miss Daltrey, you said that "another business" came up so it got put to one side.'

'And when we were talking about the Leary family earlier,' said Charlie, 'you seemed about to say something, then changed your mind.'

Peter Frencham thought, then seemed to decide he had no choice.

'You're too sharp for me,' he said. 'I had very much hoped to keep this within the school. Hoped too that it was on the sort of small scale that would allow me to do that with a clear conscience . . . We have this new boy, Ben Hayman, whose father, I've just found out, is the new sportsmaster at our equivalent school in Bingley, which explains a lot. Didn't want his son going to the same school, which is very wise. Ben is a nice lad, with a wicked sense of humour, but I took him seriously when he tipped the wink about drugs.'

'The usual drugs?'

'Not what you mean by that, I suspect,' said Frencham, marshalling his thoughts. 'I'm talking about performance-related drugs for sportsmen. It's a new problem for me, though obviously a big one in the professional sport field. This has always been a strong school for sport. I haven't tried to change that, though I have tried to strengthen the academic side. But sport has altered, hasn't it? In the past sport was a bit glamorous in a schoolboy's mind, it made you popular with the girls – though I don't think it ever worked in the opposite direction for girls. But now it's also money. The sporty kids dream of being top athletes and raking in the sort of sums you read about Beckham and Christie and Henman making. Ben mentioned a drug called Andraol. It's banned, and it's just about affordable

191

at street prices to a schoolkid, and apparently it's circulating here.'

'And the finger is pointing at Mark Leary and Lennie Norris.'

'Yes. Leary has always been rather a charismatic figure: good-looking, multi-talented at sports. Likes the girls and they like him. Norris worries me greatly, because drugs getting around among the thirteen-year-olds is a serious business, and it seems likely he's being used as the pusher. I need a lot more evidence, but that figures. Lennie has always been a bit of a smart-arse. Now he's going round with the sort of clothes and gear and appendages that I know his parents can't afford – though as you may have gathered they're silly enough to give them to him if they can afford them.'

'Mark's parents, on the other hand, have money.'

'They do. Mark has always been under strong pressure from his father. The man's an achiever, and he expects his son to do well in sport, and academically too. It may be that Mark started taking the drugs for the usual reasons, then started supplying them to get himself a lot more pocket money . . . But I don't think this can be anything to do with the Horrocks murder, can it?'

'It's hard to see how,' said Oddie. 'But I think you'd be well advised to put this in the hands of the local police. OK, OK, I would say that. But think of the sort of stink there's going to be if this drug – and heaven knows what else – is being passed around in your lower forms, and you've tried to keep it an internal matter.'

Frencham looked worried, then nodded. He ushered them out of his office and they began the walk back to their car.

'This boy Ben Hayman – is he around?' asked Charlie, as they emerged into the playground. Frencham stood scanning the noisy, crowded space, then altered his course slightly. They landed up eventually by a gangling black teenager doing brilliant physical rolls and jerks and handstands on the bare tarmac – more circus acrobatics than gymnastics.

'Hi, Ben,' said Peter Frencham. The boy did a brilliant jump to right himself and land on his feet in front of them. His eyes immediately showed he knew who he was talking to.

'Hi, Mr Frencham.'

'How are things? You never told me your father was a teacher at Bingley Morton Road.'

'I couldn't stand the shame, sir.'

'Oh, being a sportsmaster is a lot less shameful than any other kind.'

'Well, that's true. And a lot less than being a headmaster . . . We're living in temporary accommodation at the moment.'

'Oh,' said Frencham, obviously wondering what was coming.

'Really cramped. I mean, sharing a room with my kid sister! I'll be glad when we get something bigger . . . Lennie Norris has a room all to himself at home.'

'Quite a lot of children have that these days, with smaller families.'

'And his parents are never, ever, allowed over the threshold,' the boy said, looking straight at Oddie and Charlie. 'Wow!'

And Ben scurried off to join his friends.

'We've been given a tip-off,' said Charlie.

'We all have,' said Peter Frencham, and he took them to their car and said goodbye.

'I'd be willing to bet he's going straight back to his office to ring the Shipley station,' said Charlie.

'Let's go back there and find out. They'll need to search the Leary boy's home as well, but it sounds as though he's using Lennie Norris's place as his store, and the boy as his fall guy. Probably his own hands are kept lily-white.'

'I suppose this is hardly our business, and we ought to leave it up to them,' said Charlie. Oddie detected a wistful note in his voice.

'I can't see any connection with the Horrocks murder that might give us a let-in. On the other hand both boys belong to families that are in our frame. What's your interest?'

'I'm just remembering what you said about the nervousness of the boy's mother, Mary Leary. I don't suppose that was connected with this, but on the other hand this could be a catalyst to bring it all out. What *is* griping her?'

'Maybe we could get you a watching brief with the Shipley force while I go and talk to the Bishop – if His Lordship is willing to talk to me. I can't see him being enthusiastic.'

But when he rang the Bishop's office, on their return to the Shipley station, he encountered a cool courtesy on the part of his secretary, something obviously laid down from above. The Bishop was not sure how he could help, but if the Superintendent was sure it was important the Bishop would alter his schedule for a brief talk.

Oddie said it was important.

CHAPTER 18

Episcopal

The woman in reception at the Bishop's office was sweetness itself, though it was the sweetness of honed steel.

'You must be Superintendent Oddie,' she said, coming forward to shake his hand. 'I'm Bernadette Cullen. I'll tell the Bishop you're here. He'll want to see you as soon as possible, because he has a lot on.'

The manner was much warmer than the guarded, cool response on the phone an hour before. A decision from above, presumably. Her boss had, on reflection, decided on a policy of delighted co-operation. An authoritarian Bishop who made PR-based decisions on the grounds of expediency had the hackles of Oddie's neck twitching from the start. They began rising in earnest a minute or two later when the man emerged from an inner room with two priests and one wispy, gingery little layman of middle age and middle stature. Oddie had been briefed by Charlie about Julie Norris's account of the investigating committee she had been interviewed by. This was it.

The Bishop was tall, lean and fit, with fair hair and assertive features – a figure that commanded respect, with the accent on the command. He kept people in their place by expecting, even assuming, that they knew it. The fact that he was currently exhibiting geniality and openness did not change Oddie's assessment that he was not likely to brook opposition, and not likely to suffer fools at all.

'Father Maclise, Father Donovan and Gerald Beany. This is Superintendent Oddie. These three gentlemen are the committee investigating the allegations against Father Pardoe. Since they were meeting here today anyway – quite independently of me; I have nothing to do with the process – I thought I'd interrupt them and bring them along in case you had any questions for them.'

Oddie made a gesture of denial. He had no wish to be associated with the disciplinary process initiated by the Bishop.

'No, no. Your procedures are entirely your affair. Horrocks was – well, let's call him an investigative journalist. No doubt he had been involved in probing into all sorts of people and situations recently. The story about Father Pardoe was simply the one he happened to be running at the time he was murdered. It may be entirely irrelevant.'

'I'm sure that will turn out to be the case,' said the Bishop.

'I have spoken to the woman who wrote to you,' said Oddie, making it clear he was choosing his words with care and addressing the Bishop alone. 'It's a type that's dying out, though it's one that when I joined the force was well known to the police. We had dealings with many such. I imagine you have some stronger evidence than hers.'

'You have the advantage of us in having met her,' said the younger of the two priests, Father Donovan. 'We made the decision that our job was simply to look into the truth of the allegations.'

It was as close as he could come in the Bishop's presence to an admission that they had no stronger evidence than Doris Crabtree's. Oddie raised his eyebrows.

'I'm told by my sergeant that the young woman – Julie Norris – is living in very straitened circumstances. Out and out poverty, to put it bluntly. I'm sure she told you this herself, but his observations back her up.' He turned to the Bishop. 'But the Fund is something I should talk to you about, isn't it, My Lord?'

The geniality was perceptibly decreased in the Bishop by now, and, tight-lipped, he nodded and said: 'If you've no questions to ask the committee, perhaps you'll come through to my office. Mrs Cullen will bring us coffee.'

He led the way, his back unbending, down a passageway and into a comfortable but not lavishly furnished office, large enough to allow medium-sized meetings or impromptu gatherings to take place there. He waved Oddie to an armchair and took his place at the desk, where he loomed even larger over the just-regulation-height policeman. Mrs Cullen fussed round for a minute or two with coffee and cream and sugar, then she tactfully withdrew without a word.

'Just to wind up on the matter of the committee,' said the Bishop. 'Father Pardoe is talking to them early next week, then they will be sieving the evidence and coming to their conclusions. I have no idea what those will be.'

Oddie nodded a kind of acceptance of this. He had noticed the older priest who had said nothing during their encounter, and he had concluded that Julie was right, and that the Bishop worked through him. What was not so clear was what made the Bishop tick. Or rather, in a man who clearly loved power, what had made him exercise it so emphatically in this particular case then claim to be no part of the process.

'As I said, the committee is not really my business,' Oddie resumed, 'but what they are investigating is, or may be. When what they call "human interest" stories are blazoned through the popular press, people get hurt. It's not too far-fetched to wonder whether one of the people involved may have wanted to hit back.'

The Bishop considered, his fingers formed into a pensive triangle.

'I'd be the last person to try to teach you your business, Superintendent, but wouldn't something closer to home be more likely?'

'His family, you mean? His colleagues at work? A great many people are suggesting that. I've just come from a matter connected to his family, and my sergeant was in the Midlands yesterday on a matter relating to his work. In a case like this you have to juggle with a lot of balls, keep them all in the air.'

'Of course, of course.'

'When you suspended Father Pardoe, did you anticipate the sort of press interest in the matter that in fact there has been?'

A slight touch of the turkey-cock appeared in the Bishop's face.

'Not at all! I tried to combine discretion with a proper investigation of the allegations. I take it very badly that Pardoe has seen fit to go public. We have an obligation to be careful not to bring scandal on the Church itself.'

'Just to correct you for a moment,' said Oddie, holding up his hand, since there seemed likely to be a flow. 'I feel pretty sure that Pardoe never spoke to Horrocks at all, and only to the *Telegraph and Argus* after the scandal broke. All indications are that Horrocks got on to the story by listening to two St Catherine's parishioners scandal-mongering about it in the dining car of an Inter-City train from London.'

'Oh.' The turkey-cock exhaled, and looked deflated.

'And of course, for all the discretion of the authorities, there have been several cases recently when scandal has been brought on the Church, has there not? The Scottish Bishop with the illegitimate children. Many really disgraceful matters coming to light in Ireland. Those cases probably whetted the press's appetite. But I suppose it was precisely scandals such as those that made you careful in the Pardoe matter to set up a committee of enquiry.'

'Certainly this was the first time I'd done any such thing. I decided the proper procedure was to establish the truth first, then decide on a course of action.'

Instead, thought Oddie, of assuming Pardoe's guilt and moving him swiftly to another parish. That was probably what would have happened ten years before. His purpose in talking more freely than he usually would was partly to undermine this domineering man's faith in his own judgements. Oddie felt the Bishop was already showing signs of being rattled.

'But the reason I wanted to talk to you was not the sexual side of the allegations against Father Pardoe,' he said, 'which I suppose you have no more special knowledge of than anybody else. It was the matter of the Father Riley Fund, which is also the subject of the committee's enquiries.'

'Ye-e-es.' The fingers triangularized themselves again. 'The two matters were of course closely connected. The charge is that he used the Fund for the benefit of this young woman that he's been – that he may be involved with. That I can discuss. Otherwise it's a question of diocesan finances, and those must remain confidential.'

Oddie left a few seconds' pause.

'I'm afraid it's not as simple as that.'

'Oh?' He spoke magisterially.

'I gather from the article in the *Telegraph and Argus* that the Fund was set up by a will, and was to be administered by the priest of the day at St Catherine's for the benefit of the poor of that parish.' The Bishop cautiously nodded his head. 'That brings the Fund and its administration within the orbit of the law. Now, I gather that there was a decision to use the Fund not just for individuals in need, but for wider projects of general benefit and usefulness.'

'Yes. That is the case.'

'Two things occur to me about that. I gather Father Pardoe felt that larger projects were rather outside his competence, and he preferred to leave decisions on them to you and the two lay trustees. But was any legal effect given to this decision, or does Father Pardoe still technically have responsibility for the Fund?'

This time it was the Bishop who left a long pause.

'I suppose technically he remains responsible.'

'No legal steps taken to alter the terms of the will.' Oddie looked steadily at the Bishop. 'Yet Father Pardoe in the interview in the *Telegraph and Argus* seems vague about any uses the Fund has been put to, which suggests he was not only not consulted, but not kept informed. He was technically responsible for a large sum of money, but was kept totally ignorant of any uses it was put to. That could put you in a very difficult position, particularly if he were relieved of his parish and decided to take civil action against you.'

'An absurd speculation. It would never happen.'

'He seems to feel strongly that he has not had natural justice. Then there is the matter of the will. It apparently specifies the beneficiaries are to be parishioners of St Catherine's – in other words, basically, Catholics in Shipley. Either the money should be used for Shipley people or, with the extension you have made, probably justifiably, to projects in Shipley. So the question arises, has the Fund been used exclusively within the parish?'

The silence the Bishop left seemed endless.

Charlie stuck rigidly to his watching brief when he accompanied two uniformed officers from the Shipley force to the Norris home. He admired the approach of the young sergeant who seemed to have the sort of dogged, unfazed tenacity that any good policeman should have. He listened through all the 'Lennie would never forgive us'es and the 'he's been a wonderful son to us'es that the bemused and genuinely distressed Norrises could produce. Charlie wondered how in the world they had become such terrible parents.

His own situation struck him forcibly. He and Felicity were about to produce a child. He refused to believe that they could treat any child in the way the Norrises had treated Julie – as if they had a grudge against her rather than a duty to her. Nor could he see himself and Felicity spoiling the child rotten, as the Norrises had their son.

But nevertheless . . . Policemen's children, like clergymen's, were notoriously prone to go off the rails. The fact that their fathers were never there at the points in their lives – high points as well as low points – when they were needed was an obvious factor, as was the fact that, like clergymen, they had a sort of aura of probity that acted as a sort of challenge and was something any child of spirit felt it had to react against. Pillars of the community ask to be pulled down by their offspring.

But how could he bear it? What if the signs started showing that he or she was going off the rails, and *still* he was not there at the crisis moments? Then the serious trouble comes, and still he's not there. How could he bring a young life into the world but have such a nebulous responsibility for what happened to it? Rather than that, he'd leave the job he loved, was good at, felt committed to.

Sergeant Bingle had got his way. Reluctantly professing their total confidence that they would find nothing in Lennie's room, the little party began to make their way upstairs.

Simon Norris, who had already told them he had no key, gestured to a door, and Bingle cast an expert eye on the lock. Then he took out a formidable bunch of keys and selected a range. The third one he tried turned, and he swung open the door. The parents held back, as if nervous even then of their son and how he would react. The two Shipley policemen and Charlie went in.

It was not a small room, but with the three of them inside it felt cramped. Their first impression was of a modern-day Aladdin's cave. The walls of the room were piled high with boxes, cassettes and videos. When Bingle went over and swung open the wardrobe door it was packed full to bursting with the teenage equivalent of designer clothes, including trainers, block-soled shoes, track suits and the latest Leeds United and England strips. Charlie, out of the corner of his eye, saw the parents' eyes widen: they'd known he had a lot of good clothes, but not so many. What could he do with them all? Bingle went over to the videos and took one up. He flashed it in the direction of his fellow constable and Charlie: a blonde who was all breast and heavy make-up with her legs outstretched left nothing to the imagination.

'Here –' began Mr Norris, then spluttered into nothing.

Bingle muttered, 'Seems to cater for all tastes,' then settled down on his haunches. He pulled at two boxes at the bottom of the stack.

'This'll be the Andraol,' he said.

Charlie meanwhile had gone over to the window. On the sill he found two files. The top one was marked in uneven childish capitals BUSINESS. He took it up and flicked through it. Just a glance told him the sums involved were enormous for a child. Then he took up the other. It was marked in the same hand PERSONAL. And when he began to examine that one he really drew in his breath.

Eventually the Bishop made a feeble attempt to regain ground.

'I really do not see why we should be discussing this matter.'

'Don't you?' asked Oddie, hardly bothering to disguise his

scepticism. 'I grant that normally I don't suppose we would consider that this is a matter we should investigate – unless someone, for example a Shipley parishioner, was insistent that we should. But the Horrocks story was two-pronged: there was the sexual side, which was the main thing that made it of interest to the national tabloids; linked to that, though, was the financial side, the alleged misuse of the Father Riley Fund. We've touched on the sexual side outside. It's not for me to give an opinion, but I expect you registered that I was surprised you gave such a strong response to what was after all nothing but a single muckraking letter.'

'You don't realize how *careful* –'

'Of course you're right. You have to think of the Church. But let's leave that and come to the financial side. It occurs to me that if the provisions of the will had been followed unchanged, Father Pardoe could hardly have got in any trouble. In order to provide this girl – who had been cast off by her own family – with a washing-machine, a television, or whatever, he would simply have consulted the two trustees, told them what he wanted, who he wanted it for, and he would have got the go-ahead.'

'You seem very knowledgeable about what he used the Trust for.'

'That, and to provide free heating for a very old lady, he told the *Bradford Telegraph and Argus*. Nothing very exciting. It could hardly have been much more, certainly not cash for Julie Norris to live riotously, because he would have had to go to the trustees to get permission to give cash, and I pay you the compliment of saying you're not a fool. You would not have given it.'

'I fail to see where this questioning is leading.'

'I'm not questioning, I'm theorizing. Let's continue with that. It's fairly well known that the finances of the Catholic diocese are in pretty poor shape. Land has been sold, school playing fields, disused orphanages and nunneries have been sold off as soon as they have outlived their usefulness to be used for speculative building, and so on. I wonder whether, just possibly, the Father Riley Fund hasn't somehow disappeared – not through any dishonesty, in the usual meaning of the word – but into the general morass of diocesan funds. And with the consent, tacit or explicit, of the two other trustees. So that when Father Pardoe started using it again, feeling that Shipley had got very little out of the new dispensation, and it was time to reassert its original purpose, there was a degree of panic, which was probably not caused by the relatively small sums involved, but by the prospect of his resuming control of the Fund, which he had every legal right to do.'

'You are accusing me of something very base,' said the Bishop, slowly and softly. 'Of using accusations against Pardoe to cover my own misdeeds.'

'I am not accusing you, I am speculating. And "misdeeds" is too strong a word. The Church has many obligations, many charitable concerns, many pressing and legitimate calls on its funds. A will that was itself charitable in intent may have seemed a legitimate means of funding these activities.'

The Bishop shook his head, as if in sadness.

'I wonder where these speculations are leading, and when they will end.'

'I may say,' said Oddie, ignoring him, 'that I think it was unwise to bring the Fund into the accusations against Father Pardoe, because it drew attention to it. But the Catholic Church is not yet used to scrutiny of its doings or questioning of its hierarchy, is it? I can bring these speculations quite speedily to an end.'

'Please do.'

'I think there are two options open to you, if my theories bear any relation to the truth. One is that after the committee has put in its report – which on the financial side at least must surely be in Pardoe's favour – you call the man in and tell him what happened to the Fund, and invite his understanding of how it came about.'

It will never happen, he thought, not in a million years. The man doesn't have the humility in him, and apart from that he would have to face Pardoe's suspicion, or near certainty, that his whole ordeal had been part of a ploy to cover up the Bishop's misuse of the Fund. Even if the suspicion remained unspoken, both men would know it was there.

The Bishop's expression remained studiedly blank.

'The other course would be effectively to recreate the Fund. I don't need to use terms like "creative accounting": in complicated financial organisms money can always be shifted here and there, a bit lopped off this area of expenditure, a bit shifted from that contingency fund. It doesn't even need to happen all at once, because Father Pardoe is unlikely suddenly to have a need to draw on the Fund. But when he did have small charitable uses for it, and when perhaps he made enquiries about the Fund, its extent and the uses it had been put to, he would find at least it was *there*. Reassuring for him – reassuring for you too.'

Oddie got up from his chair. Rather uncertainly the Bishop got up too, and put out his hand.

'Thank you for talking to me, My Lord,' said Oddie, his voice unshaded by any emotion.

'Er . . . can I assume your interest in this matter is now at an end?'

Oddie left a pause, with a reluctance unusual in him to let this particular big fish off the hook.

'I never believed in the Fund as a motive for murder, you know. It just isn't a big enough thing. And policemen don't go around looking for least likely suspects in murder cases, not in real life. Most such cases are simply a matter of a killing and arrest, but where there is doubt and mystery much of our time is spent clearing away side issues, so that we can concentrate on what turns out to be the central question. That, I suspect, is what it will turn out I've been doing with you today.'

'Quite.'

'As to whether our interest in the matter is at an end, I think that is mainly up to you.'

And he turned and left the room, walked swiftly down the corridor ignoring all attempts to usher him out, through the main office where Mrs Cullen rose and started to make noises that almost immediately she suppressed, then out into the bright spring sunshine.

'I wonder why I did it,' he said to Charlie later, back in the Shipley station, where Lennie Norris had been processed, and was now waiting (and shouting) in the cells while the custody officer put in train calls to satisfy his demands for a lawyer. 'I went way over the borderline. We'd normally regard what happened to Church funds as out of our field, unless there was evidence of someone with their hands in the till for their own benefit.'

'Which there wasn't here?'

'No way. Unless the man and the Church had become indistinguishably mixed up in his mind.'

'You probably put the fear of – well, not God, I suppose, since he ought to have that already, but of the law into him. These people who value their own dignity highly can be very vulnerable. That will put a stop to any further shenanigans of a financial nature he may have had in mind.'

'So what I did was the equivalent to preventive medicine – preventive policing, shall we call it? I hope so. But I don't think that's why I did it. And I don't think it was because I liked Father Pardoe and didn't at all like the Bishop. Do you think I can suddenly have developed a passion for abstract justice?'

'Stranger things have been known. Mind you, coppers with a passion for natural justice usually never get beyond constable rank.'

'How do you work that out?'

'It plays havoc with their conviction rate.'

'Cynic. Come on, let's see if the Shipley people would agree to our going to the Learys and bringing in their promising son.'

CHAPTER 19

A Sporty Family

Charlie and Oddie heard the voices as soon as they got to the front gate.

'I just want to know what's biting you – what I'm being accused of.'

It was a loud, assertive male voice.

'I'm not accusing you of anything.'

'Mary Leary,' mouthed Oddie to Charlie. The latter raised the latch of the gate with the utmost care, and the two slipped like cat burglars into the evergreen-shaded cover of the front garden.

'Don't give me that. I know you when you've got a funny idea. You go all quiet and sullen. You suspect I'm up to something.'

'I always suspect you're up to something, and you usually are.'

Then there came a younger, female voice.

'You're getting it wrong as usual, Dad. That's not what's biting her, because this is different. Mum, something's eating away at you, and it has been for days. I think you're *afraid*.'

'Don't be silly, Donna.'

'I'm not being silly, Mum. For God's sake, I've *seen* your hand shaking. You've got some idea, and it's driving you crazy. Knowing you, it's got something to do with this family, and if so it's got to be one of the men in it.'

'Donna! I've never made any distinction –'

'Mum, don't worry. It doesn't bother me. It's made me freer. But I do know, however you might resent it now and then, and however you may hate Dad's roving eye, it's the men who count with you.'

'Well, you could have fooled me,' said the male voice, with

the practised tone of one airing a grudge and avoiding the main issue. 'Half the time I think the two of you are ganging up on Mark and me.'

'Don't give me that!' said Mary Leary, her voice suddenly suffused with bitterness. 'You two do exactly what you want – Kings of the Castle. The men in your family always have, Con. And the women cook and wash and iron and *take* whatever you care to dish out to them. I'm fed up with taking.'

'Mum, you're changing the subject too. What we want to know is, what's up with you?'

'Nothing's *up.*'

'All right then: why have you been going so often down to the basement? What's so fascinating about the sports cupboard?'

'Donna, don't even –'

At that point, seeing through the laurels a tall, well-built boy or young man loitering up the street, a worried expression on his face, Oddie regretfully rang the doorbell. The voices immediately ceased. The next sound they heard was not footsteps down the hall but the raising of the gate latch. Charlie stepped forward, his ID held at eye level.

'We're police officers.'

The boy's expression suddenly changed. From mere worry the look involuntarily changed to fear.

'What is it? I thought you'd talked to Mum. Is it about Julie Norris?'

Charlie was saved from replying by the door opening. The man in the entrance was an older version of the boy: not so tall, though, and with a much more assertive manner.

'We're police officers,' said Oddie, and again both presented their IDs.

'Police officers? But you've talked to Mary, haven't you? I've nothing to add to what she's told you. I don't get involved in parish politics. It's enough for me if I go to Mass once in a while.'

'Could we come in please?' said Oddie, unalterably polite. 'It's not about parish business we've come. We need to speak to more than your wife, sir.'

The man reluctantly stood aside. As they walked down the

207

hall and turned to the left, into the room from which the voices had come, he kept up a litany of complaint, which, as often happened, was progressively rolled into a great ball of grievance.

'This is very inconvenient. Can't you make an appointment? I was planning to go back to the shop and work late. And I expect Mark is off to cricket practice.'

'I am,' said Mark.

'You're not,' said Oddie. The boy's brief spurt of aggression gutted and went out.

'Then will you tell us what all this is about?' demanded Conal Leary. They were standing round in a group, the Learys facing the two policemen. Oddie did not suggest that they all sat down.

'Let's be clear,' he said. 'This family is involved in our enquiry, an important one, and much deeper than just in a fringe way. I don't know, Mrs Leary, if you told your husband about our earlier talk?'

She swallowed.

'Only in a general way.'

'Then let me tell you, sir, that we are now fairly sure that the dead man, Cosmo Horrocks, first got on to the Father Pardoe story by hearing you and a friend of yours, Derek Jessel probably, swapping gossip over lunch on a train.'

'What? But that's impossible. We kept our voices so low –'

'Sometimes low voices carry just as well as raised ones, particularly if the voices are naturally loud ones.'

'Anyway, what of it? What are you accusing me of?'

'Nothing. But you can't be happy, I should have thought, about having started a process that led to murder. Your son –' he turned to Mark, who was standing over by the window trying to suppress an expression of alarm on his handsome face – 'is involved in a variety of offences, some trivial, some serious; some nothing to do with the Horrocks case, some very much to do with it. He is in deep trouble, and I shall be taking him immediately to the Shipley station. As I believe he is still a minor –'

'Sixteen,' said Mark, very quickly.

'Sixteen – then you will have the right, sir –' he had

turned back to Con Leary – 'to sit in on the questioning, you or your wife.'

'Are you going to *charge* my son?'

'At the moment we're at the stage of questioning. Let's take things one step at a time. I shall take your son to the station and hand him over to the Shipley force. I suggest the best thing, sir, is for you to follow in your own car. My sergeant here has things he'd like to ask your wife. If she wants to be at the station –'

'Of course I want to be with my son!'

'Then I'm sure Sergeant Peace will bring you along when you're finished with him. Shall we go, Mark?'

He looked at the boy. Suddenly he seemed remarkably unattractive. The best features and the most even tan don't help when fear is contending with petulance in your face, and lurking behind the eyes there is an incipient impulse to blub. For the first time Oddie realized he ought to think of Mark Leary as a boy. It seemed to Oddie, remembering the conversation they had just overheard, that he had been brought up to think of himself as cock of the walk, and now at the first major crisis of his life he was showing just how uncertain and inadequate that indoctrination had left him. He put out his hand and took him by the arm.

'Come on,' he said, and led him out to the car.

Conal Leary's tendency to fume and shout, which had been kept under control while Oddie was still in the room, now began to rear its head again. He turned on Charlie, his face getting redder and redder by the second.

'Can you *tell* me what all this is about? I mean, am I allowed to have some *idea* what my son is supposed to have *done*? Or am I just some bloody member of the *pub*lic who pays your bloody *wages* and is treated like *dirt* for the privilege?'

'Con –' said his wife. He whipped round at her.

'Oh yes, and am I supposed to slip off meekly down to the police station while you and this black –'

'That's enough,' said Charlie, taking a step towards him. 'Don't say anything you'll regret later. You'll need to be as together as you can be. I can't tell you what your son is being

209

questioned about, but I can say he's in a lot of trouble, with a variety of possible charges, and you really should be down there with him, not making things worse by saying things you'll regret later.'

'Con, please go. So you're there for him.'

'Your wife is right. He needs you now.'

Con Leary looked from one to the other. He was in uncharted waters, and like his son completely out of his depth. Suddenly he barged through them, fumbling for his car keys, and out of the front door.

'*Please* don't mind him,' pleaded Mary Leary. 'He's not really racist –'

'Water off a duck's back,' said Charlie cheerfully. 'If I got steamed up about that sort of thing I'd be going off like a whistling kettle all day. I just wanted him to do what is most useful to you all at this moment.'

'Could I sit in when you talk to Mum?' asked Donna, emboldened by his cheerful mood.

'*No!*' said her mother.

'No, you can't,' said Charlie. 'You're getting it the wrong way round: your mother can sit in if I want to talk to you about your brother. Because you did know something about what's been going on, didn't you?'

'No . . . Just suspicions. There are lots of rumours at school.'

'Well, we'll probably see how we go with what we've got already, and maybe talk to you later on. I'm sure you hate the idea of women being sent out of the room to make a cup of tea, but you are the only possible pair of hands at the moment, and a cup of tea would be very welcome to me, and I suspect to your mother. So –?'

Donna stood stock still for a moment, her brow lowering, then she turned and left the room.

'Now,' said Charlie, gesturing Mary to a seat and sitting down himself to face her, 'tell me what it is that's been worrying you these last few days.'

'Nothing's been worrying me. Where would you get that idea from?'

'From my boss, who talked to you, from your friends, who

are puzzled, from your family. Why have you been going up and downstairs to the basement?'

She did a double take, then exploded.

'You listened! You stood outside and listened to a private conversation.'

'We were outside, and we overheard. OK, we listened. This isn't scouting for boys we're engaged on, you know. Now tell me what's been of so much concern down in the basement.'

She launched herself straight into the most obvious of lies.

'Nothing! It's where all the sports gear is kept. The summer season is just starting, and both Con and Mark are keen sportsmen. There's a lot of stuff to wash and iron and put away.'

'Mrs Leary, I don't get annoyed at being called a black bastard, but I do get itchy when people treat me as if I was a fool. Now, tell me what it is in the sports cupboard that has been worrying you.'

'Nothing has. It's just all their clothes –'

'Or maybe something that should be there that isn't?'

'Everything's there that should be.'

'*Now*. That's it, isn't it? Something was missing from the cupboard and now it's back. Mrs Leary, it would be much better for your son if you told us what it is that went missing.'

She looked at him fiercely.

'How could it be better for Mark? Betrayed by his own mother. Anyway, this has nothing to do with Mark –'

'Did you suspect whatever it was was missing had been used by your husband? Is that it?'

'I don't *know*!' she wailed. 'I don't know anything. But I do know all about Con and women, I know someone had connected him with this Julie Norris, and that he'd been talking about the Pardoe case and his connection with her on the train, and somehow I thought – well, I just jumped to the conclusion he must be involved in some way. He usually is. I thought it might be financial too, because Con is up to any trick going. Of course I wondered about Mark, but

I couldn't think of any connection at all between him and this murder.'

'Right,' said Charlie, as she dried up to a halt, 'you have a choice, Mrs Leary. Either I phone the local station and we get a couple of uniformed helpers and we take everything from the sports cupboard for forensic examination. Or you take me down there and you point out what went missing and has now been put back. It's up to you.'

Mrs Leary sat there, her hands clasped, her head bent – sat there, it seemed, for an age. Donna came in with a tray, and suddenly her mother got up, looking away from her daughter to shield her eyes from her, then led Charlie down the hall to a little door under the stairs. She switched on a light, then led the way down bare wooden steps. As they came to the bottom Charlie saw a snooker table, body-building equipment he recognized from his days as a gym attendant, and a cheerful mess of sporting this-and-thats: a putter, wicket-keeper's gloves, a punch-bag. Mary Leary led the way across the basement, bumping into things her eyes were so full. Then she threw open a cupboard door, and Charlie saw shelves of sports clothes, a golf-bag bulging with clubs, cricket bats and a snooker cue. Mary Leary pointed to the murky depths of the cupboard's interior.

'The Indian clubs?' Charlie asked. 'Don't see them much these days.'

'No. They've just sat there for years. They were Con's father's, or grandfather's, I don't know which.'

'And one of them was missing?'

'Yes. What can you do with *one* Indian club?'

'But it's back now.'

'Yes. It was put back a couple of days ago. But there . . . seem to be stains on it. And I've been so afraid that Con, with his temper, and having been involved with that woman – that Horrocks was on to it, and . . .'

Charlie didn't voice the suspicion that Mary Leary had got the whole thing very muddled, and that when she found out who was actually involved with Julie Norris her present worry and fear was likely to be redoubled.

* * *

In the car taking him to the Shipley police station Mark Leary remained silent. His face, Oddie could see out of the corner of his eye, was working, and still behind the eyes there was the tendency to cry. Poor blighter, thought Oddie: pity he can't come right out with it and sob his heart out. Probably in his family it's thought to be unmanly. He could sense that Mark was aching to say something, ask him something. Possibly he was afraid that if he did that he would reveal some aspect of his multifarious wrong-doing that the police hadn't already cottoned on to. He had only had time for the briefest of conversations with Charlie, but it was already clear that the boys were into so many scams – and worse – that they would put to shame the average small-time shyster and petty criminal in the Leeds area.

Oddie pulled into the small yard of the Shipley station.

'Come on,' he said. 'Let's get you processed.'

He always tried to keep things as neutral as possible with the more vulnerable suspects. It seemed to help them, and there were limits to the amount of involvement in a case that the investigating officer should allow himself. And of course the fact that Mark was still a boy did not in itself guarantee vulnerability. Children these days grew up and became streetwise horribly early. What Mark had done, he suspected, had been totally unchild-like.

He led him through the back door of the station and into the reception area. As they went through the door he felt in the boy's body a sharp intake of breath. Going through the far door to the cells was an even younger lad, and Oddie recognized Mark's playground companion of earlier that day.

'Lennie!' called Mark. The boy swung round and slipped the guiding hand of the uniformed constable leading him and ran up close before the man caught him again. His sharp, near-adult face was twisted into a sort of grin, and his dark eyes gleamed.

'Tell it like it was, Mark,' he shouted, and then was led away.

The processing took some time. Five minutes into it and Oddie was told that the boy's father was in the station's waiting area; twenty minutes after that he heard the mother had arrived too. He took the opportunity to have a word with Sergeant Bingle about Lennie Norris.

'I picked him up at the end of school,' the young man said. 'It wasn't how I wanted it to happen, just how the timing turned out. I didn't want him to go home, that was the main thing. After a lot of initial bluster he seemed to think the whole thing would give him enormous prestige, and he came along without protest.'

'Kids – I'll never understand them,' muttered Oddie.

'This is one you wouldn't want to,' Bingle said. 'When he got to the station he demanded a lawyer, and said he didn't want his parents – "those two no-hopers" he called them – sitting in on the interview.'

'He's inherited the family charm.'

'In spades. Do you or your sergeant want to sit in on the interview?'

'I don't know . . . What I want now is to talk to young Mark Leary on the Horrocks business and surrounding matters. Then we could hand him over to you for the drugs and the other things. He's the obvious ringleader, but I've got to go carefully because, though he doesn't look it, he's still a minor.'

Bingle nodded. 'Here's your sergeant now,' he said, and stood by while Oddie and Charlie talked.

'What Mary Leary was worried about was a possible murder weapon,' Charlie explained, 'an Indian club. One was missing from the cupboard in the basement for several days, though no one in the house had used them for decades. We'll take it to Forensics. Looks to me as if there's blood on it.'

'But *why* did she straight away jump to that conclusion?' pondered Oddie. 'It seems a massive jump.'

'She knew, or thought she knew, that her husband was or had been involved with Julie Norris. She thought Horrocks might have been on to him.'

'And was the unlovable Con having it off with her?'

'It's my guess it was the son. You may not have heard, but Mark immediately jumped to the conclusion that it was to do with her when I flashed my ID at him. Probably saw us as an arm of the Child Support Agency.'

'The father of the forthcoming child, then?'

'I think so. Julie said she prefers younger men, so it fits. She hadn't seen or heard from him since she gave him the news. Seems like a really caring type. Caring for his own skin.'

'I'm quite looking forward to seeing what makes him tick. Do you want to sit in on Bingle's interview with young Norris?'

'Wouldn't miss it for the world. I'd welcome any clue as to how that family got into the psychological mess they are in.'

When Oddie sat opposite Mark in the interview room, a uniformed Shipley policeman by his side, Mark's father by his, it was a long time before he could get beyond that care for his own skin that Charlie had mentioned, and that perhaps didn't mark him off from most teenagers. Mark seemed determined to put his worst foot forward.

'You thought when you found out we were police officers that it was the Julie Norris connection we were on to you about, didn't you?' The boy nodded. 'Why that?'

'They chase up the fathers these days, don't they?' He pulled himself up, from an instinct, perhaps sporting, of conceding nothing. 'If I am the father. I've only got that slag's word for it, but they'll probably believe her.'

'How did this heartwarming teenage romance start?'

'Are you being sarky?'

'Yes. Answer the question.'

Mark's father's hand went to his arm, and the boy sat back in his chair.

'She came to the Youth Club – the one Father Pardoe started. He thought it would give her an outside interest, but she felt like a fish out of water, so she told me. Like having a baby, living on her own like that, made her feel quite different from us. She felt she was mixing with children again. I walked her home and showed her she wasn't.'

He tried to hide the smirk on his face, but it forced its way there, and nothing his father's greater sexual sophistication could do could stop it. Oddie felt he was being told the story just in the way Mark had told it to his mates at school. Probably over and over.

'How long did the relationship last?'

'A few weeks. One night my dad and mum were going to be away overnight, and I stayed over with her, and we got careless and . . .' Con Leary hid his face in his hands. Oddie thought it was a sort of gesture, that he was not in the least ashamed of the boy. Mark gave him a glance, then went on: 'When she told me I couldn't believe she would refuse to get rid of it. But she did. You'd think she would have learnt after the first time, wouldn't you?'

'Maybe. Perhaps you both should have known more than you did. Was it a factor in the relationship that she is the sister of your – let's call him your friend, Lennie Norris?'

Mark gave a man-of-the-world shrug.

'No. Why should it be? The family had chucked her out a couple of years before, and she seemed to prefer it that way. It was nothing to do with Lennie. She was just a good lay. I can have anyone I want of my own age, but she had more experience. I liked her. I might have known she'd turn out to be a gold-digger, like all the rest.'

'In fact, Julie refuses to name the father. Us coming after you has nothing to do with her.' The boy remained silent, either sceptical, or fearful of what was to come. 'Let's start with Andraol.'

'That's Lennie's scam.'

'Come off it. It's you who's the sportsman.'

The boy reddened with indignation.

'I don't take the stuff! Test me and you'll find that out. I'm hoping for a trial for the Yorkshire Under-18s eleven. I'd be mad to take anything that would show up on a test.'

'Are you saying you don't take it but you push it?'

'No, I'm not. Ask Lennie about it. It's his scam.'

'Come off it. You're sixteen, he's thirteen. You're the great sportsman, the sort who gets to know about things like performance-enhancing drugs. You'd know the potential market as well, wouldn't you?'

The boy was silent, not knowing how much to tell. Then he said:

'There's plenty that are interested.'

'And you could supply them.'

'I'm not saying any more about that.'

His father, a shadow of his former self, felt he had to chip in at that point.

'Have you any evidence my son is supplying drugs?'

'That's really a matter for the Shipley police,' said Oddie. 'I'm sorry if I've got in first, but I'm really interested in the relationship between these two boys. Because a close friendship between an older and a younger boy might mean two things. And since your son is undoubtedly heterosexual, that leaves one: he's using him. Using him to store the pornographic videos he'd got hold of, for example, because Lennie has got his parents terrorized and you and your wife keep a much sharper – but not sharp enough, I'd say – eye on what your children are getting up to. I would guess those videos found a market all the way up the school. As to the other scams – minor blackmail, protection and so on, maybe the two boys were on a more equal footing. Maybe in the cheap designer labelware scam Lennie used some of his father's dodgy contacts. All this is up to the Shipley police. What I'm interested in is the Father Pardoe matter.'

The boy's face fell.

'Did that stupid nerd put that in his book?'

'Father Pardoe's temporary address, yes.'

'All that was Lennie's business. I had nothing to do with it.'

'Really? Yet Lennie's family were hardly more than nominal Catholics, whereas yours are prominent ones, with a strong interest in the parish and influence too. I think it was you who found out the address.'

'He couldn't have from me,' said Con Leary.

'Yes, I did,' said Mark, turning on him. 'You told Mum, coming out of church one Sunday. I wigged school and went over and kept watch there in Pudsey. When he came out to go on a walk I knew the exact street number. That was one up on Lennie. He's such a smart-arse, with such a high opinion of himself. I had something to tell *him* for a change.

All the rest was up to him. I wouldn't have anything to do with it.'

Oddie leant back in his chair, looking at the discomfited father, and the whiter-than-white cricketing hero. It was a very uninviting prospect.

CHAPTER 20

Favourite Son

It seemed to Charlie, sitting silent through Sergeant Bingle's interview with him, that Lennie Norris did not have downcast in his repertoire of emotions. It was as if his arrest was what he had been aiming at all along, a true climax to his grubby nefarious activities. He sat there oozing self-approbation, a smirk never far from his lips. Attempts by his lawyer to advise him or enforce the discipline of silence were brushed aside with a gesture worthy of a Gladstone interrupted in full flow in the House of Commons, and he himself was never far from taking complete control of the session.

'Now I want this clear,' he said, wagging a finger in the direction of Sergeant Bingle. 'These were my schemes, all of them. My ideas – got that?' He shrugged off his lawyer's hand on his arm. 'I brought Leary in on the Andraol, because he had all the contacts and went to sports meetings with other schools. I don't waste my time on that sort of crap. But I got the supplies, I held the purse strings. Leary tried to nose his way into other things as well, and I let him if I needed a bit of muscle. But I thought up all the scams, and I was the brain behind them all.'

'Right,' said Bingle quietly, 'so the sums of money you got out of your fellow schoolkids for not blabbing their little secrets –'

'Blackmail. It's called blackmail, Thicky.'

'– that was your idea?'

'Yeah.' Lennie grimaced. 'It tailed off after a time. People got cagey. And you need to hear things right at the beginning, before anybody else gets wind of whatever it is, otherwise it's useless. I was thinking of having a go with Miss Daltrey over her pash for Samantha Horrocks, but before I could work out how to approach her they were tittering about it all round the school.'

'Tough,' said Bingle, with irony doomed to go undetected. 'And the designer goods business?'

'Mine. I used Leary with some of the sporting stuff, but I never let him in on anything else. Why should I? That was a much bigger earner. Those clothes brought in real money.'

'Where did you get them from?'

Lennie put up his hand, in an adult gesture that looked comic from him.

'Never reveal sources of supply. Of course a lot of them were not *real* designer goods, but those kids are too dumb to realize that, and most of their parents too. Tell people they're getting something cheap and they lose all common sense. My dad told me that. About the only thing that no-hoper ever did teach me.'

'When did you realize there might be something for you in the Father Pardoe story?'

A shade of caution came over his face, but it could not entirely obliterate his bumptiousness.

'Right from the start. That was my idea too, don't let anyone tell you anything else. I brought Leary into it because his family is in the thick of all that Catholic Church stuff, but he worked at my direction. I thought it was a potential earner right from the word go. Catholic priests and young chicks – bound to be a chance for blackmail there. I set Mark on to pumping the girls at the Youth Club, but he was useless. Got nothing at all. But I knew there had to be something, it stood to reason. If he was having it off with one there had to be others, sure as eggs.'

Charlie touched Bingle's arm, and the sergeant nodded his permission for him to intervene.

'Didn't it help that Mark had been having it off himself with your sister?'

'Don't call her my sister!' said the boy, with whiplash fierceness. 'That hopeless cow's nothing to do with my family any more. I wouldn't nod in the street to a pathetic slob like her – I'd be afraid of catching a whiff of baby's pee. And it didn't help, not one bit. Don't you understand the principle,

220

you black thicky? Once a thing's generally known it's no use any more. Anyway, Mark wasn't willing even to go and talk to her. She's preggie again, the stupid git, and he was afraid he'd get handed the bill for the maternity clothes and the little knitted things. He's dead ordinary, Mark, and a bit of a coward. If it'd been me I'd have chucked the bill in her face. Who knows how many men she's been going with? Half Shipley if I know her.'

'But it was Mark who came up with the information about where Father Pardoe was living, wasn't it?'

Lennie gave an ugly grimace.

'Oh yes. Just happened to overhear it from his prick of a dad. Clever big-boy even went and checked it out over at Pudsey and came to me with it, like it was an egg he'd just laid. Hadn't the first idea what to do with it. Thought we might be able to screw money out of Pardoe not to spread it around. I've hardly been to church, but I know he isn't the type to let himself be blackmailed about a little thing like that. Chicks was a possibility, an address, never.'

'So it was your idea to approach Cosmo Horrocks?'

'Who else's? I tell you, Leary's just brainless muscle. I had the idea, and I made the phone calls. I'd done it before with the boys I'd screwed money out of. Sort of whispered, half-male, half-female voice, with a lot of menace in it. It disorientates them. Scares the life out of them.'

His self-love was apparently undentable. Charlie said:

'I don't suppose you scared the life out of Cosmo Horrocks.'

'Had him guessing though,' said Lennie, with a cat-like smile. 'Didn't quite know who or what he was dealing with.'

'But you came to an agreement with him.'

'After a time. Had to play with him a bit, leave him to stew. Second time I rang we struck a bargain. I'd have kept him on the hook longer, because he was dead keen, but if Mark's stupid Dad knew, it could have been round the parish in no time.'

'How much did you get out of him?'

'A hundred. Not bad for a bit of paper with an address on it.'

'And how did you receive the money?'

'He handed it over – in the park at Saltaire. It was late, ten o'clock, and practically dark. I can get out of and into my room at home whenever I like – just down the kitchen extension roof my stupid oldies had built a couple of years ago. Most of the time they don't know if I'm at home or not. Anyway, I insisted he wouldn't get the address until he'd handed the money over. He huffed and puffed, but in the end I had him cornered, he wanted it so much. I used Mark's name, because he knew all about the Learys. Told him he'd be along, and he was a champion athlete.'

'And he did come along, didn't he.'

''Course. I wouldn't have gone without back-up.'

'And in the end Horrocks handed over the money and you handed over the address.'

'Yes.'

'And then?'

Lennie blinked.

'Then nothing. He nodded and went off to his car. I gave Mark his wage and we went home.'

'You didn't split fifty-fifty?'

'Just for standing there? You must have taken leave of your senses, black boy.'

'So what else happened with Cosmo Horrocks?'

'Nothing else happened. Over. Finished. Kaput.'

Charlie raised his eyebrows.

'Tell me about the Indian club from the Learys' sports cupboard.'

'Indian club? Don't know what you're talking about.'

'An Indian club went missing from the Learys' cupboard, and was put back after the murder. I think you took it.'

'Give it a rest! Why should I do that? And why would I want to murder the git from the *Chronicle*? I just made a packet out of him.'

And that, Charlie thought, was really the nub.

Mark Leary was sweating now. He had had an hour back in the cells and his brain, which was self-obsessed but sharp where his own interests were concerned, had as the minutes ticked by come to terms with the mess he was in. Unfortunately it had not come up with any fail-safe idea of how to get himself out of it.

'Now, Mark,' said Oddie quietly, 'I don't think you should keep up this pretence that you had nothing to do with the Father Pardoe business. We know from Lennie that you were on hand when the cash and the address were exchanged.'

Mark put on an expression of hauteur.

'Lennie would say that.'

'Would he? My impression from Sergeant Peace is that he's quite willing to claim sole credit, if that's the word, for most of his scams.'

'Stupid berk. That's what comes of getting involved with kids.'

'You could be right there. I think you'd better tell us exactly what went on in Saltaire Park.'

Mark thought it over, and looked at his father, who shook his head. But when the boy spoke again it was clear he'd decided that Oddie was right.

'I just went along as observer, that was all.'

'What exactly do you mean, as observer?'

'To see fair play. To make sure he didn't pull a fast one. If he had done, I'd have stepped in.'

'But he didn't.'

'No.'

'I'm having difficulty with this, Mark,' said Oddie softly. 'Because there's this matter of the disappearance of the Indian club from your basement cupboard. Now, I'm willing to bet that when Forensics go over that, there will be things that tie it in with Lennie that they will pick up, but nothing that will have been left on it by you. That is unless you picked it up to examine it after it was returned.'

There was silence, and then Mark said: 'I didn't. I was scared. I didn't want to have anything to do with it.'

'That's about the first wise thing I've heard of you doing. What I'm wondering is why you're holding back on me, why you're shielding this boy if you yourself weren't involved in the most important thing that we're investigating.'

Mark muttered something. Oddie couldn't quite hear, but it sounded like: 'He's gruesome.'

'Come on – tell us what happened. In Saltaire Park, or afterwards.'

Mark swallowed. Oddie guessed suddenly that he was afraid.

'It happened like we planned – Lennie planned – up to the handing over. There was a bit of argy-bargy, then Horrocks agreed to hand over the money and then be given the address. We were all standing by one of the seats, well away from the road or railway line. He handed over the money, Lennie gave it to me, and I retreated under a tree in case he tried any funny business. Somehow you could tell he wasn't just going to accept tamely anything Lennie told him to do. Lennie puts people's backs up. He puts mine up.'

'I can understand that.'

'Then Lennie got the address out of his pocket and handed it towards Horrocks, and as he took it with his left hand he grabbed Lennie's arm with his right and sat down on the seat. He dragged him across his knee and began spanking him.'

'*Spanking* him?'

'Yes. It was brilliant. Like he was just a little kid. Lennie went spare. He screamed blue murder and kicked and spat, and I just saw the funny side of it, this smart-arse kid with the big opinion of himself being treated like what he really was – no more than a child. I roared with laughter. It was just what Lennie needed.'

'It was very clever,' agreed Oddie. 'Cunning too. That's what Horrocks specialized in: humiliating people. Bruising their egos at the most sensitive point.'

'Eventually he just chucked Lennie away and walked coolly off. I really admired him. But Lennie was exploding with rage. His face was brick red and he was crying, and he started shouting at Horrocks's back: "I'll get you, Horrocks. You're a dead man. Start counting the days." Stuff he'd heard on television. And then he turned on me, and started pummelling me in the chest. I took it for a bit, and then I pushed him away too. But he was terrifying. His language was like I'd never heard it before – it was so intense, so –

crazy, almost. Horrocks was "dead meat", he was going to get more than a spanking back, he was going to die face down in a pool of his own blood. Then he'd turn his fury on me and say I'd pay for laughing at him, not coming to his rescue. "Don't think you'll get off scot free, you useless git" – that kind of thing, but said in such a way that . . . it made me shudder, somehow.'

'Why on earth did you let him into your house after that?'

'He came up to me in school next day, said he was going to forget about the whole thing, after all we'd got the money, hadn't we? So things went back to normal. All the things I'd been imagining seemed – well, a bit far-fetched. A day or two later we'd been playing snooker in the basement and I went upstairs for a leak. When I'd finished I came out on to the landing and saw him going out the front door, walking a bit funny. I guess that's when he took it. He was holding it in front of him.'

'And when did he return it?'

Mark swallowed.

'A couple of nights ago. Came round when he knew I would be at home, and tapped a little grille that gives out on to the front garden – that was our usual procedure, because I was always down in the sports room after I'd finished my homework. I went up to let him in, and he marched past me and down to the basement, carrying the club. When I got down there he was putting it back in the cupboard. He turned round and said: "Just borrowed it for a bit of practice," looking me straight in the eye. I was terrified. What can you do with one club? Anyway Lennie wasn't interested in sport, or anything like that; said it was just for kids. He kept on looking at me for what seemed like ages, then he marched out, up the stairs, and left the house. I just stood there – it was like my blood was frozen. I knew what he'd done, what the club had been used for, but I didn't know what to do.'

'So in the end you did nothing.'

'Yes. What could I do?'

He spoke with the naivety of his age, looking down at his father, who had his head in his hands. To Oddie Mark seemed the perfect example of a man without principles who has got himself well out of his depth. But there was one unusual ingredient added: the odd spectacle of a confident near-adult who could not disguise the fact that he was terrified by a child.

When Lennie came back into the interview room two hours later with his lawyer he had lost none of his swagger. In fact, being investigated and interrogated, having the details of his petty-criminal schemes laid out before him, seemed only to have ministered to his monstrous self-love. Oddie had joined the Shipley investigating team, now that it was clear Lennie Norris was into something much deeper than school playground scams. He chose to talk to him in the tone that would aggravate him most – the tone of talking to a naughty boy.

'Well, Lennie – things are becoming a bit clearer to us now.'

'Good, then you can let me go.'

'I don't think that will be on the cards for quite a while yet. After all, you haven't been straight with us, have you?'

'Straight as you fucking deserve.'

'For example, the exchange of the money and the address didn't go as smoothly as you said, did it? Or as painlessly, you might say.'

The boy looked at him hard, his face becoming brick red, his eyes dilating.

'What's that berk Leary been saying?'

'What we've heard is that when you came to hand over the address, Horrocks took it, but took you as well, and put you over his knee and gave you a jolly good spanking.'

At this the boy exploded. He erupted out of his seat and stood flaming with rage and wounded vanity, stabbing his finger in Oddie's direction as if it were a stiletto.

'And he fucking paid for it, didn't he? I said he would and he did. Thought he could treat me like a kid. I showed him I wasn't a kid, didn't I? I said he'd die face down in his own blood, and that's what he did. That's what happens to people who mix it with me. You'll find that out, dickhead. That clown Leary would have been next. Will be next. I'm already thinking out what I'm going to do to him, and I'll do it, however long they put me away. Am I the youngest murderer you've ever arrested? The youngest ever? I'd like that. People are going to have to take notice of me. You'd never have caught me if it hadn't been for that arsehole Leary. I'll know next time: act on your own. Keep everything in your own hands. You'll be hearing from me in future. You'll be hearing from me for the rest of your fucking career.'

But Oddie felt he had heard more than enough already.

'Interview terminated at nineteen forty-three hours,' he said, and switched off the tape.

CHAPTER 21

Afterword

Some days change lives: other days seem to symbolize the fact that some lives will never change.

The days after the arrest of Lennie Norris, and of Mark Leary on less serious charges, were just such days for many of the people in Shipley. Many of them had only the vaguest idea of what was going on, for the papers were circumspect in not naming anyone 'for legal reasons'. Parents were forced for once to listen to their children's stories, especially if they went to Bingley Road Comprehensive, or had played cricket or other sports with the older of the boys. The news passed from mouth to mouth in a pre-twentieth-century fashion.

Two people whose lives were changed were the Norrises. The day of Lennie's arrest was the day their world collapsed around them. When, after three days of terrible suspense, he finally consented to see them, the interview was so terrible as to invade every minute of their waking days thereafter, and form the stuff of their nightmares: the abuse, the contempt, the vile language, above all the cockiness about what he had done and the boasting about what he would do. Norris was a broken man. People even stopped coming into his shop out of curiosity, because the spectacle was too painful. Bettaclothes just waited for an opportunity to sack him without attracting adverse publicity. Mrs Norris flitted to her nearest shops and straight home again, not attracting adverse comment now because she was obviously a shattered wraith. Aunt Becky suggested they should get in touch with Julie, but Daphne vetoed this. In any case, she would probably not have responded.

Janette Jessel's life also changed dramatically. She moved into the guest bedroom, and when her husband asked her why said she was fed up with being married to an adultery addict. It might suit the American First Lady, she said, but after twenty-five years she had decided it didn't suit her. She added that she was contemplating a more decisive break, particularly if she could get a job. When Derek made feeble (and rather ignorant) remarks about her faith she said her faith was not such an ass as to condone the sinner and condemn the victim of the sins. She hoped she was right.

Other lives resumed the course that the Father Pardoe case had interrupted. Miss Preece-Dembleby swelled with gratitude that family disgrace was not about to overwhelm her, and that the murder had been found to be nothing to do with her brother and the Father Riley Fund. She reflected, though, that men, as exemplified in her brother, seemed to need all kinds of inducements to stay on the straight and narrow, and that even so all kinds of precautions needed to be taken to ensure that they did so. They were, she concluded, undoubtedly the weaker sex morally. She had in fact decided this in her late 'teens, and recent events only strengthened her attitude and her thankfulness at her escape from the closest kind of involvement with them.

Mary Leary spent the days in feverish activity on behalf of her son. Her daughter Donna regarded her – initially distraught, but then determined and effective – with an amused exasperation. Both women knew she would never change: that she would go on – knowingly, regretfully, reluctantly – in the paths she had been trained up in, ministering to a man's world, accepting all it threw at her. Her brief days of militancy had been not an advance but an aberration.

Father Pardoe, when he attended the interview at the Bishop's office the following Monday, was surprised at the perfunctoriness of the questioning, astounded when, at the end of the session, he was told by the chairman that his account of the matters under investigation was entirely consistent with everything else the examining committee had been told, and that he was free to take up his duties in Shipley at once. In the outer office he had his hand shaken by the Bishop, who said they would need to have a chat in the near future. Pardoe responded gravely, but with few words.

He packed his few possessions, said goodbye to Margaret, and was close to tears when he kissed her goodbye inside her front door. There were so many things that both of them could have said, but there was absolutely no need to say them. Pardoe felt he had never known any woman so well. And if Margaret felt for the first time that there was cruelty in a system that kept apart two people so well suited to each other as they were, her upbringing and her natural discretion ensured she remained silent. They arranged to have a meal together every few weeks.

Some days later, when he had seen Father Greenspan off to a small and undemanding parish in super-rural North Yorkshire, he went in his old way to visit Julie Norris in the early afternoon. He cherished her smile as she opened her front door. She put Gary down on his little bed, but said: 'Better not draw the curtains.'

'Of course you must draw the curtains,' said Father Pardoe. 'He'll sleep better. And not drawing them would be like an admission of guilt in the past.'

Then they went into the kitchen, and over endless cups of tea talked and laughed about the Bishop's committee, about people's reactions to the newspaper stories, about Julie's parents and her prospects in the world. Doris Crabtree, going a very long way round on her way to visit her friend Florrie Mortlake, saw them through the kitchen window and curled up her lip in a gesture of contempt. They didn't fool her!

Cora Horrocks was relieved at the arrest, though she was unwilling to admit that it lifted from her mind a burden of doubt and uncertainty. She had already become aware of the paradox that Cosmo's death made her and her daughters more of a family, not less. One night, after Adelaide had gone to bed, Samantha confided in her the truth about herself and Cassie Daltrey, and her determination not to be hurried into a relationship that might be contrary to her nature and spring from a sort of adolescent hero worship. Cora, with her past, was fairly unshockable in sexual matters, but warmly seconded her daughter's decision. She too began wondering what jobs might be available to a woman of her age and lack of training.

And one night, when all the case's paperwork was done, Charlie and Felicity sat over a bottle of wine after a good meal cooked by her and talked about the future.

'It frightened me, that case,' said Charlie. 'That terrible boy: how did he get like that? All those parents cut off from their children, knowing nothing about them. How did that situation develop? How can I make sure it doesn't happen to me and him-or-her?'

'It won't. You're not that kind of person.'

'But they're perfectly normal people. Not the Norrises – they're weird – but Mary Leary, for example. Typical old-fashioned mother, but she produces this narcissistic prat of a son.'

'There are a hundred ways of being a bad parent, but I'd guess that there are a hundred ways of being a good one too. Tolstoy got it all wrong, as he usually did. There are infinite varieties of happy families, as well as infinite varieties of unhappy ones.'

'I just hope you're right.'

'I'm going to be here for him-or-her, but I'm not going to be a smothering, overwhelming parent either.'

'We both come from pretty odd home backgrounds,' Charlie said. 'Who knows: that may be an advantage.'

'It's something to cling on to, as a hope.'

'And no, you mustn't be overwhelming, mustn't be too much around, when what he-or-she needs is space. It's a good thing that you'll have a bit of academic work to do, if things work out.'

'Maybe . . . Actually I'm reconsidering on that. I'm thinking of writing a book.'

'Oh good. But no money in that.'

'A novel.'

Charlie's mouth fell open.

'A *novel*! For Christ's sake! Hasn't your father put you off that?'

'My father writes rotten novels. Crap. Mine is going to be a good one. Maybe there will be more than one. There certainly will be more than one child. Now, getting down to the actual wedding . . .'

Later that night Charlie awoke from a very strange dream indeed, in which he and Felicity and the several children she had foreseen were out on a picnic and the whole thing was like a cosy advertiser's film of pretty people in pre-Raphaelite green fields being gooily happy together with cows looking benevolently on. Sleepily Charlie felt across the bed and settled his hand on Felicity's stomach, wondering if he could feel the little one's presence yet. He decided he couldn't, but was pleased in the knowledge that it was there.

'You're going to have to get used to more reality than that,' he said. 'Life's not going to be all green fields and cows, little him-or-her.'